P9-DBQ-275

"I can't, Katherine, I can't. I've made too many promises."

A stolen moment from heaven as they stood in the darkening room, caught between the past and the future. Then gently but firmly, Daniel set her aside.

He knew he was at a crossroads. Walking out alone, he would be leaving behind the young man who had entered that room an hour before, leaving behind the riotous colors of his youth. And leaving behind, too, nothing as simple as love, no, but something bigger, a part of him that would determine how the rest of his life would be—or not be. Though he would have a good life, he knew— there would always be something missing.

His grief palpable, Daniel took a deep breath and left the sewing room.

Katherine was not so complicated.

Memorize the feel of his kiss she told herself as she lifted her hand to her lips. It had to last a lifetime.

Dear Reader,

I'm delighted to introduce Barbara Gale, whose intense story *The Ambassador's Vow* (SSE #1500) "explores not only issues involved in interracial romance, but the price one pays for not following one's heart." The author adds, "Together, the characters discover that honesty is more important to the heart than skin color. Recognizing the true worth of the gold ring they both sought is what eventually reunites them." Don't wait to pick this one up!

Sherryl Woods brings us *Sean's Reckoning* (SSE #1495), the next title in her exciting series THE DEVANEYS. Here, a firefighter discovers love and family with a single mom and her son when he rescues them from a fire. Next, a warning: there's another Bravo bachelor on the loose in Christine Rimmer's *Mercury Rising* (SSE #1496), from her miniseries THE SONS OF CAITLIN BRAVO. Perplexed heroine Jane Elliott tries to resist Cade Bravo, but of course her efforts are futile as she falls for the handsome hero. Did we ever doubt it?

In *Montana Lawman* (SSE #1497), part of MONTANA MAVERICKS, Allison Leigh makes the sparks fly between a shy librarian and a smitten deputy sheriff. Crystal Green's miniseries KANE'S CROSSING continues with *The Stranger She Married* (SSE #1498), in which a husband returns after a long absence— but he can't remember his marriage! Watch how this powerful love story unites this starry-eyed couple.... Finally, Tracy Sinclair delivers tantalizing excitement in *An American Princess* (SSE #1499), in which an American beauty receives royal pampering by a suave Prince Charming. How's that for a dream come true?

Each month, we aim to bring you the best in romance. We are enthusiastic to hear your thoughts. You may send comments to my attention at Silhouette Special Edition, 300 East 42nd Street, 6th Floor, New York, New York 10017. In the meantime, happy reading!

Sincerely,
Karen Taylor Richman
Senior Editor

Please address questions and book requests to:
Silhouette Reader Service
U.S.: 3010 Walden Ave., P.O. Box 1325, Buffalo, NY 14269
Canadian: P.O. Box 609, Fort Erie, Ont. L2A 5X3

The Ambassador's Vow

BARBARA GALE

SPECIAL EDITION™

Published by Silhouette Books

America's Publisher of Contemporary Romance

If you purchased this book without a cover you should be aware
that this book is stolen property. It was reported as "unsold and
destroyed" to the publisher, and neither the author nor the
publisher has received any payment for this "stripped book."

To Larry, who, in so many ways,
helped me to write this book.

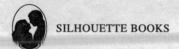 SILHOUETTE BOOKS

ISBN 0-373-24500-9

THE AMBASSADOR'S VOW

Copyright © 2002 by Barbara Einstein

All rights reserved. Except for use in any review, the reproduction
or utilization of this work in whole or in part in any form by any
electronic, mechanical or other means, now known or hereafter
invented, including xerography, photocopying and recording, or in
any information storage or retrieval system, is forbidden without
the written permission of the editorial office, Silhouette Books,
300 East 42nd Street, New York, NY 10017 U.S.A.

All characters in this book have no existence outside the imagination of
the author and have no relation whatsoever to anyone bearing the same
name or names. They are not even distantly inspired by any individual
known or unknown to the author, and all incidents are pure invention.

This edition published by arrangement with Harlequin Books S.A.

® and TM are trademarks of Harlequin Books S.A., used under license.
Trademarks indicated with ® are registered in the United States Patent
and Trademark Office, the Canadian Trade Marks Office and in other
countries.

Visit Silhouette at www.eHarlequin.com

Printed in U.S.A.

Prologue

The choice is partly cultural, partly social, and partly political, but it is mostly affectional. One selects a milieu. It is a choice not about where one lives or how one votes but whom one loves.

Stephen L. Carter

Standing tall and regal in a tuxedo carefully tailored to stretch across his broad shoulders, Daniel thought suddenly of Katherine. Positioned at the head of the receiving line, in the midst of greeting three hundred guests who had come especially to honor him, the air redolent with perfume and filled with the carefully pitched laughter of wealth, Katherine's elfin face unexpectedly materialized. And with her image, a familiar frisson of loneliness.

The irony was inescapable.

There he was, Daniel Sheridan Boylan, the first African-American ever posted to a major embassy, hosting a ball to celebrate his tenth year as Ambassador to France. The most desirable position the diplomatic corps had to offer. Living in the most elegant mansion in the most elegant city in the world.

Lonely in Paris.

Was it possible?

Not that the job was without gratification. He was a damned good diplomat, with always a clear eye on the horizon. Long-sighted, as a good politician should be, and patient but firm, as behooved an ambassador. But lately he'd been feeling restless. Just the other week, he'd chewed the ear off of one of his friends till the wee hours. Last night he'd made three staffers stay up well past midnight running nonsensical errands they didn't dare refuse. Apologizing profusely when he finally realized the time, he himself couldn't slow down till well past four.

And now, his face carefully schooled as his guests whirled past, chiffon and taffeta a palette of pastel, Katherine Harriman had inexplicably come to mind. The girl he'd left behind when the gold ring was dangled before him. He'd grabbed for the ring unthinkingly, well, certainly not thinking of Katherine, persuading himself she was an infatuation he'd outgrow. Except that every once in a while, like now, even though it had been ten long years, there she was, an unexpected vision surfacing in his mind's eye. Katherine in red velvet, gazing up at him, the light of promise in her beautiful green eyes. She was his one and only regret, he thought sadly, as he watched his secretary hurriedly approach, a long white envelope in hand.

"Sorry, Mr. Ambassador, but this letter came in yesterday's mail pouch. I had set it aside to deliver it to you myself, but it was inadvertently shuffled beneath another pile. I deeply apologize for the interruption, but if you would take a quick look, it is from the States."

"Nonsense, Philippe, you are paid an exorbitant salary to read my mail. Go ahead and deal with it yourself," Daniel ordered. "We are at a ball," he added.

"Believe me, sir, I thought twice about this, but the letter is marked Personal and Urgent, and in red ink."

Daniel examined the lightweight envelope. It showed his name, the embassy address, and, as Philippe had observed, the words *Urgent* and *Personal* were scrawled large in red ink, clearly meant to catch someone's attention. Definitely mailed from the States, the return address had been smeared and the postmark was almost illegible. Curious. But just then the massive gilt doors of the ballroom swung open. Tucking the letter into his pocket, he carefully wiped all expression from his face as he watched a woman in her late seventies slowly mount the grand staircase. She steadied her fragile frame with the aid of an ornate, jewel-encrusted cane. A gauzy cashmere shawl draped across her shoulders protected her from possible chill.

Daniel bowed low over the thin, veined hand she offered, her fingers knobby with arthritis, but still heavily adorned with rings. Daniel sighed for her vanity, but his smile was courteous. "Madame Beaucart."

The old woman nodded, his homage taken for granted, as he bowed low over her hand. "*Bon soir, Monsieur l'Ambassadeur.* And good evening to you, also, Monsieur Philippe," she said, smiling past Daniel's shoulders. "Ever-faithful, handsome, and vigilant, as always."

Daniel's secretary bowed low, but kept correctly to the background.

"*Tiens,* Monsieur Boylan," she said, tapping Daniel's hand with the black lace fan that dangled from her wrist. "Are you surprised to see me? I am not dead, yet, my friend. Did I not promise to attend the social event of the year?" The widow of a French courer, Berenice Beaucart was well-versed in the obligations of the diplomatic circuit.

Daniel smiled, his amber eyes alight with mischief. "Madame Beaucart, we are both long past the age of surprise. Although, if anyone could surprise me, it would be you."

"*Tiens,* such grace, such wit!" she exclaimed. "Oh, Daniel, do stop fawning over me. You know better than anyone how I abhor it. And I dislike it intensely when you pretend that you are my age, instead of the thirty-something we all know you really are. Or perhaps you have reached forty and I didn't notice?''

"Not yet, but close."

"Truly an ancient, *non?*" Berenice teased. "But it is too late, if you are trying to annoy me to distraction. I saw Philippe hand you that letter," she informed him slyly. "Duty knows no bounds, eh, *Monsieur l'Ambassadeur?* Or is it the handsome Philippe who is the harsh taskmaster?''

"Those keen eyes of yours miss nothing, Berenice. They are definitely France's best weapon." Daniel spoke kindly to his longtime friend, the formal tone they used for the public gone, his affection for the old woman risen to replace it. Ten years ago, when his inexperienced feet had landed at Orly Airport, Berenice Beaucart had literally adopted him. He was a born diplomat, but without her support, he would never have survived the maze of French society, and he had never forgotten his debt to her.

"Not true, my son, but so nice of you to say so. Alas, things are not as they were in my day. Technology makes fools of us all, *n'est-ce pas?* Nowadays, it is all fax this, fax that, or, how do you young people say, *le i-mail, non?*"

"E-mail, Berenice, e-mail."

"*Mais oui, le eee-mail,*" she drawled. "Everything must arrive yesterday, *et tout est trés important!*"

"*Mais oui, madame, c'est necessaire, non?*" Daniel countered, slipping into French because he knew how much it pleased her.

"Perhaps, Daniel, perhaps. But sometimes I am not too sure. Well, I won't keep you, read your very important letter, then," she said with a pointed glance at Daniel's pocket. She knew that Philippe would never have dared to interrupt Daniel with anything less than an emergency. When Daniel saw the direction of her inquisitive eyes, he shook his head.

A knowing smile spread across her wrinkled face, but she let the matter drop with a Gallic shrug. She would dearly have loved to be the first to know the contents of that letter. Whatever the news was—it had been so boring in Paris this past spring, and summer was fast approaching with as much ennui—she would never allow herself to be accused of bad manners. Besides, there were other ways of finding things out. Less obvious, *and* more fun. "Only promise, then, *Monsieur l'Ambassadeur,* to find me later. For a waltz, Daniel," she said, meeting his suspicion with irony. "You really do waltz divinely, *mon ami,* one of the few who do. Someday, you must remember to thank your mother for me."

Daniel looked at her, puzzled.

"For all those wonderful dancing lessons she no doubt forced on you, when you were a child!" Berenice explained with a hearty laugh as she walked away. She never noticed her near-collision with a young couple who stepped aside as she sailed into the ballroom, her glittering head-plumes waving as she nodded this way and that. When Berenice Beaucart entered a room, everyone made way.

Noblesse oblige, Daniel thought, fascinated as he watched Berenice make her grand entrance. Having long since cultivated a certain ageless innocence, fine-tuned with a surfeit of power borrowed from her late husband, the heady combination opened doors for her everywhere. He had to admire her knack of making everyone feel like her long-lost friend. Intimacy was not one of Daniel's strong points. He would have preferred it differently, having been accused too many times of exhibiting a perfunctory sort of personality. Respected and revered, but cold, standoffish—just this side of being a cold fish, he remembered hearing someone whisper. But he had long since lost the art of laughter.

Katherine had stolen his smile.

He frowned. What an odd thought. And unfair. But there she was again, and that was unfair, too.

With a shake of his head, Daniel pushed away her memory, an art he had mastered long ago. He would not have survived in the public arena without enormous personal discipline. Sometimes he believed *that* was the real criticism lodged against him. He had given up a lot to attain his present position, if people only knew. Though he supposed no one would ever thank him—and why should they?—for having no personal life whatsoever: no wife, no children, not even a mistress, which the French would certainly have understood. Of course, these were his choices. If he ever stopped to wonder why he had made them, he would tell himself he was being maudlin. He damn well knew he wouldn't have changed anything, if he had to do it over. Feeling the crumpled envelope he'd stuffed in his pocket recalled him to the present.

Peeling open the missive, he removed a single sheet of familiar-looking paper. Loose leaf paper! He smiled. How...American! It had been years since he'd seen a sheet of loose-leaf paper, perhaps as long ago as law school. Observing its meticulous print of neat lettering, he sighed. He received tens of these a week, fan-mail hype. Philippe should have known better, but apologies to Philippe, it had been a sealed envelope. Quickly, he read.

Dear Daniel,
    My son is desperately sick and I have no where else to turn. Please help me.

                                            Katherine Harriman

Good grief, Katherine Harriman! How odd, his having just been thinking of her. Her son? She had never mentioned having a son, when they'd met last year...

The shock must have registered because although he quickly cleared his face, Philippe moved forward.

"Is there some sort of emergency, sir?" he asked quietly, alarmed at a possible dereliction of duty. He had hopes for his future.

Unsure of what to say, Daniel hesitated as he handed the envelope to his aide. But he was careful to keep hold of the letter. "Philippe, this...this letter. It might be serious. Try to get more information on the address. It's almost illegible, but not quite. Harriman is the name, Katherine Harriman. Last I…heard…she lived just outside Phoenix. What and where. You know the sort of thing.''

"Immediately, Mr. Ambassador.'' Philippe hurried away, but was back within minutes, visibly agitated.

"Sir, you have a call in the library!''

Daniel's brow rose, a faint smile on his lips. "Surely you don't expect me to leave the ball in order to answer the telephone?''

Philippe was insistent. "I understand, sir, but it's trans-atlantic, and the operator said it was urgent. From Phoenix, Arizona,'' he whispered.

Daniel froze. "From Arizona? You must be joking.''

Philippe took a deep breath, knowing Daniel wasn't going to like his next words. "From a Miss Harriman, I believe the operator said. A Miss Katherine Harriman,'' he repeated, careful not to meet Daniel's eyes. In all the years he'd worked for the embassy, he'd never known the ambassador to be even remotely indiscreet, but if anything ever sounded like… Well, one could never be too sure.

Directing Philippe to take his place at the reception line, Daniel hurried down the hall to the library, his mind reeling as he closed its heavy door against intrusion. He stared unseeing at the hundreds of books that lined the polished shelves, ignored the deep-set sofa where one often found him at the end of the day, a small brandy at hand as he wrapped up the day's business. But now, he had eyes only for the huge desk situated at the far end of the room, laden with manila folders and neatly arranged stacks of papers, everything meticulously grouped according to priority by the ever-scrupulous Philippe. He could see the late-afternoon's mail, carefully slit, organized alphabetically, ready for his attention over tomorrow's morning coffee. And resting to one side, a bank of telephones studded with dozens of dull red buttons.

One was winking. Tiny, bright, blood-red and ominous, compelling even from this distance, more of a priority than any single sheet surrounding it. He knew exactly how much it had taken Katherine to make that call. Suddenly, he felt sick, wanted to weep for the pain that scored his heart.

Her son.

My God, Katherine, he breathed, what have you done?

Chapter One

New York—Ten years earlier

Daniel scanned the rolling lawns as his limousine took the last mile to his parents' home. Squinting against the glare of the latest snow to fall on Long Island, he was unable to stop the frown that wrinkled his thick brows and dulled the light of his amber eyes. God, how he hated parties. Give him a good, solid forum and an audience of three hundred, fine. But small talk was not his chosen art form, it was torture, plain and simple.

Between his mother and his sister Deirdre, half the state of New York must be in attendance, half of New England, maybe, judging by the parking lot the lawn had become. College-age boys dressed in green uniforms looked as if they were having a really good time parking all those BMWs and Jaguars and Corvettes. And, my God, more reporters! He groaned. What a fool he'd been to think he'd lost them at the airport. They were here ahead of him, that's all, crowding around the massive iron gate, ready to pounce. Sitting stiffly, he stared straight ahead while the guards unlocked the gate, his driver managing to negotiate the limo past the throng of photographers as they shoved their cameras against the car window. Their flashes exploded in his face, incendiary— false fireworks that celebrated nothing. When the car pulled to a halt at the top of the driveway, Daniel climbed out with a sigh. It was going to be a very long day.

Just beyond, he could see the house lit up like the Fourth of July, every window ablaze. The high ring of girlish voices outdistanced the loud barks of male laughter coming from the mansion, and, even at this range, he could hear an obnoxious-sounding DJ hard at work. Deirdre had probably insisted on one, and when Deirdre insisted, everybody obeyed. More than once he had marveled at how she did it. He never had managed to master the trick. Something to do with pouting, spoiled minx that she was. Daniel smiled. Anyone who knew him knew that he adored his baby sister, that he was unusually close to his family and that he kept a watchful eye on the whole clan even when he was thousands of miles away.

Dismissing his driver, he strode up the wide expanse of stairs swept clean of the recent snowfall. Judging by the gloomy overhang of clouds, there was more to come. No doubt his mother had left a standing order to sweep the stairs even as the snow fell, should snow have the bad manners to fall the day of Deirdre Sheridan Boylan's engagement party.

Smiling at the thought, anything to bolster his spirits at the ordeal ahead, Daniel raised his hand to lift the brass knocker, but the door flew open before he could knock. A little girl stood before him, dressed in fluffy pink organza and patent leather, her black braids embellished with matching pink ribbons, her toothless, six-year-old smile wide as she ambushed her favorite uncle and threw herself into his arms.

"Uncle Dan, I just knew it was you! I was watching the whole time. What took you so long? Did the plane crash?"

she asked with childlike relish. "Did you get a flat tire and fall in a ditch and have to be towed? Gramma said maybe you had *'cause you're so damn late*. Gramma said a cuss word, didn't she? I pretended not to hear 'cause I wasn't supposed to be listening. Did you bring me a Christmas present? Mommy said you would, even if you couldn't get here in time for Christmas Eve."

"See here, Kiesha!" Daniel laughed as he scooped up his niece for a hug. "Whatever happened to hello?"

Kiesha dutifully wrapped her arms around his neck, squeezed extra hard and gave him a big sloppy kiss on his cheek. "Is that good?"

"Yeah, that's better, honey," he smiled, "but now I think you broke my neck! So, where is everybody? And where is Jeffers? I thought the butler was supposed to open the door, not little girls!"

"Grandma asked Jeffers to watch the party. She said there were too many strange people walking round and she didn't want them to get lost."

"You mean strangers, not strange." Daniel chuckled.

"No, I meant strange. That's what Grandma said. I know, 'cause Jeffers said that's what Grandma got for letting little miss invite every—"

"You know what, princess? I believe you." Daniel chuckled, easily able to imagine the conversation between his mother and their morose but loyal butler, Jeffers. He'd witnessed many, and it was always a draw. "But hey, tell me, what did Santa leave you?"

"Santa Claus? Oh, please, Uncle Dan." Kiesha groaned, rolling her eyes. "There is no Santa Claus! I've known that forever! Just ask all the kids in school."

"What school do you go to, Kiesha?" Daniel frowned. "Juvenile Hall for Jaded Pre-adolescents?"

"Oh, Uncle Daniel!" Kiesha giggled. "I go to Miss Dexter's School! You know that!"

"Well, I think I better go have a talk with this Miss Dexter, find out what she's teaching you kids. But, hey, if you don't believe in Santa Claus anymore, maybe I shouldn't, either.''

''Exactly,'' she agreed in her most adult voice.

''And if we don't bother to believe in Santa anymore, then maybe we ought to skip Christmas. I mean, what's the point? And all those presents in my car...'' Daniel shrugged. ''I guess I'd better send them back to Santa Claus.''

Startled, Kiesha thought quickly, her nut-brown face an open book as she tried to work her way around that idea. Daniel had to bite his lips to keep from laughing.

But a true Boylan, she was quick on her feet. ''You love me, so you bring me presents! And anyway, you always do,'' she announced with smug satisfaction.

Daniel thought hard, scrunching up his lips. ''Well, honey, I do believe that if I rummaged about in my bags, I might— no promises, now!—but I just might have something a pretty little girl might have some use for.''

Kiesha beamed. ''See! I told you so!''

''So you did.'' Daniel smiled gently. ''But you'll be getting nothing from me right now, Miss Kiesha, not until later when everyone's gone home.''

''But everybody's been here for ages!'' Kiesha wailed. ''They may never go home!''

''Yeah, I know how you feel, kid, but that's the deal.''

''And I've been waiting here for you forever!''

''But I thought that was because you loved me and I'm your favorite uncle!''

''I suppose,'' she agreed reluctantly, not entirely convinced.

Her grievance was short-lived, as Daniel set her down and insisted they go in the house. ''I don't want your mother blaming me if you get a cold!'' But Kiesha never heard. She was already halfway down the hall, anxious to be the first to announce Uncle Dan's arrival.

Following her into the house, Daniel was dismayed to see a small crowd milling about in the foyer. Heads turned in curiosity, subdued into silence when they saw who it was.

Standing six feet and one inch, Daniel knew he made an entrance. He had presence, his sister May, liked to say. He dismissed such talk as nonsense, but somehow, whenever he entered a room, a path did clear, and, even now, the small crowd watched him closely, nodding and smiling, their champagne glasses raised in salute, each one hoping to be singled out.

Thus, the advantage of a poker face, Daniel thought wryly, as he measured the tenor of the room. Good lord, how they stared! Well, what could he expect, the way his face was in all the newspapers, lately? A pity. They ought to have something better to look at than his ugly mug. A stony mask, classically un-handsome, he thought with dry humor.

In truth, though, his face wasn't nearly as bad as he made out. A profile of strength and character, his dark skin stretched smoothly over the high ridges of his cheekbones while a patrician nose settled majestically above a generous, well-defined mouth. Deep-set amber eyes took in a world he viewed with faint misgiving, which accounted for that brooding look he'd once been told women found so attractive. He'd laughed hard at that one because, personally, he likened himself to those huge chicken hawks that owned the skies of upstate New York. Enormous black hawks that swooped down low over cornfields—seeming to float, utterly graceful and vaguely disturbing. Predatory, he was thinking, as he closed the massive oak door, only to collide head-on with a lithe female body, her thick mane of blond hair softening the blow to his chin.

"Oops. I'm so sorry. Are you okay?"

Apologizing profusely for his clumsiness, Daniel steadied the young woman he'd stumbled against, only to find himself grow still. The world lost its clarity as he stood enthralled, arrested by the serene innocence of a pair of green eyes that met his with curious good humor. Instinctively, his fingers tightened, digging into the woman's shoulders. But it was she, tiny mouse, who captured the hunter.

Disarming him effortlessly.

Waving away his embarrassment.

Captivating him with her wide smile and the charm of a rosy blush spreading across her cheeks. Her face a perfect oval, her nose short and straight, it was her hair that drew him, a wealth of heavy yellow silk that refused to be tamed. The silver filigree barrette she wore seemed to be of no use, the whole pile threatening to come undone at any moment. He had an impulse to help it along. Used to perfectly groomed women, Daniel was intrigued. And more, he found her very appealing, dressed as she was, head to toe, in an old-fashioned red velvet gown. Perhaps it was those eyes, the twinkle in their mossy depths.

"Hello, Mr. Boylan." Her soft voice brought him back to earth, her mouth a sweet smile. Dropping his hands, Daniel stepped back, appalled at where his thoughts had drifted.

"You don't remember me, do you?" The beauty grinned, unaware of his turmoil. "Not that I'm all that memorable, I know."

Daniel had the grace to look uncomfortable, but for the life of him simply could not come up with a name. And wouldn't he remember such a face?

"Deirdre and I roomed together at Sarah Lawrence in our senior year," the young woman prodded.

Daniel was mortified, but fortunately, the woman had more presence of mind than he.

"No bells going off, huh?" She grinned. "I've stayed here a few times, as Deirdre's houseguest, but, well, you were always in such a rush, it's no surprise you don't remember me. Actually, I'd have been more surprised if you did remember me, the way you were always hurrying off somewhere. No time to notice your baby sister's girlfriends. I remember once feeling quite envious that someone could be so busy, that anyone could have so many friends and so many things to do!"

Holding out her hand, she teased Daniel into a handshake, her small hand lost in his large paw. "I'm Katherine Harriman, the soon-to-be-slightly-famous pianist whose face you will then remember...I hope!'' she added with a grin.

"That name seems familiar," Daniel lied diplomatically. "And now that I look at you—really look at you," he cleared his throat, glad that she couldn't tell that he was blushing, "you do seem familiar. Perhaps you've changed your hairstyle?" he asked hopefully.

"Well, okay," she smiled, mischief in her eyes. "I'll throw you some slack, but only because I usually don't wear my hair up like this."

"Yes, that's it!" Daniel smiled, grasping gratefully at the straw she offered.

Katherine wasn't fooled, but she was willing to be generous. "It really is good to see you again, Daniel," she said, her voice suddenly earnest.

"And you, too, Katherine," he said, matching her tone, "now that my memory is beginning to work. I do believe we did meet a while back, one weekend when I was picking Deirdre up from school. It was snowing, I got stuck in a drift and you both stood there laughing hysterically. I couldn't decide who to be more angry with—Dee, her ditzy friend or that damned snow."

Katherine brightened. "Yes, that was me, but it was very funny, you up to your knees in a snowdrift, trying to dig out your fancy Jag. You were so angry, acting as if the snow were a personal affront."

"Well, if memory serves me right, I was wearing Italian loafers that night."

"Your first mistake," Katherine told him firmly.

"And my second?" Daniel asked, straightfaced.

"Why, trying to go anywhere in six inches of fresh snow, and in a Jaguar!"

"You're right! I should have taken the Porsche," he said agreeably, his mouth quirked in good humor.

"A hard-won lesson, was it not? For goodness sake, Daniel Boylan, don't you own anything as pedestrian as a Jeep?"

And now they were two strangers standing in the middle of the foyer, laughing quietly at an absurd memory.

"Well, I'm glad you remember me," Katherine said cheerfully. "I wouldn't want you to think I was some silly groupie."

"A groupie? On my account?" Daniel asked, incredulous.

Katherine's green eyes danced with excitement. "If what I hear is true—and it's what everyone here is saying—then the idea isn't all that outlandish, Mr. Ambassador!"

An uncomfortable glance past her shoulder told Daniel she was right. People were still staring. Christ, everyone must know what was up. Well, damned if, in future, he wouldn't be more selective what he told his family. It sure seemed they didn't know how to keep a secret. Katherine found his irritation puzzling.

"Why the surprise, Daniel? Those reporters at the gate, the extra security guards your dad hired. You didn't really think that was all for Deirdre's engagement party, did you? Your mom's been in a flutter all day, the way the phone's been ringing off the hook, and your dad can talk of nothing else except his son, *the ambassador*."

"It would be nice to allow the president of the United States to do his own appointing and not my parents!" he observed with heavy irony. "I'm not even sure of the appointment. There are two other men who are also in the running and they're every bit as qualified as I. And anyway, I don't want this to interfere with Dee's engagement announcement."

"As if she'd care!" Katherine scorned, "with her big brother about to become the next American Ambassador to France!"

"Maybe!" Daniel sighed, weary of the argument.

"All right, *maybe*!" Katherine allowed, her pretty green eyes rolling heavenward. "Look here, Daniel, why don't you get rid of your coat, and I'll help you search for your mother. She's put everyone on red alert for your arrival, and you'll only hurt her feelings if you don't say hello to her first thing.''

Relinquishing his coat to an unfamiliar servant hovering nearby, he scanned the hall, looking for a familiar face, but he didn't recognize a soul.

"You aren't shy, by any chance?" Katherine asked doubtfully when she saw the way his eyes darted about.

Surprised, Daniel shook his head. "No room for that in my profession. If you want the truth, I just don't like parties all that much.''

Katherine was openly amused. "An unfortunate cross for an ambassador to bear! Are you sure you're going into the right profession?" she teased as they threaded their way through the small crowd to stop beside an elegant paneled door.

A good question, Daniel thought as the high pitch of female laughter reached his ears.

"This is where we part company," Katherine said, motioning toward the door. "You're on, Mr. Boylan.''

"Aren't you coming in with me?" he asked uneasily.

"This is your show, Mr. Boylan. Oh, no! Don't tell me you're nervous! Where's all that savoir faire and charm diplomats are so famous for?''

Daniel smiled as he reached out to give a gentle tug to one of Katherine's errant golden curls. "You misunderstand the situation, Miss Harriman. I can face down the president of the United States, the vice president, and even his cabinet, if need be. But that's...that's my mother in there!''

"And that's what mothers are for!" Katherine chuckled. "To make grown men tremble!''

"Will you be that kind of mother?''

"No question about it!''

"No question?''

"Daniel, you're stalling!''

"So I am." With a resigned but comical twist to his features, Daniel turned the doorknob. "All right, here goes. But wait! I want your word—promise to find me later.''

"You mean if you survive?" Katherine teased.

"Will you promise?"

"You're stalling!"

"Promise!"

"Okay, okay, I promise!"

He watched, charmed by the little wave she sent him as she backed away into the crowd. He felt fortified by her promise. If he survived the hour, Katherine Harriman would be his reward.

Katherine hadn't gone far, just around the bend, before she collapsed against the wall in a heap of breathless confusion, wondering what had just happened. *Tall, dark and good-looking, that's what!* she berated herself. With a pair of puppy-dog eyes that made you want to scoop the man up and cuddle him to death. The very idea made her laugh. As if! The puppy topped six feet!

Considering he was about to become a Very Important Man he seemed strangely unhappy. What on earth had happened to Daniel Boylan since she'd seen him last? He'd been such a social animal, way back when, running around just as she'd described. At least he'd seemed to be enjoying himself, which he was definitely not doing today!

Thirty minutes later, Daniel was inching toward the door, living proof of Katherine's intuition, as he wiped his brow. His mom had done all he'd dreaded, embarrassed him completely as she showed him off to all her friends. It wasn't until Deirdre chanced to put her head in the door that he had the excuse he needed to escape.

"Hey, Dee," he called, and Deirdre's chocolate-colored eyes lit up.

"Oh, Daniel! You made it!"

"Of course I made it," he said, rushing from the room. "Did you really think I'd miss my baby sister's engagement party?"

"Last I heard, most of the airports were closed because of snow."

"Not the airport in Paris, goose. But I made sure to catch

a flight into Kennedy, after I heard the New York weather report, even if it took a little longer to get here. My limo driver was an expert.''

''You hired a limousine?'' Deirdre grinned. ''My, my, aren't we getting a bit extravagant?''

''How else did you expect me to get here?'' he asked defensively. ''Or were you planning to pick me up?''

''Oh, Daniel, I'm only teasing. You're so sensitive.''

''You think so?'' he asked laughing, ''Did I miss anything?''

''Yes! The first three hours of my engagement party! And don't tell me you couldn't help it!'' she said with a threatening finger. ''You've known about it for at least two months! And if I know you, you were getting ready to give me some hogwash excuse for being late! And just look at you.'' Her lips pursed, Deirdre studied her brother with the critical eye of a sister. ''Gray tie, gray shirt, gray silk suit. Is gray the latest color in ambassadors?''

''I hope that black is the latest color in ambassadors,'' Daniel teased. ''But that was supposed to be a secret, something the family seems to have forgotten.''

''Sorry, Daniel, but it's way too late. Didn't you see the *Times* today, and maybe every other newspaper in America? Or the television news? Or listen to the radio, even?''

Deirdre was astonished when her brother shook his head. ''I slept most of the way over. The plane was pretty empty.''

''That's because anyone who was supposed to be somewhere today was already there!'' she told him pointedly.

Dutifully, Daniel bowed his head. ''I stand before you, chastened, bereft of any excuse for being late and truly apologetic.''

Deirdre Boylan's elegant, thin brows arched. ''Are you making fun of me?''

Daniel stepped back, palms up, his smile tipping the corners of his mouth. ''Never, sis, never!''

A thoughtful smile curved her own mouth. Her brother knew exactly how to work the charm, when it suited. It was a large part of his success. Oh, he could say what he wanted about his ugly old mug, but she knew what she saw, and what she saw was that women couldn't keep away from him, and that men deferred to his authority, authority that was about to realize its full potential under the aegis of genuine power. Heady stuff for a black guy from Long Island! But she knew he could handle it. Not a moment's doubt. Helping herself to a glass of wine a passing waiter proffered, she handed one to Daniel and raised her own in a toast. "Daniel, it may be that even as we speak, I'm looking at America's next Ambassador to France! And if it's true, I want to be the first to drink to your health."

"Dee," Daniel warned, "you're looking at the underdog. Harvard law isn't enough. I hear tell that my age, or lack thereof, is working against me. The White House is looking for someone older, more mature, and with a whole lot more experience. Someone who's paid his dues."

"Well, I hear tell differently and so has everyone else at this party. Oh, Daniel, get real!" Deirdre chided when she saw his face fall. "Everyone in this house is talking about nothing else! Better go check out those newspapers. There are at least a dozen copies in the library. It seems that while you were sleeping on that plane, your friend in the White House attended one of those fancy D.C. parties, where they must have been serving the same whisky as Daddy. Seems like the president was persuaded to reveal the names of three main contenders to the ambassadorship and yours was number one. I can't even remember the other names," she said with a dismissive wave of her glass. "They don't count anymore because you were the only black man on that list. It's all over the radio this morning how the White House switchboard is being bombarded—bombarded, brother mine!— with phone calls. From black bigwigs all over the country! They're insisting how it's high time an African-American be appointed ambassador. It's long overdue, which everybody knows, anyway, and it's time to do something about it!"

Daniel swore, suddenly feeling uneasy. He wanted the

ambassadorship on his own merits, not because a black caucus pressured for it.

"And," Deirdre added smugly, "those calls aren't only from those Jesse Jackson-type power brokers, but from regular folks—black and white!—all over the country, from Mississippi, the Ozarks, California, and, oh, everywhere, Daniel, just everywhere! Isn't it wonderful? They want a black man in that old embassy, Mr. Boylan, and I do believe they are about to get one. So, the only thing I want to know is, when is the announcement going to be? Or can't that white man in the fancy White House get up the nerve to let a fine, upstanding African-American like yourself through the front gate, for once, instead of the back door?"

Daniel glanced around the crowded hall, wondering if anyone was listening. Deirdre peered at him suspiciously. "Can't I say what I want in my own house?" she asked indignantly.

Daniel looked at the feisty young woman who certainly had a right to speak her mind anywhere, and often did. "Frankly, no, Deirdre, not when you have every Tom, Dick and Harry crossing your doorstep, one of them probably a reporter! Ten of them, more likely."

"Is that the way it's going to be, then?"

Daniel grinned crookedly. "Only if you want to visit me at the American embassy in France."

Deirdre studied her brother, understanding full well that he stood on the threshold of history. She would do nothing to hurt him, there were enough people waiting in the wings to do just that. "All right," she shrugged, "not another word. We'll go find Daddy before this crowd notices you're standing still."

"Thanks, Dee, and don't worry. I'm sure you'll know who the new ambassador is before I do. Probably before the *Times* does, too," he added with a laugh. "So if you'd let this all go for a few minutes, I would like to meet the reason for this party. I must be the only one in the family who hasn't met your fiancé."

Daniel smiled at the uneasy look that crossed his sister's face. "Has your fiancé abandoned you already?"

"Pops stole him!" Deirdre bristled. "He's hiding out in the library with Daddy and his friends, smoking those smelly cigars and drinking that fancy whisky just as fast as they can pour it. And if I know Henry, he's probably sick to his stomach by now! I heard Mom complaining, too."

"Kidnapped from his own engagement party? This doesn't bode well, Dee," Daniel teased.

"Oh, Daniel," Deirdre explained patiently, as they headed for the library, "everybody knows that engagement parties are for girls. The guy is just window dressing."

It took them a while to get there, everyone wanting to welcome the newest star on the horizon. The party wasn't half bad, once Daniel had armed himself with a cold beer and allowed Deirdre to take him in hand. He knew she was dying to show him off. Half of Sarah Lawrence was there, and he was glad he had that beer in hand. It made it easier to nod and smile, which was all he had to do. Everyone crowded around him asking so many questions, it was impossible to answer any single one. Everyone apparently had read the morning papers, just as Deirdre had warned. The president was obviously out to garner some free publicity while he kept the country guessing. Well, hell, the president of the United States could do whatever he damned well wanted, couldn't he? Daniel supposed, and wondered if the other men on the short list were as embarrassed as he by such public juggling. It was possible that, like the president, they enjoyed the limelight.

With Deirdre talking a mile a minute, Daniel found he didn't even have to speak, just stand around, look good and smile agreeably. In silence there was greatness, Daniel surmised ruefully. Most of the guests just wanted to shake his hand, anyway, then go brag how they'd met Daniel Sheridan Boylan. Name-dropping was a popular sport. For sure, they didn't want to talk about the drought in the Sudan. Then his eyes met a pair of dancing green ones, clear across the room. A smile crossed his face as he raised his glass.

"You remember Katherine Harriman?" Deirdre asked in surprise when her eyes followed his.

"I do," he said as he strode across the room, leaving Deirdre to trail behind.

"Alive and well, I see, Mr. Boylan." Katherine grinned as she met them halfway.

"And I'm glad to see you kept your promise, Miss Harriman."

"Truthfully, it wasn't planned."

"But I would have made sure."

"Would somebody mind telling me what's going on?" Deirdre asked, confused by their conversation. "Did I miss something?"

"Katherine was at the door when I arrived, so we had time to renew old acquaintance," Daniel explained, his eyes never leaving Katherine.

"I didn't know there was anything to renew," Deirdre said, her eyes shifting from one to the other.

"There wasn't, at first," Katherine agreed, "but I managed to jog Daniel's memory." And she was glad. She studied his large frame, broad shoulders, the taut pull of muscles that his suit couldn't hide. She colored fiercely when she raised her eyes to find him watching her, in turn, amusement in his dark eyes.

"Hold on here, guys. I must be having a senior moment!" Katherine laughed gently. "Oh, you remember, Dee. The night Daniel came to pick you up and there was that sudden blizzard and his car got stuck?"

Deirdre wrinkled her nose. "Yes, I remember. What's so special about that?"

"Nothing!" Daniel and Katherine answered in unison.

Oh, my, Deirdre thought, when she saw the sheepish smiles Daniel and Katherine exchanged. Looks like something else got jogged besides Daniel's memory! She took an experimental step back. Yeah, they didn't even notice. It was almost like watching a play, the way Daniel placed his hand on Katherine's elbow, steered her to an alcove, turning his back on the room.

If she'd been privileged to listen, Deirdre would have laughed at the nonsense they spoke, these two highly educated creatures. Nice party. Pretty dress. Great food. Yes, his mother had been tolerably nice. Their eyes did all the real talking—admiring, intent, discreetly appraising. Two people, well-met, at a fancy dress ball—until Deirdre intruded.

"I'm glad you two are getting along so well," she said cheerfully. "But if I can tear you away, Daniel, you still haven't met Henry, my fiancé. You know, the guy I'm engaged to? What this party is all about?"

The blank look he gave her was replaced with chagrin, while Katherine scrambled to her feet. Deirdre felt as though she'd interrupted something personal, the way they were carrying on, and she was barely able to keep the laughter from her voice. "You know, Henry knocked me down, too, the first time I ever met him." She was delighted by the look of surprise they sent her. Katherine was a very good friend and a really nice person, and Daniel could definitely use a really nice person in his life, with what he was about to go through.

"No, no, he really did!" she laughed, enjoying their innocence. "He literally knocked me down, rushing to some old lab. He's always rushing to a lab. He's a chemist—did you know that, Daniel?—studying for his Ph.D. So there it was, a classic episode in the life of the absent-minded professor. Really, guys, it was so-o-o trite! And what was worse, by the time he helped me sort my books and papers, I was in love."

"Oh, come on, Dee," Daniel said, disbelieving, until Katherine spoke up.

"She's right, you know. Just wait till you see them together!"

Her arms folded across her chest, Deirdre eyed him fondly. "That's right, brother mine, love at first sight. It happens, you know. You'll see. And when it happens to you," she predicted gloomily, poking a perfectly filed fingernail into his chest, "remind me to be somewhere else. I hate the sight of blood." She snickered.

Daniel was caught unawares by the fantasy Deirdre's warning triggered, a blurry image that oddly, included Katherine. *Shrugging off his overcoat as he came home from work to find her studying a recipe, nuzzling at her neck, pushing aside the cookbook, persuading her to start dinner with dessert. Turning her in his arms, her laughter egging him on as she melted against him. Soft, sugary kisses, creamy arms wrapped about his neck, her sweet curves neatly pressed to his....* Horrified, Daniel quickly shrugged away the thought. It meant nothing, just a result of Deirdre getting dramatic while he filled in the empty spaces.

"Oh, well," Deirdre declared, thoroughly satisfied with her handiwork. "Time to go. If it's okay with you, Katherine, we'll catch up with you later?"

Katherine wanted a chance to pull her thoughts together. She watched them walk away with relief. Something had just happened but she couldn't figure out what. She'd been invisible to Daniel Boylan for years, but now, tonight, suddenly he saw her, actually saw her, and she was hard put to understand why. An uptown guy going places, it was too late for a flirtation! She was just a small-town girl trying to make a living in the big city—no important plans for her future, and none wanted, thank you very much! It would be best for her to remember that and not let herself be diverted by a pair of playful golden eyes. Playful, yes, that was it! It was a lovely night at a lovely party. Guests were supposed to be merry and enter into the spirit—and she and Daniel had—no more than that.

Daniel could smell the acrid smoke of cigars before he even got close to his father's library, and it was a blue wall they faced when Deirdre peeked through the library door.

"Guess what?" she whispered over her shoulder. "I do believe there's a bachelor party taking place in there."

"Now, that's more like it." Daniel grinned. "Okay, sis, go on back to your party. I'll scope this one out for myself. You wouldn't enjoy it, anyway, all those stockbrokers soused to the gills."

"And don't forget the half-dozen lawyers lurking in the background, scrounging around for stock tips. Okay, I'll go, but only because you promised to stay the night. I have about a thousand things I want to tell you."

"If you're planning to wax enthusiastic about Henry Cobbs, you can forget about it," Daniel teased. "And I'm letting you know right now that I'm heading for D.C. first thing in the morning. The French delegation took great pleasure in dragging out that conference in Provence—"

"Ah-ha!"

"Okay, okay, I admit I was late! But I also haven't been home in two weeks. I need to check my apartment, look over the mail, that sort of thing."

"Daniel Boylan, just listen to you talk. *Check my apartment. Look over the mail.* It doesn't sound like much of a home to me."

"It's what I call home."

"If you had a wife, she'd make you a real home," she persisted, not afraid to speak her mind.

Daniel sighed. When Deirdre was on, there was no stopping her, and her next words justified his fear.

"Too bad you don't have nerve enough to ask Althea Almott to marry you."

"Deirdre!"

Deirdre didn't bat an eyelash. He was the one in the diplomatic corps, not her. "I wonder if she's here, yet," she mused, a mischievous gleam in her eyes. "I'd guess not, since you were hanging out with Katherine!"

"Deirdre!"

"Okay! Okay! Go smoke those yucky cigars and make yourself sick. But I'm only giving you half an hour! And you can tell that to Mr. Henry Cobbs, too!" Deirdre shouted after him as he disappeared into the smoky library.

Men of every size, shape and color filled the library, and when they saw who had entered, all rose to their feet to applaud, while Daniel's father hurried to his side.

"Daniel, Daniel, welcome home, son!" Throwing wide his long arms, James Boylan enveloped his son in a bear hug. "Gentlemen, I know I'm not supposed to say this, but since you've all heard the rumors...I give you my son, the American Ambassador to France!"

"Pops!"

But the room only roared louder.

"Come on, Dan," someone shouted, "we all read the morning papers—"

"Or cruised the Internet!"

"Congratulations, Danny-boy. Your name's on the front page of every Web site known to man."

"Yeah, let your father enjoy you, kid," an old family friend advised, clasping Daniel's shoulder. "It's all he has left in his old age. Or so he's been trying to convince us over the last couple of hours."

"It's the truth," James Boylan insisted mournfully. "This morning, when I woke, my heart was beating like I'd just run a marathon."

"Aw, that was just Mary handing you the bill for this shindig."

"Yeah, Jimbo! Just wait till you get dunned for Deirdre's wedding! Oh, yeah, you're gonna be one happy camper then, my friend, let me tell you!"

"I tell you, gentlemen, I'm not long for this world!" James groaned. "Where's the damned brandy?"

The whole room laughed as they watched him fill his glass and fill one for Daniel, too. James Boylan might be gray, but at fifty-some-odd years, he was hale as any forty-year-old and knew it. But he loved to complain, and everybody knew that, too, so they humored him, and dismissed his worry as so much talk. Besides, picking his son's brain about the president of the United States was much more exciting.

Giving up any illusions of secrecy he'd cherished, Daniel

allowed them to ask, but he was careful not to reveal anything of value. Having lived in the limelight since becoming a partner in a prestigious New York law firm, he was always on the alert, wary and apprehensive about the notoriety thrust on him. Famous to the point of obscenity, in his personal opinion, when all he'd ever wanted was to study law and aim for a judgeship somewhere down the line, he was sometimes accused of being overly sensitive, and not only by Deirdre.

He knew better.

Let down his guard and he was fair game. A black man from a wealthy family, he was a special target with every move he made. When he was in the mood, he was philosophical about his celebrity status. He tried to tell himself it was no different than any movie star's or athlete's—black or white. Or serial killer's, he told himself in his more cynical moods, because fame was a harsh teacher. Equanimity was hard to maintain when one found oneself cornered by the press in a hotel bathroom! But raised to be kind, he'd learned early on to become deft at skirting issues. So that now, settling into a comfortable armchair and lighting a cigar, he was easily able to deflect the barrage of questions his father's friends hurled at him, without hurting anybody's feelings. By nodding affably. By sipping a beer. By insisting on an introduction to Deirdre's fiancé.

"Well, sure enough, son. I'd forgotten you two gentlemen had nevah met. Hey, there, young fella," James Boylan called to a group of men in the corner. "C'mon over here, son, and meet your future brother-in-law."

Daniel loved when his father got that southern accent going, as if he'd left the South only last month instead of forty years ago, with Yale University in between!

But *My God!* he thought, unable to hide his shock when a slight young man rose to his feet and extended his milky-white hand.

"Pleased to meet you, sir," the young man said softly.

Daniel looked into Henry Cobbs's pale-blue eyes and marveled at the secret his family had managed to keep.

"Ah, er, gentlemen," James Boylan said, turning to his guests when he saw the look on Daniel's face. "I would like to ask you all, um, would you excuse us for a moment?"

The room emptied at once, the guests, understanding that the Boylan men needed time alone, urged out by the promise of another large selection of whisky to be found in the den down the hall.

"Yes," said James Boylan heavily. Daniel's dismay was evident as the door closed behind the last guest. "I know exactly how you feel, Daniel. He's all the wrong color!"

His hand on Henry's shoulder, James eyed his future son-in-law with something akin to amusement. "And rest assured, we've had that out, a number of times! An interracial marriage." He sighed. "Who'd have thought? But I have to warn you, he's grown on us."

Henry faced Daniel bravely, and Daniel felt a twinge of sympathy for the guy. But not much; he felt his temper rising as Henry tried to explain, ever so reasonably, how things stood.

"Deirdre and I fell in love just like any other young couple. Our skin color was never an issue. It all happened too fast. I was looking in her eyes when Cupid shot his bow."

"He really does talk like that," James warned his son as he handed Daniel a bourbon.

Imperturbable Henry continued. "Oh, I know I don't meet with your family's requirements. In particular, I know I fall sadly short of your parents' expectations, which were perfectly legitimate. They worked hard to raise Deirdre with a careful and studied consciousness of your race, one that no doubt precluded marrying out of it. Ah, yes, I can see the shock on your face. One shouldn't speak of these things. But one should, they exist! And we are talking about it in the context of matrimony. This party means nothing, no matter what Deirdre says. If you are so against our marriage, I will bow to your wishes. This is too big not to be an issue, and

I would not see her split from her family. It would not bode well for our future.''

"Hear! Hear!" That from James.

"But you're…you're white!" Daniel said, stunned.

"Yes, I am, aren't I?" Henry agreed wryly. "Look, Daniel, it's no secret that everyone in the family is concerned about Deirdre marrying me. No more or less than many a white family would feel about a black man wanting to marry their daughter. Please, Mr. Boylan, don't deny it, it's true!" he said gently, when James shook his head.

"No, Henry, I won't deny it, but close up and personal, things tend to take on a different slant. Daniel, Henry's credentials are impeccable. Nothing could be less offensive than a chemist. His career is secure, and Deirdre's absolute adoration of the boy has been impossible to ignore. And you know Deirdre," James left off with a shrug.

Daniel didn't know what to say.

No way?

Where is Deirdre, I'd like to kill her?

Nothing suited. Most certainly not snowy-white Henry Cobbs. Dee couldn't have found a whiter white boy if she'd tried! Henry looked as though he hadn't seen the light of day since birth. Oh, yeah, the chemistry factor. All lab and no play.

"Well, hell, Pops, since I don't know what to say," Daniel said softly, trying to contain his temper, "why don't one of you explain why I wasn't told earlier on?" His voice spoke to his father, but Daniel's eyes were glued to Henry Cobbs.

Henry might be short and skinny but he was no coward, not even in the face of Daniel's anger. "It was expressly my wish not to keep you in ignorance," Henry said implacably. "I wanted to tell you—and everyone—from day one, when Deirdre and I began dating, but Deirdre wouldn't hear of it. She wouldn't tell anyone at first, but when we began to get serious, I absolutely insisted on telling her parents. I threatened to break things off if she refused," he said sententiously, "and she only agreed when she saw I was a man of my word. But Deirdre absolutely forbade anyone to tell you. She insisted you had a habit of browbeating her, and she didn't want you to interfere. I did point out that her reasoning was insufficient, that you were just representing a more worldly position. As her brother you had every right to do so. Indeed, she should be grateful that you care enough to do so. But she said that was exactly what she meant."

"What she meant?" Daniel repeated, thoroughly confused, and not a little hurt by Deirdre's decision.

"She said," Henry explained quietly, "that you cared too much, that you sometimes tried to run her life. The baby-sister syndrome." Henry spread his hands wide. "I could hardly insist, in light of her having informed your parents. One must pick and choose one's battles, you know, especially with Deirdre. To tell the truth, though I love your sister dearly, I do foresee a future in which I must tread carefully if I wish to assure us of any sort of connubial bliss."

Past Henry's shoulder, Daniel could see his father threatening to burst with laughter, but he himself was not so inclined. One look at his father told him that James was used to Henry's speechifying ways, and more importantly, was reconciled to the marriage. So the ball was in Daniel's court. Would he like to throw or pass?

Daniel threw. "Henry Cobbs, are you for real?"

Henry's smile was benign. "I agree with your graciously unspoken question, Daniel. The truth is, I don't know what Deirdre sees in me, either. And I know your family has wondered, also. But I love Deirdre, and I can promise you that if Deirdre honors me with her hand in marriage, I will cherish her all the days of my life. She will never regret her decision. And it will be for life. I don't believe in divorce, as I have told her. This will be a long engagement, at least a solid year, so Deirdre will have plenty of time to reconsider. Of course, your parents are excellent role models for the sanctity of marriage, so I have hopes. But we will have the additional stress of an interracial marriage.'' Henry shrugged. "It will be a very long engagement.''

"And your family?'' Daniel wanted to know.

"My family is three thousand miles away. Having been informed, and been unamused, they wished us luck and sent a check. A small check, I might add.''

"And you, Henry Cobbs? Do you know what you're doing, marrying the original African-American princess?''

Henry smiled with genuine amusement, and Daniel caught a glimpse of what Deirdre might see in him. "I love Deirdre to distraction but that doesn't mean I have blinders on. She's quite spoiled…er, rather…she's a bit untidy in her ways,'' he amended when he saw James glare. "But that sorts itself out with maturity and children—don't you agree? As to her color,'' he said, looking Daniel straight in the eye, "I won't hold it against her. She looks good with a tan. A whole damned sight better than me.''

James could contain himself no longer. He shook with laughter, his eyes streaming, while Henry sent him a look of long-suffering tolerance.

Daniel guessed that was how Henry planned to deal with his future family-in-law, speechifying with fancy words until they were numb.

"Is this about money?'' Daniel demanded coldly. At which Henry finally showed some color—beet red—and temper—white hot—as he jumped to his feet.

"I will forgive you that insult because I know you don't know me, and I assure you with as much vehemence as I can muster that this is not about money! I have already proven to your father—to his complete satisfaction, I might add—that as I am a tad older than Deirdre, my money has long been carefully and conservatively invested. Our finances will never be an issue, you may rest easy on that point. We will never ask you for a sou.''

"Nor a dollar?'' Daniel muttered, rubbing his tired eyes.

"And any money your family wishes to bestow on Deirdre will go directly to her and our children, as she sees fit.''

The room waited in silence.

"In the end, it's not a matter of color, you know," Henry said quietly. "You may not like it and you may try to stop it, but you cannot help it—the heart wants what the heart wants."

The heart wants what the heart wants.

Henry's words gave Daniel pause. And wasn't it so true? Obliged to attend a law chambers' party a few years back in a major Manhattan club, hadn't he been hiding out in a corner with a friend, trying to ignore the major headache the band gave him, when a magnificent woman passed by? Matchstick thin, tall and elegant, her ebony skin incandescent against the gold lamé of her gown. Not the sort of woman he was wont to date, but how to explain the impulse?

"There goes Althea Almott," his buddy had whispered in awe. "One of the hottest models in the business. They call her the Goddess of Night."

Daniel had laughed so hard that Althea had turned to look his way, her million-dollar cat eyes zooming in on him. He still marveled at how she'd walked up to him, wordlessly taken his hand and led him to the dance floor. Thank goodness the band was playing something slow and mellow. Pretty soon, they were looking for their coats.

And that was that.

Daniel liked being seen with Althea, maybe his only vanity. A star in her own constellation in a notoriously tough industry, Althea Almott had it all. Intelligent, gorgeous, energetic and self-made. Daniel counted himself lucky to have attracted her interest at all. When duty had forced him to behave like a social animal, he'd called her up more often, relied on her social acumen to see him through many a torturous party. And damned if she didn't seem to know everyone. It didn't matter if they were in New York, L.A., London or even Paris, where his office had begun to send him more and more. Everyone knew her, and he rode her coattails. He could depend on her, so he did.

And now, at that very moment, Althea Almott sailed into

the silence of the library, invading their territory, as he had no doubt she was aware. Daniel had to admire her nerve, but then, he knew that very little fazed Althea.

"Daniel, finally! Darling, I've missed you so much." Her eyes warm and glowing, Althea wrapped her arms about his neck, her graceful figure almost matching his in height so that it was no effort to kiss him soundly.

Daniel cringed. He hated public spectacles, even if only in front of the family. But Althea was a creature of fame, utterly comfortable in the spotlight, almost relishing it, so his discomfort went unnoticed. Or rather, ignored, because they had talked about it many times. Out of the corner of his eye, he could see the approving glance of his father. James adored Althea and Daniel supposed his dad was right, he was a lucky man. Why then, he wondered, didn't he rush to marry her? Why did he hesitate, keep everyone, including Althea, guessing, cautiously advising himself, *not yet*.

Her low, gravelly voice, the one that sent shivers down the spines of most red-blooded men, demanded his attention. "How long do you have this time, darling?"

He knew exactly what she meant. They'd had words over the brevity of his free time. "I have to be back in Paris by Tuesday."

"So soon?" she frowned. "Don't ambassadors get any time off?

Daniel felt his face grow hot. "Nothing has been announced," he said in a clipped voice, suddenly fed up with everyone's grandiose assumptions about his career. Untangling himself from Althea's arms, he was brusque. "No matter what everyone here seems to think, I'm not an ambassador yet."

Althea brushed aside his denial with a short laugh. "Oh, honey, it's just a matter of time. Everybody says so, don't they, Mr. Boylan?" Althea asked, appealing to James for support. She hated arguing, it wasted too much energy, and she especially hated fighting with Daniel. He always seemed to win, his fancy Harvard words and cool, rich-boy demeanor no match for her inner-city high-school diploma. Besides, it had been weeks since they'd seen each other, and she didn't want to get off on the wrong foot. Until three days ago, she'd been on location in Brazil, too far for Daniel to commute, something he often did when she was in Europe.

"Pops, I'm warning you, I'm low man on the totem pole."

"Oh, please, Dan," his dad protested. "Everyone knows you're first in line for the job."

Only Henry said nothing.

That settled, Althea flashed the Boylan men a megawatt smile and asked to steal Daniel away, something she knew they would allow, because no one refused Althea anything when she smiled. She had long ago mastered the art of making one feel complicit, the only one who would understand whatever it was she wanted you to understand. Hours late for a shoot? I am so sorry, she would apologize and trot out that famous grin, earning instant redemption. More than once she had used it on Daniel, and he knew the goofy way even he fell for it was no different from any of those poor saps who wrote her frenzied love letters every time her picture appeared on the front page of a national rag. Even now, knowing full well that he was annoyed with her, he still let her grin seduce him as she dragged him down the hall.

Until she stopped and turned in her tracks to give him a soul-searing kiss. She grabbed hold of his lapels and gave him a full-bodied, full-blown, full-mouth kiss, just the thing to make him burn.

With embarrassment. Her eyes might be closed with passion, but his were wide with apprehension. Any number of reporters could be lurking about, and he really would rather not give the press a field day with a vulgar, lip-smacking photo for tomorrow's front page! Especially if he were to win the ambassadorship! And he had long since learned that, like God, the press moved in mysterious ways. Glancing down the hall to see if anyone was watching, he was flustered to glimpse a bit of red darting round the corner. Silently, he swore. "Come on, Althea, let's find someplace more private."

Amused, she let him lead her down the hall, but as they turned the corner, they realized that they didn't have a chance. Deirdre's engagement party had spilled over into the hallway and up the gleaming marble staircase. Guests perched in twos and threes on the treads. The long balcony, too, was filled to capacity with young, handsome, laughing faces, their hands flapping, their conversation animated, their beautiful, sleek bodies draped along the gleaming banister as they sipped champagne and called out to their friends below.

Sarah Lawrence at play, Daniel mused as he and Althea carefully picked their way through the crowd.

And suddenly, he felt old.

A rush of inexplicable sadness enveloped him. He felt as if he were suffocating in the youthful ocean of laughter surrounding him. He and Althea didn't belong, they were too old, no longer on the brink, not in the same way these youngsters were. He found himself propelling her forward, overwhelmed by an odd urgency to leave. But someone spotted him from the balcony and frustrated their escape.

"Daniel, Althea! Hey, you two, up here!"

Daniel looked up to see Rudy Pierson waving wildly from the balcony and directly behind him Rudy's wife—Daniel's older sister, May—frowning down at them. Following Althea up the stairs, he was careful not to step on any fingers, nodding to the few faces he recognized. Or who recognized him. Deirdre was always dragging someone home for the weekend. Like Katherine. The one face he wished he'd remembered.

May Sheridan Boylan Pierson was accounted the beauty of the family, and, seeing how she glittered in that slinky blue dress, Daniel thought it was probably true. She greeted him with a warm hug, although she was very careful not to let him ruin her lipstick or muss her hair. On the other hand, her cool salute to Althea was no threat to her perfection, and no surprise to Daniel. Rudy had long since confided May's dislike of Althea. And since the feeling was mutual, Althea's makeup also stayed intact.

"Hey, Danny, my man, how's it going?" With absolutely no agenda other than to be likeable, Rudy greeted his brother-in-law with a mighty backslap. "Sorry, Danny-boy, did I hurt the merchandise?" He laughed, massaging Daniel's massive shoulders playfully. A weight trainer by profession, Rudy's massage hurt even more than his backslap, and he knew it. And, as ever, he took great pleasure in ruffling his staid brother-in-law's carefully arranged feathers.

But, genuinely liking Rudy, Daniel was tolerant of his clowning. And, safe in the knowledge that he himself worked out religiously, he dared to tease Rudy back. "Hey, my man." Daniel grinned. "Are you asking me to go one-on-one? Do you really want to head down to the basement gym and see who's made of brown sugar?"

"Anytime, Danny-boy, any old time you think you're ready. Just make sure your will's in order," Rudy warned, giving Daniel's bicep a hard squeeze. "Skip our morning workout, did we?"

"Geez, Rudy." Daniel groaned in not-so-exaggerated pain. "Do that to your clientele and you'll empty that brand-new fancy gym of yours in no time flat."

"Don't worry, bro', I save all the pain for you. I treat my clients with kid gloves. Gotta pay the rent, dude!"

"Well, I've got some new moves I want to show you personally, dude!"

"No problem, dude! Maybe later on tonight?" Rudy said, with a swift glance at his wife.

"Under orders, Rudy?" Daniel teased, knowing how hen-pecked Rudy was.

"Very strict orders," May answered for her husband as she joined them. "And so are you, my brother, so no disappearing acts."

"Oh, May," Althea cut in, "Rudy's a grown man. Shouldn't he be able to do what he wants?"

"My husband knows that he can do whatever he wants," May retorted, her smile arctic, "as long as he has my permission."

"Do you think that's wise? A man needs space to breathe. I try to give Daniel the most freedom I can."

"A wise idea," May murmured.

Her mouth a thin line, Althea looked sharply at May, but before she could say anything, Deirdre appeared, Henry in tow.

Deirdre stood before Daniel, a warning light in her eyes. "Look, Daniel, I forgot to show you my ring. Isn't it just the most beautiful thing you ever saw?"

"Honesty is a beautiful thing, Dee."

"Daniel! Look, I know you're angry. Henry told me. But not now!"

"Not ever! Because you know what? You're right. You're a grown woman. You can make your own decisions. I'm just hurt you didn't confide in me. Maybe it was my fault."

"I would have, Daniel," Deirdre swore, instantly contrite. "But I didn't know how you'd feel about Henry and I didn't want to take any chances. I love him, I really do. Forgive me?"

Daniel took Deirdre's hand and lifted it high to get a close look at her diamond. The solitaire was huge, for a college professor's fiancée. "This diamond must have set you back quite a bit, Henry."

"Deirdre is worth it," he said solemnly.

"Yes, she is," he said quietly, and Deirdre knew she was forgiven.

"Thank you," she whispered as she threw her arms about his neck. Behind her, Althea beckoned to a nearby waitress. They would have a toast.

At first, the young woman didn't move, but as Deirdre turned and gave her a wide smile, she walked over to the Boylans, her tray a shaky affair.

"Thank you, my dear," Althea said, helping herself to a fluted glass.

"Althea!" Deirdre giggled. "Oh, Katherine, I'm so sorry! Althea, you just mistook the Sarah Lawrence class valedictorian for a waitress! For mercy's sake, Katherine, what are you doing with that silly tray?"

Katherine looked down at the tray she was holding. "I was helping out a waiter," she explained with a wry smile, "who was helping Charlie Tweed beat a hasty retreat to the men's room, bless his drunken heart."

"Charlie, that monster! I just knew I shouldn't have invited him. Was he really being sick?"

"Very!"

"Oh, how gross!" Deirdre groaned. "Well, you'd better get rid of that tray, Katherine, put it on that table over there, before someone else says something stupid. Oooh, I'm sorry, Althea." She blushed. "But you know what I mean."

"Well, I didn't realize. How could I have?"

"You couldn't have," Katherine defended Althea. "I understand perfectly." She knew she looked like a ragamuffin, but clothes and things were not a high priority for her. Her hair had refused to cooperate, her dress hung in all the wrong places, and fire-engine red was maybe the worst color in the world for her. Lifting the heavy skirt slightly, she smiled. "Something borrowed...from the wrong person, I guess. Next time, I'll call you, if I may!"

"We're not exactly the same size," Althea observed with a faint smile.

"Too true. Well, then, I guess it's a good thing I don't go to that many fancy parties." Katherine grinned. "And, hey, Princess Deirdre, what was that about waitressing, you little snob? It's a perfectly honest living!"

"Maybe, but it's not yours," Deirdre retorted, unrepentant.

Bored with the barely civil civilities, May roused herself. "My, my, will you just look at that?" she said, pointing to the sprig of mistletoe hanging high above them. "Katherine, you've gone and got yourself trapped beneath some mistletoe. I wonder who the lucky guy's going to be?'' she asked loudly.

Giving her brother a sharp jab in the ribs, May turned an innocent eye on Althea. "You don't mind if I borrow Daniel for a moment, do you, Althea? I believe you said something a moment ago about freedom?"

Althea burned. Knowing precisely what was coming down, she was powerless to stop May unless she wanted to make a scene. She would have dearly loved to put May in her place, and could have easily, but Daniel was another matter. He would never forgive her for making a scene at Deirdre's engagement party. And right now, their relationship was at a critical stage. She was sure he was on the verge of proposing, and she didn't want to make waves, not even ripples. "Of course, May, you do what you want. I trust Daniel."

Foolish girl, May thought.

"Daniel?"

If Daniel could have killed May just then, he would have, gladly, and he promised himself the pleasure next time they were alone. Damn that old mistletoe! Overlooked all afternoon, now it was found, and everyone wanted to share in the joke. By God, he would make sure May regretted her little trick. Katherine's embarrassment was as great as his, he knew, seeing the scarlet tint of her cheeks.

"Don't worry," he whispered. A smile plastered to his face, he cheered, "For Father Christmas," and pressed a light kiss to the corner of Katherine's mouth. The touch sent a jolt through his system.

"You call that a kiss?" someone hooted and Daniel spun round, ready to commit murder.

The hall went ballistic! This was the best way to end the party and they would have their ounce of Daniel's blood, on Katherine's lips, yes, they would! They started chanting, hooting, laying odds. Damn it to hell, Daniel thought, May must be suicidal, the way she stood there not doing a thing to help them out. Silently, he implored Rudy to put a stop to his wife's nonsense, but Rudy, a born coward, only laughed.

"Oh, yeah," someone called up. "We want a real kiss. Come on, Katey! Go, Danny, go!"

"Passion is all," May said quietly, her arms crossed, her smile so...feline.

"Go on, Androcles, give the crowd what it wants," Katherine said quietly. "I promise I won't bite."

"And I promise you that I will feed May to the next lion I meet," Daniel swore.

His hands moved gently down the small of her back and drew her into his arms. She smelled so good that Daniel automatically pulled her closer. Pliant beneath his hard grasp, she was a delicate sprite, her mouth its own tantalizing persuasion. Desire began to overtake him, he no longer needed the crowd to egg him on, as his mouth swooped down to cover hers.

Katherine, too, had felt the wave of passion roll between them. When his tongue brushed the seam of her mouth, her response was instantaneous. Her lips parted; she was helpless as his tongue searched hers out, devouring its softness. She clung to his lapels, shocked by her own eager response, suddenly knowing how it felt to free fall—mindlessly frightening and beyond exhilaration. When he finally raised his mouth and gazed into her eyes, she knew desire.

A cannonade of applause brought them back to earth. "Crowd control," Katherine murmured and started to smile. It died at the sight of Daniel's face, at the dismay he was trying to hide. Bravely, she threw back her shoulders and walked over to May, leaving Daniel to the crowd that swallowed him up.

"May Pierson." Katherine smiled, but her voice was a low threat. "What devil has inhabited your soul?"

Incorrigible, May laughed. "Blame it all on that witch, Althea," she whispered back. "She's got her claws dug so deep in my brother, it makes my blood boil. I just wanted to rock her boat. Sorry, Katherine, but you were in the right spot at the right time.''

"For you!''

"All right. I owe you big-time.'' May admitted. "But please don't be too angry at me. I couldn't help it. I love my brother so much, and he's throwing away his life. I just don't seem to be able to get through to him! I thought this might shake him up. I hope so, because I don't know what else to do!''

Katherine shook her head. She had been friends with the Boylan girls since her freshman year at college when Deirdre had dragged her home one long winter weekend. The whole family had adopted her, loving her soft-spoken ways and gentle demeanor, except for Daniel, a busy young lawyer for some fancy New York law firm, who had no time to spare for unfinished college girls.

That had been seven years ago. Long enough for him to forget the half-woman, half-girl, mostly scrawny waif who'd left her heart on his doorstep.

Chapter Two

Overwhelmed by the raucous crowd and stunned by his response to Katherine's kiss, Daniel bolted.

He sped down the hall to his old room, knowing that his mother kept it dusted, always in readiness for his visits home. But when he reached the door, something made him keep walking, steered his feet toward his mother's tiny sewing room, her inner sanctum, as she liked to call it. No one outside the family knew it existed, but then, no one outside the family knew her for the expert seamstress that she was. He slid through the door. It was getting late, but the bay window had never been curtained, so the room wasn't entirely dark.

A huge, old-time Singer set in a massive wrought-iron base, complete with treadle, was the center attraction. Bolts of cloth, in a rainbow of bright colors, were strewn across a long Formica worktable. A cupboard stood ajar, overflowing with spools of thread in every color imaginable. Measuring tapes, packets of needles, jars of pins, scissors of every type, fabric binding, zippers and little piles of buttons, boxes of buttons, jars of buttons, all the accoutrement of a seamstress, littered the room. His mother staunchly defended her right to the chaos, and no one questioned her because they knew that beneath the chaos was order. Besides, they loved it, too. As children, he and his sisters had adored the kaleidoscopic disorder and brought their toys here to play by her feet while she sewed, the soft hum of the Singer a comforting, industrious sound.

Crossing to the window, Daniel felt a piercing longing for those days, when life had been simpler. He sighed as he gazed out at the lawn of snow. Memories as vivid as the colors of thread that lay at hand, surrounded him. May, the beautiful teenager, reading the latest fan magazine while she polished her nails, more interested in movie stars than the homework that lay abandoned at her feet. Deirdre, tiny baby Deirdre, her black curls bobbing as she made endless secret pacts with her Barbies. His mother, hunched over her beloved Singer as she stitched together curtains, dresses, shirts and pillows that she could easily have afforded to buy. And Daniel, long past the age of toys, sprawled out on the rug, his homework a neat stack at his fingertips. A little bit of an outsider, the family scholar who didn't say much as he scribbled and indexed, he never missed a beat of his family's lazy, hazy conversation. And he was still able to keep one ear cocked for his father's footsteps, that his mother somehow always managed to be the first to hear.

But now, perched on the seat of the huge bay window, watching as fresh snow began to fall, Daniel forced himself back to the present. The party must be winding down—and none too soon, he thought, his mouth a grim line as he watched a young couple hurry to their car. Though the last thing he wanted to think about was what had just happened, the sight of a beautiful pair of green eyes had been branded on his soul. He was sure only he had seen, he had prayed only he had seen the unmistakable sheen those eyes had betrayed.

And good lord, Althea! She must be furious! And not only with May. Even if she hadn't been aware of his response to Katherine, she had been May's intended victim, and the slight to her pride would not go unnoticed. With justification. This past fall, May had waged a campaign against Daniel and Althea's possible marriage, but with this last maneuver, May had gone beyond bounds. Even if she hated the idea that Daniel would consider a loveless union, it was his decision. Wasn't that why Deirdre had kept her own affair with Henry a secret, to minimize family interference? Exactly as May was interfering now.

And if he really were going to be offered the European assignment, it would be best to go with a wife. He would need a hostess and no one could handle that job better than Althea. Besides, he wasn't getting any younger and neither was Althea. Her eyes were wide open, they had talked about having a family. May would have to be told in no uncertain terms to mind her own business. He would have to—

The squeak of the door, a shimmer of red.

"Excuse me, Daniel?" Katherine called softly.

Daniel turned to stare at the young woman peering around the door. Wary, her hand grasping the knob, she seemed ready for flight.

"Yes?"

"I don't mean to intrude, but—"

"But?"

"I'd like to talk to you for a minute, if it's okay?"

"How did you know where to find me? How did you know about this room?"

"Your mom showed it to me, once. She told me it was the family's inner sanctum."

"*Family* being the operative word," Daniel said tersely.

"I know," Katherine admitted, feeling a little guilty as she slid into the room. But closing the door, she didn't move far. "I had a hunch you'd head this way, as far from the party as possible. Daniel, I feel terrible about what happened out there, and I just couldn't leave things the way they were.''

"'Things' aren't anything," Daniel snapped.

"Well, that's good. At least, I guess so…" Katherine trailed off uncertainly. His body a stiff silhouette against the huge bay window, she was unsure how to continue. She was even more uncomfortable when he turned his back and spoke to the gray winter sky.

"Look, Katherine, I know it wasn't your fault. You and I were part of a…a plot.''

"A plot?" she repeated, with a small laugh of surprise. "How melodramatic.''

His face grim, Daniel turned to Katherine. If Katherine had been hard put to gauge his mood before, she wouldn't be now. "I know for a fact that May is mad at me—never mind what for—but this was her way of sending me a message, and you were her courier, Miss Harriman. Pretty heavy-handed, I know, for a family famous for diplomacy, and May owes you an apology. I'll make sure you get it, you can count on that, but for now, well, I apologize in her stead. And I hope that puts an end to the matter.''

Good grief! Katherine marveled. *What an apology! I'm glad nobody was murdered!* But who was she to argue? "Apology accepted," she agreed with a soft smile. "But May and I do go back, and to be honest, I'm sort of used to her jokes. Anyway, she already said she was sorry. That said, what on earth are you doing holed up in here?" she asked, shivering at the dark shadows closing in on them. "Kind of gloomy for a celebration, don't you think?''

She was right, Daniel thought as he followed her eyes. Not the most festive place for a celebration. Deirdre would be angry that he'd disappeared on her. "You have a point," he agreed. "Let's get the hell out of here.''

But Katherine heard the irritation in his voice. "Oh, you're still angry! You can't go back out there in a temper.''

Daniel smiled unpleasantly. "In a temper? How quaint. Well, hell, why shouldn't I be in a temper? My loving sister just made me the laughingstock of the party, embarrassing me into that little scene…kissing you.''

"A fate worse than death?'' Katherine smiled, she couldn't help it, he was being so stuffy. "Daniel, it was only a kiss, for goodness sake!''

Only a kiss? Now, that rankled! "Well, lucky for you, little miss, you seem to have a better sense of humor than me.''

"You're being silly!''

"Silly?'' Daniel was appalled. He didn't think he'd ever been called silly in his life, much less behaved that way. He didn't think he even knew how to be silly. "Look, I admit, it took me by surprise, the way it felt to kiss you. It was nice, very nice, and if that's what you came to hear, consider it heard. But you're the one who followed me, not the other way around!''

Katherine's brow furrowed in surprise. It was slowly dawning on her that, among other things, Daniel's pride was very much at stake here. If he was willing to be so rude to salvage it—at her expense, too—it must be a very fragile thing. "Frankly,'' she declared, in the haughtiest tone she could muster, "I'm not in the least interested in what you think. About how I kiss, I mean!'' Katherine was grateful that the room was getting dark. He wouldn't be able to see how red-faced she was, talking so brazenly. "If you really want to know, I only followed you to smooth things over for the sake of your family.''

"Ah, my family, again.''

"Family is everything!'' she said. "If you didn't have one, you would understand! You know, you really are making this very difficult. I just thought that since I'm close friends with Deirdre and May, and since you and I might run into each other from time to time, I would make this effort. I didn't want what happened to mushroom, although I think I might be too late. I'm trying to be a good sport, but since you're being so crabby that we can't even have a decent conversation—''

"I am not being crabby, and since we've never talked before, I don't see why it matters, now."

"Oh, but it does matter. Your sisters and I are good friends. How's it going to be when I visit Deirdre and May, wondering whether you'll be here and how you're going to treat me? Look at how you're treating me right this second, for goodness sake!"

The more she said, the angrier Daniel got. "May should have thought of that before she played her little trick." But this wasn't the heart of the matter, at least, not for him. He felt impatient, his palms itched, and he knew why. The fact was, he had spoken the truth when he'd said he'd liked kissing Katherine.

Hell, he'd more than liked it.

His world had sort of...swayed. He'd never, ever, felt anything like it before. Didn't this sort of thing only happen in books? And all the time the little minx was standing there, mouthing off, all he could think was...would it happen again? If he kissed her again, would the earth tilt? And because he wanted to know so badly, he was furious with himself.

And terrified. She was right, his perspective was gone. May was right, too, passion was all. Only, it had come too late for him and with the wrong woman. And it made him lash out, when that had not been his intention.

"Katherine, where are you going with this?" he asked with a cold smile. "Do you dissect every kiss you get, or just the ones you get from black men?"

Heartsick, he watched her flinch, but refused to relent. It was the right path to take, to abort his inexplicable attraction to her. For God's sake, she was white! Wasn't one in the family enough? "Embarrassed again? My family has embarrassed you a good deal, this evening, hasn't it? Chalk it up to high spirits, the excitement of Deirdre's engagement to Henry. If you girls are such old friends, you can be a bit forgiving."

"Daniel, this is not about embarrassment," Katherine said

quietly. "At least, not the kind you mean. And it isn't about the color of skin, at least, not for me."

Daniel couldn't let that go by. It was always about the color of skin—when you weren't white—and he wasn't going to let Katherine get away thinking otherwise.

"Katherine," he said gently, "this most certainly is about the color of skin—mine and yours. Even admitting there was some sort of connection between us, back there under that ridiculous mistletoe... Okay, I'd even go so far as to say it was nice, very nice, and if you were black, or I were white, we might have something going here. But, you are white, and I am black. End of subject."

Black and white. End of subject. Katherine didn't know which part made her angrier. "The almighty color line! Is that what this is about?"

"Give the girl the gold ring!"

Katherine sighed. "Maybe you're right. Maybe it does come down to that, if it's so important to you."

"I'm glad you finally understand," Daniel said, feeling depressed. "Now, may we go?" He took two steps but Katherine didn't follow.

"I didn't see, at first," she murmured, a thoughtful look in her eyes. "Honestly," she swore as she lifted her face. "I didn't think about color, I mean."

He read the truth in her eyes, but it didn't matter. "Fine. I've had enough practice to last us both a lifetime. And don't tell me you don't understand what I'm talking about!"

"Oh, I understand, I'm just a little slow. Not that you'd believe me!" she said indignantly. "But then, the subject never arose before."

"What subject?" he frowned.

Katherine was candid. She had nothing to lose. "My being attracted to a black man. That is what we're talking about, isn't it? And if we're being really honest, my being attracted to a white man, either. I don't have much of a track record, if you must know," she confessed, her face pink.

Daniel was furious. Even her honesty was a burden. "Don't touch this, Katherine. Don't go near it."

"Oh, for God's sake, Daniel! I'm only twenty-four. Why do I have to learn this now?"

"Lady, this is one lesson you should have learned light-years ago, at your mother's knee or your father's. Someone's."

"It seems I missed a lot of lessons," she said sadly. "Color me...blind."

Grabbing her by the shoulders, Daniel lashed out at her with expertly arranged words. "Don't you talk to me that way, lady! You talk white, you think white, and you know nothing, absolutely nothing, about being black. You want to count how many black ambassadors there are in this country? Hell, we can hardly elect a black mayor before some damned poky town has a goddamned riot! Is it so wrong for me to want to be something more than the MVP for the National Basketball Association?"

He read the hurt in Katherine's eyes as they stood battling in the twilight, the room not dark enough to mask his rage. He wondered if she could see beyond it to his dread of their attraction to each other. His terror at the sparks flaring in the shrouded room, like rockets on the Fourth of July, celebratory, flagrant, unmistakably erotic. His fear of the fact that, despite his rage, his long, brown fingers savored the feel of her soft shoulders.

Katherine's look was searching and sympathetic. "I can understand your wanting to be your best, Daniel, but why are you so angry? The world is at your feet."

Daniel's eyes narrowed. "Katherine, do you know what could happen if the press ever got wind of that little mistletoe scene? It would be on the front page of every paper in America, by morning, not to mention the six o'clock news."

"And?"

Daniel was incredulous. "You really don't understand, do you? It would be a scandal," he explained harshly, giving her a little shake. "Ruinous."

"A scandal? Ruinous? Oh, come on! Your reputation isn't that flimsy!"

Releasing Katherine, he turned back to the window, to the gray picture it framed. Rubbing his neck, he shook his head, exhausted. "No, I know it's not," he admitted, his voice low and weary, "but, Katherine, you see before you the blackest man in America, and I'm not only talking skin color. I'm the original African-American dream, black man scaling the very white cliffs of Dover for God and country. Everything I do is watched, by my race, as well as yours. So many hopes are pinned on me. I'm a model for black youth. My picture hangs in schoolrooms all over the country, for Pete's sake! And you'd better believe that I certainly never asked for this. All I wanted for my old age was a judgeship. Never this, I swear it! But someone had an idea, and I was it. Now, I'm being groomed, my life is in the spotlight. There will be no mistakes! Not having come this far! I accepted a trust, and I take my responsibilities very seriously."

"I see," she said slowly. "Then it's true, what everyone here has been whispering today, that you're about to receive the ambassadorship?"

"To France."

"And kissing a white woman would be the absolute worst publicity?"

"Really bad publicity!"

"Worse than kissing a black woman?"

"Apples and oranges, sweetheart."

"That would be okay?"

"Definitely a different take."

"Black manhood asserting itself but crossing no lines, knowing his place. We can trust him."

Daniel spun round, his face hot with anger, as he seized her by the shoulders. "How dare you!"

Katherine looked at him, her eyes filled with tears. "Wrong take, again?" But beyond his anger she saw the turmoil in his soul and the pain in his eyes. She raised a hand to cup his cheek. "Daniel, aren't you afraid to pay too much for somebody else's dream?"

He wanted to brush her warning aside, but watched instead, mesmerized as she toed up to press her mouth to his. The glancing kiss of an angel. "Katherine," he begged, his voice a ragged whisper. "Don't do this. This is nowhere, nowhere!"

But words didn't matter, desire overwhelmed his will. The crush of velvet was sensuous beneath Daniel's sensitive fingers. Only her skin would be softer. Wanting badly to know, his hands circled the tiny expanse of her bare neck, skimmed her firm jaw, memorized her downy cheek. He was right, her skin was satin. Trailing her body, his hands sought her breasts, their heavy curves filling his palm. Even through the velvet she couldn't disguise her body's reaction, her breasts surging at his touch. His own body was hard with response.

In a deliberately crude display meant to hurt and have her at the same time, he lowered his head and covered Katherine's mouth with his own, forcing her to endure his punishing kiss. He was experienced, he'd had many women, so it was easy to detect her untutored surprise. But beneath her inexperienced response, he felt the disquiet of her passion, and it tore at his defenses. Wild with desire, he felt his heart shatter, irretrievably lost, but it couldn't quell the resentment he felt as he lifted his head.

"Happy now?" His voice a hoarse whisper, he resisted the confusion in her eyes. "This is why you followed me, isn't it?"

His scathing tone was cold water in Katherine's face. Where was her pride? Tucked away, behind her humiliation. "I'm sorry, I'm so sorry." Her voice a low sob, she pushed him away and stumbled toward the door.

Watching her run blind, Daniel was appalled. Catching her wrist, he dragged her back. "Jesus, Katherine, don't make me out to be more than the bastard I am. I'm the one who should be apologizing."

"No, no, you're right," she gulped hard, swiping her wet

eyes with the back of her palm. "And it doesn't even matter whose fault this is."

"That's what I've been trying to tell you, but it doesn't have to earn me brownie points in hell." Gently, he buried his long hands in her golden curls. "Ah, Katherine, you didn't deserve any of this."

His lips brushing hers, he swore that he was sorry, begged her to forgive him, and read the compassion in her brimming eyes. Surrendering to the gift she made of herself, he caressed her unpracticed mouth, his tongue searching the shy contour of her lips, dueling with her timidity. They were so close, he wondered they could breathe. Surely the good Lord hadn't sent Katherine here tonight simply to tantalize him. She was a gift, a few, sweet moments he was meant to enjoy, before…the rest of his life.

Slowly, almost of their own volition, his hands explored her warmth. Traveling down her spine, he traced the lines of her waist and hips in a brazen flash of need to feel her everywhere. He pulled her close, though it wasn't really possible to get much closer, just in case she doubted what she made him feel. Bursting at the seams for her, wondering what bargain he could make with the devil for just one night in her bed.

Her answering desire was the sweetest torture. Inarticulate and shy, her body was pliant and willing beneath his hands. Lightly, she raised a hand to explore the contour of his face, stroke the bristle of his five o'clock shadow, his brow, the seam their mouths made, her hand finally feathering his jaw. She hadn't meant for things to go this far, but kissing him was its own seduction. It erased all her doubts and fears, became its own complete moment where nothing else existed except the man folded around her.

Overwhelmed by the reverence in her touch, Daniel felt her tenderness replace their passion with something more delicate. Her soft form molded to the contour of his body. Her head fitted perfectly in the hollow of his shoulder as he held her tightly, his face buried in her hair. "I can't, Katherine, I can't. I've made too many promises," he whispered as he held her fast. A stolen moment from heaven as they stood in the darkening room, caught between the past and the future. Then gently but firmly, Daniel set her aside.

His fist tight around the doorknob, he paused, knowing he was at a crossroad. Walking out alone, he would leave behind the young man who had entered that room an hour before, leave behind the riotous colors of his youth. And leave behind, too, nothing as simple as love, no, but something bigger, a part of him that would determine how the rest of his life would be—or not be. Though he would have a good life—and it would be a very good life, he knew—there would always be something missing.

His grief palpable, he took a deep breath and left the sewing room.

Katherine was not so complicated.

Memorize the feel of his kiss she told herself as she lifted her hand to her lips. It had to last a lifetime. And knowing that the sensation of his lips upon hers wouldn't last the evening, she caught the treasure to her heart.

"Ah, there you are, son," James Boylan called out, spotting Daniel dashing down the hall.

Daniel looked down over the balcony rail to see his father standing arm-in-arm with Althea.

"We've been looking all over for you. You can come down now, it's safe," James laughed. "The party's about over, most everyone is gone. I might have known you'd be hiding out. Not that I'm one to criticize, mind, but I sure wish I'd remembered that old sewing room a couple of hours ago."

Daniel glanced back over his shoulder to see if Katherine had followed, but she was nowhere to be seen. It made him sick to think of the way he'd left her, standing alone in that gray chamber, cast off like the rest of the stuff crammed into the sewing room. Forcing a smile, he joined his father and Althea, waiting at the bottom of the stairs. "Stealing my girl, Dad?'' he managed to say, thinking that if tickets were sold for one-way trips to hell, maybe he'd just purchased one.

His father clasped an arm around his son's shoulder and draped the other round Althea as he led them to the library. ''Now, there's a good question, son.'' He chuckled. ''Is she, or isn't she? Maybe it's the brandy talking, maybe I'm putting you on the spot, but hell yeah, I'm asking straight out— when are you going to make this little lady one of the family? I doubt if she'd refuse the next Ambassador to France, if that's what you're afraid of. There, I've said it. My son, the Ambassador to France! What do you think, Althea?'' he winked. ''Would you refuse a proposal from an ambassador?''

Her lips pursed, Althea looked thoughtfully at Daniel, as if she were seriously considering the idea. ''I think the wrong Boylan is proposing.''

''True enough.'' James snorted. ''Daniel, you frown any harder, you'll crack all the mirrors. You've made this pretty lady wait long enough. She's not going to wait forever, ain't that right, honey?''

''Dad, in case you're forgetting, this is Deirdre's special day, and Henry's. I wouldn't want to infringe.''

''Well, heck, son, we aren't talking anything formal here, just a simple yes or no will do.''

''Dad, you're embarrassing Althea!''

''Althea's used to my ways, aren't you, honey? I don't mince words for anybody, especially not my son. And as for your sister, why, Dee and Henry couldn't care less if you and Althea got engaged today! Of course, if you're telling me you want to put a hold on your engagement until the president's announcement, well, I can't see why,'' James argued. ''Can't ever be too much good news, I say. If that's the reason, though, I guess I can respect that.''

''Why, thank you, father,'' Daniel said wryly. ''But I meant it when I said it was Henry and Deirdre's day. Althea and I have plenty of time to decide when and where, so to speak.''

This much concession was a lot for Daniel, and Althea didn't want to crowd her future husband. He had come this far, she would handle the rest. "Daniel's right, Mr. Boylan," Althea said agreeably. "We must let Deirdre have her day." Ignoring the swift rise of Daniel's head, she sent him a wide smile. "We have all the time in the world to make it official."

But to James Boylan, the word *official* was relative. He strode ahead of them into the library where the family and the last of their guests were collapsed in a state of happy exhaustion, enjoying a last brandy. "Ladies and gentlemen, listen up, I have news," he shouted, flinging his arms wide. "Hand me that tumbler and pour me a drink. I want to toast the newest wannabees to the family. I give you Daniel and Althea, the most semi-engaged couple in the U.S.A.!"

"Dad!" Daniel's grip tightened on Althea's arm and she pressed her hand over his.

"Let me take care of this, Daniel," Althea whispered and turned to the others. "We weren't really ready to announce anything," she said softly. "Mr. Boylan is jumping the gun."

"Ah, but who's holding it?" May muttered into her glass, while Deirdre threw her arms around her brother. The leftover guests stood to applaud the couple lightly and even sleepy little Kiesha, cuddled in her daddy's arms, had something to say. "Oh, Althea, can I be a bridesmaid?"

Henry politely shook Daniel's hand, Rudy hugged him with his free arm. But May was furious. "Not written in stone, I hope?" she hissed.

"In blood, May," Daniel returned quietly, his eyes clouding over as he looked past her shoulder. May followed his gaze to see Katherine Harriman walk into the library, smile as Deirdre ran up to her, and blanch when she heard the news.

"Oh, you are a bastard!" May whispered to her brother as they watched Katherine pale.

Daniel smiled and smiled as his jubilant family closed in. He watched Katherine discreetly back out of the room, his pain visible to anyone who cared to look past the carefully pasted smile on his lips.

It was another hour before the last guest departed and the exhausted Boylan family was finally alone. Drooping, surrounded by empty wineglasses, abandoned buffet plates, and crumpled napkins, the family congratulated each other on a fine party and its equally fine aftermath. Mary Boylan, Deirdre and Althea joined in a thorough dissection of who wore and said what while the Boylan men sat quietly, nursing generous snifters of brandy.

The call came much later, around two a.m. after everyone but Daniel and his father had gone to bed. James had just uncorked a bottle of cognac, an extravagant purchase made years ago at a wine auction and squirreled away for just this occasion.

"Guess I owe you an apology, son." He grinned sheepishly as he threw another log on the fireplace.

"About what, Dad?" Daniel asked, gazing into his untouched brandy.

"Oh, the way I manhandled you and Althea into getting engaged."

"Guess you do," he agreed quietly. "But I let you. I could have stopped it."

"Now, son, don't be that way."

"What way?"

"Carrying on like this. Hell, everyone knew you and Althea were going to get hitched. I just helped you two along."

"You certainly did do that," Daniel allowed sadly.

"Well, maybe I was a little, er, premature. Like I said, you have my apology. But I'm a very proud man, today, and you're a big part of it."

"You drunk, Pops?"

"No, I am not!" James denied, deeply offended. "It

doesn't hurt to tell your kids you're proud of them once in a while.''

Daniel raised his eyes to smile at his father. "Kids?"

"Yeah, kids! Always." James grinned. "Don't get me wrong, Daniel, I can see the man you have become. You've done the family proud, son, real proud, fit-to-burst proud. Why, hardly a day goes by, I don't see your name in the paper. Mr. Boylan said this, Mr. Boylan ate here, what Mr. Boylan wore—and they aren't talking about this Mr. Boylan.'' James laughed as he thumped his chest. "Hell, son, it's even affecting my business! Lately, my clients aren't calling to place in a stock order, they just want to talk about you!''

"Must be boring for you.''

"Yeah, right! And now, tonight, getting engaged to that beautiful little girl.''

Mr. Boylan's voice became a low hum as Daniel, awash with guilt, thought about another beautiful girl. He wondered what his father's conversation would be like if Daniel had announced his engagement to Katherine. Sure as hell Pops wouldn't be breaking out the Napoleon and joking about grandchildren while he warmed his feet by the fire.

James was so much at one with the world that, when the phone rang, he jumped. But when he put down the phone, he was somber.

"That was Stamford Hospital. It seems there's been an accident. A car skidded on ice. Mandy Kaplan was driving, got herself a broken rib or two. And Deirdre's little blond friend, it seems she was in the car, too. But they say she's okay, too, just a few bruises.''

"Katherine? Katherine Harriman?" Daniel asked calmly though his knuckles had a death grip on his glass.

"Yes, that's the one. The police want someone to come and get her. Seems she's in a bit of shock but refuses to be admitted. Insists she's all right, stubborn little thing, and since there's nothing really wrong with her, they have to let her go. But when one of the doctors heard the girls had been guests at our party, he thought we'd like to know what happened." Mr. Boylan rose from his leather chair with a sigh. "Well, I guess I'll go get her and see about Mandy Kaplan, make sure she's getting good care."

"Don't be ridiculous, father," Daniel said, scrambling to his feet. "You're half asleep. If I take the Porsche, I can be there in under an hour. And I've hardly touched my brandy," he said, with a glance at his father's empty glass.

"True enough, but you might want some company. It's a bit of a drive."

"On the contrary," Daniel assured him. "I like driving, and I could use a late drive after today. It will give me time to think."

"Ah, yes, about that young beauty you're finally going to marry," his father winked.

"Sure, Pops," Daniel smiled, ignoring the wrench of his heart.

Hospital lights were a beacon in the night, as they were meant to be, Daniel mused as he pulled into the empty parking lot an hour later. Directed to Mandy Kaplan's room, he found her sleeping peacefully, her head bandaged, with an IV in her arm. She had obviously been sedated.

Katherine had also been given a mild painkiller, according to the night nurse, and had nodded off in the chair by Mandy's bedside. She looked like an angel, a bruised, rumpled angel, he saw, as he knelt beside her. Searching for signs of blood, he was relieved not to see any. Gently, he touched her shoulder and watched her stir. "Daniel! What are you doing here?"

"Hey, take it easy!" he whispered. "The police called the house and I drove over to help. Are you okay? Nothing broken, is there? They said you were okay, that Mandy took the brunt of the accident."

"I'm fine, really. Just going to be sore for a few days. Nothing a hot bath won't cure. It's Mandy who was really hurt, but not too badly, thank goodness. Banged her head and bruised a few ribs, but if you saw the car, you'd know she was lucky. We both were. They want to observe her a day or so for internal bleeding. Oh, I feel like such a fool!'' she cried and burst into tears.

"Why, for Pete's sake?"

"I fell asleep, that's why!"

"You mean you were driving?" he asked, horrified as he thrust a tissue box in her lap.

"No, but I was supposed to be riding shotgun! It's all my fault!"

Relieved that she hadn't been behind the wheel, Daniel briskly mopped away her tears. "Nonsense, no one's to blame for an ice skid in the middle of the night. The police called it black ice. They had the grace to blush," he teased, but it had no effect on Katherine.

"Look, Katherine," he continued with a deep breath. "The nurses say I can take you home. Mandy's parents will be here in a little while, and I've arranged for a private nurse to sit with her tonight. Since there's nothing else we can do for her, how about we get you to bed?"

"Absolutely not! I'm not leaving this bedside till Mandy's parents get here!"

Daniel smoothed down Katherine's disheveled hair. "You've been in a car accident, too," he reminded her softly.

Katherine looked at Mandy, who was sleeping soundly. Even as Katherine chewed her lip in indecision, the private-duty nurse tiptoed into the room. Looking very efficient in her white starched uniform, a stethoscope dangling from her neck, she asked them outright to leave. That was good enough for Daniel, and he dragged Katherine from the room.

But Katherine was adamant about not leaving the premises, and, since Daniel couldn't change her mind, they stayed another hour, until Mandy's parents arrived. The Kaplans were grateful. They were upset that Katherine refused to be admitted, but when Daniel promised to look after her, that he was going to drive her home, they relented. Especially after they made him promise to reassess the situation, if necessary.

"Reassess?" Katherine frowned through a haze of codeine.

"Lawyer-talk for getting you to a hospital, if need be." He smiled over her head at the Kaplans, who nodded silently and let them go.

"I would never have thought to hire a private nurse," Katherine mused as they rode down the elevator. "Very generous. It was generous of you to drive here, too, now that I think about it." Loopy with medication, she shrugged away his guiding hand. "I can take care of myself now, thank you."

"Really?" Daniel asked, his mouth turned down. "Good. It relieves me to hear you say so."

"Good," Katherine repeated as they crossed the empty lobby, missing the faint sarcasm in his deep, rumbling voice. "Well, then, if you don't mind, I'll say goodbye and just grab a cab."

"But I do mind! It's five o'clock in the morning! And if I may also point out, this isn't exactly Forty-second Street, ma'am."

Dismayed, Katherine peered through the lobby windows and realized the truth of his words. It was dark and deserted. Not a car in sight, much less a taxi.

"Let me take you back to my house."

Katherine thought that was hysterically funny. "Good idea. I can bunk with Althea."

Daniel's eyes were frosty. "Look, I'm just trying to help."

"Go on home," Katherine said, with an irritable shrug. "That would be a big help. I'm sure there's a bus stop or train station somewhere in this godforsaken suburb." She pushed through the revolving door but Daniel dashed in with her. Grabbing hold of the handlebar, he pulled the door to a sharp halt, making a cage of their exit. His wide bulk took up so much space, she had just enough room to breathe. His heat surrounded her, a warm musk filling her senses. Clutching the handlebar for dear life, she pressed her head to the cool glass. "Daniel, for God's sake, let me alone!"

"I don't think so."

"Come on, Daniel, let me go."

"No! Not until we resolve this."

"What on earth are you talking about? There's nothing to be resolved. I—" Katherine wanted to argue, was perfectly willing to argue, but was suddenly overcome with wooziness. Suddenly, all that was keeping her upright were a pair of strong, brown hands. Clutching at his lapels, she could not even lift her head. "Daniel, I think I'm going to faint."

"Good, then we can skip the small talk." Grasping Katherine tightly, he rolled them through the door and scooped her up into his arms.

"Small talk," she giggled, her head rolling on his shoulder. "What a great phrase."

Daniel smiled. She was a goner. Between the long day, the longer night, the accident, and goodness knew what medication they had given her, Katherine was a hundred pounds of cotton candy. Holding her tightly, he strode to his car and tucked her in. Taking a moment to let the engine warm up, he secured their seat belts, and tried to ignore her babbling. Even though he knew the painkillers were loosening her tongue, it didn't make it any easier to bear her scorn.

"You got engaged tonight."

"Faster than the speed of light!"

Katherine shrugged. "Congratulations."

"It wasn't what I planned."

She slumped down and closed her tired eyes. "You looked pretty happy to me."

"You should have looked harder. My father sort of forced my hand."

Katherine opened her eyes and turned her head. Incredulous, she started to laugh. "Oh, Daniel, get off it! Nobody can make the future Ambassador to France get engaged! It's not in the job description. Or maybe it is! Have you read the fine print?''

Starting to speak, Daniel thought better of it and wisely said nothing. About two miles down the road, he found the entrance to the parkway and got on, heading west.

''Con-congratulations.''

''You said that already. And you're right, I bear full responsibility for the mess.''

''Oh, ho-ho! You calling your engagement a mess? Wow, you are in bad shape!'' In a moment of codeine-laced clarity, Katherine struggled to sit up. ''Does Althea know that you don't love her?''

Daniel turned and looked her fully in the eye. ''She doesn't love me, either.''

Katherine was horrified. ''Do you know that for a fact?''

Daniel felt his face burn as he shifted gears. ''I know how she treats me.''

''Oh, Daniel! How sad!''

''Hey, don't worry. It doesn't mean we don't like each other.''

''You poor man! You haven't a clue, have you? Love, passion. Don't these words have any meaning for you?''

''Of course they do!''

''Well, then, I guess we use different dictionaries.''

''Oh, Katherine—'' But he was unable to finish. Passion was a newly learned lesson still fresh in his mind. Wanting Katherine from the moment he'd seen her, he had secretly thanked heaven for that mistletoe. And in the sewing room— hell, all he'd wanted was to lay her down and make the colorful fabrics the canopy of their bed as he slowly peeled away her clothes. Even now, he ached with wanting her, had felt his heart accelerate the moment he spotted her slouched against Mandy Kaplan's bed. The impulse to lift her into his arms had been unbearable. Oh, yes, he was learning all about passion. He hadn't known a moment's peace since they'd met. Was it five, maybe six hours ago? How could a man have so many fantasies about a woman he'd only known a few hours? Oh, he knew about passion, all right.

And because her eyes were closed, her head propped against the car window, Katherine missed the anguish in his eyes. "Look," she said, the exhaustion in her voice pronounced, "I really don't want to talk about this, and it's none of my business really. Your life is your concern, as you warned me earlier this evening, and I was pretty brazen trying to lecture you. Now, all I want is to go home."

Chapter Three

Daniel and Katherine made it back to New York in time to be greeted by the worst snowstorm of the decade. The local radio station called it a blizzard. Later, Daniel would come to think of it as an act of God.

They were approaching Manhattan when it started, but by the time they arrived at Katherine's apartment on the Upper West Side, the snow had reached four inches and was still falling fast. He was lucky to find a parking spot within twenty minutes only five blocks away from her apartment. They were frozen by the time they reached her building, pre-war brick that had seen better days, but that commanded outrageous rent because of its location. Its thick, plaster walls were a major plus for a pianist, and the heat was excellent, blasting away even as they staggered through the lobby door. It kept Katherine paying rent she could barely afford. It meant she ate spaghetti for weeks on end, but she took pride in being able to cook pasta seventeen different ways.

Shivering and wet, she led the way up a dimly lit staircase

to the fourth floor, fumbling for her house keys at the bottom of her bag. She had three locks, so it took time to open the door, but when her struggle to unlock them became a farce, Daniel took possession of the keys. Her eyes closed, she leaned against the wall and tried to decide whether to offer him the sofa—it had been a hellish night for both of them—when he finally opened the door. The sight that greeted them drove all thought from her mind.

The place was a shambles. Anything that could have been trashed had been, and to make matters worse, snow was drifting in from the shattered fire-escape window to accumulate on the rug.

"I've been robbed!" Katherine cried, but it was more a groan than a shout. Daniel quickly pulled her back, out of harm's way.

"Let me go in first, Katherine. You never know, though the bastards are probably long gone."

Locating the light switch, Daniel reconnoitered, but he was right, the thieves were gone, the apartment empty. And bitterly cold, too. Gingerly, he dragged down the broken window and watched the pane splinter completely.

"It's all right, Katherine," he called. "It's safe to come in. If you don't mind the weather."

Pale with fear and shock, Katherine stumbled into her apartment and surveyed the damage with a glazed look. She watched as Daniel stuffed some throw pillows against the broken window to block the wind and snow, telling herself that everyone got robbed in New York at least once. Didn't they? It was part of living in the big city. It could have been worse. She could have been home when they broke in. And now she didn't have to wonder any longer when her number would be up. Now she was a statistic, and there was safety in numbers. After all, people didn't get robbed twice in one year, did they?

Did they?

Spinning round, she secured the deadbolts and adjusted the chainlock.

"Too bad you didn't do that to your window, before you left," Daniel said irritably.

Katherine was astounded. "You're not blaming me for this, are you?"

Daniel motioned to the window. "Well, explain to me why you don't have one of those damned fire gates that lock automatically."

"Because I can't afford one, that's why!" she retorted. "We're not all born with silver spoons!"

"You're joking, aren't you?"

"Why, Daniel Boylan, you snob!"

"Oh, come on, Katherine! Valedictorian at Sarah Lawrence! Didn't I get it right?"

"Ever hear of scholarships, Mr. High-and-Mighty Rich Man? I went to Sarah Lawrence on a scholarship! A full scholarship. Concert pianists are poor as church mice. My idea of dinner out is McDonald's, and make no mistake, I love Big Macs every third Tuesday of the month! Otherwise, it's rice, beans and spaghetti. But I play a mean concerto," she added wryly.

"Then how could you afford to go to Deirdre's party? How could you afford to buy her a present?"

"Tactful, aren't you, Mr. Boylan?" Katherine smiled as she collapsed onto her sofa. Exhaustion had caught up with her and she hardly had the strength to move. Traveling to Long Island, the party, the accident...and now, this! She was grateful to feel the apartment warming up, now that Daniel had blocked off the cold air. Not that she would thank him, since he'd been so rude, blaming her!

"So, maybe I'm behind a bill or two. Call a cop." She sighed. "I have a nest egg, I'll manage. I always do," she said proudly. "I'm well-versed in surviving. My mother made sure. When my parents were divorced eight years ago, my father did the best disappearing act this side of the Atlantic. A year later, we moved to Amarillo with her second husband, where she started a new family. And she made it perfectly clear, early on, that when I was old enough to be on my own, I'd be expected to leave. I think the French have a phrase for it—de trop. We haven't spoken since.''

So, there would be no help from her parents. Something about the way she spoke told Daniel that her nest egg was pretty much depleted. He had a hunch this burglary was a financial disaster of major proportions. She was so prickly, though, it was going to take a lot of ingenuity to help her out.

Setting a fallen chair upright, he took off his overcoat and set it on the chair. Ignoring Katherine's start of surprise, he picked up the telephone. ''First things first. Let's call the police.''

''Hah!'' she laughed. ''That's the funniest thing I've heard all day. They'll take about an hour to get here, cluck sympathetically, make a few notes, and leave. Look, Daniel, I have no insurance, so I don't need a police report filed. And you can bet my stuff is long gone, probably pawned right down the block. Maybe I'll stop by sometime, see if there's anything familiar in the window.''

She made light of it but Daniel could hear the bitterness in her voice.

''Ohmygosh!'' she cried and tripped over her feet getting to the small upright standing against the wall. Skimming the piano keys, she tested each and every one, and got down on her knees to examine the three pedals before she sat up, breathless, but satisfied. ''I can't believe I forgot to check my piano. It's only the most important thing in my life.'' Scrambling to her feet, she gently drew the lid over the ivory keys. ''I think that life as I know it would have been over if any harm had come to my piano.''

She saw Daniel's disbelief and spread her hands. ''It's how I earn my living. I have a concert the end of this very week. Music is my life. How could I function without my piano?'' Suddenly, it was all too much for Katherine. A sob caught in her throat, and she started to cry.

Startled, awkward, Daniel gathered her up and let her have her cry. ''Yeah, get it all out, Katherine. You've had a really long night.'' Scooping her up, he strode to the sofa, where they sat until she calmed down. Then he made them some tea in the smallest makeshift kitchen he had ever seen. He made sure she drank her entire cup before he led her to the bedroom. Ignoring the wreckage on the floor and the tumbled drawers, he straightened out the bed and drew back the covers. When she sat at the edge of the bed, he removed her shoes. Sopping wet. He wondered why he was shocked. Flimsy high heels, pretty as they were, were no protection against a snowstorm. In the excitement of the burglary, she'd obviously forgotten to remove them, and in the excitement of the evening, he'd forgotten that's what women wore to parties. It wasn't difficult to remain detached as he helped her remove her tattered red gown, either, they were both so tired. Tucking her in, he pulled up a chair, careful to swaddle the blanket around her icy toes.

"How about I just sit here awhile, until you fall asleep? I'll camp out on the sofa. Don't worry, I'm not leaving." He smiled as her heavy lids closed before he even finished speaking. There was no fight left in this girl.

Resting his chin on his fist, Daniel sat by Katherine's side, guarding her sleep. She was restless at first, and her tossing worried him, but eventually she settled down. Searching for food, he had to be satisfied with crackers and cheese. Then he puttered around the apartment picking up bits and pieces that could be salvaged, piling the stuff that couldn't be saved near the door. He was operating on nervous energy, and he, too, soon collapsed, exhausted, on the lumpy sofa. Lumpy, but dry, he told himself, taking wry note of the snow piling high against the window as he listened to the wind whistle down Broadway. The day's events sifted through his mind, but they were no deterrent to sleep. His tired body had its own ideas.

It was the faint clatter of dishes that woke him. And the smell of the most wonderful cup of coffee ever brewed by man, shoved beneath his nose, its steam tickling his face.

"Come on, lazybones, I've been up for hours." Katherine

laughed as she watched Daniel fight sleep, coffee winning hands down, as he pried opened his eyes.

"How are you feeling?"

"Oh, pretty stiff," she admitted with a small laugh. "But I took a long, hot bath while you snored away the morning and that helped enormously. I even went out and got us some bagels, after it stopped snowing. But I did walk very, very slowly."

Pretty eyes for a guy, she thought, looking down at him. Molten gold. Do they glow in the dark? she wondered, and realized from the way he was wrinkling his brow that she must have spoken out loud. "Your eyes," she smiled. "They look like that gemstone. Amber, I think it's called."

"I wondered that about yours, once." He smiled back. "Emeralds—and yours do glow. At certain times." He laughed when her cheeks pinked up. She rushed off, mumbling something about eggs. Unwilling to leave the comfort of the sofa, he sipped his hot coffee and listened to Katherine make breakfast noises from the tiny kitchen. If he ignored the chaos and shabby decor for the grandeur of the high, ornate ceiling and old-fashioned elegance of the apartment, he thought she wasn't so unlucky.

After a leisurely breakfast they returned Katherine's apartment to some semblance of normalcy. It took innumerable trips to the cellar with the garbage, but that done, they were able to look around the apartment with some satisfaction. At that point, Daniel informed her that he was going out to buy a security gate for her window. She backed off when she saw the stubborn line of his jaw.

"Okay, okay, I won't look a gift horse in its mouth." Katherine laughed. "But where on earth are you going to find a store open today?"

"If there is one store that will be open today," Daniel snorted, "it will be a hardware store. Selling snow shovels at a premium, I bet. Anyway, this is New York. Nothing closes down for more than an hour."

Daniel walked up Broadway to the nearest hardware store,

and although he knew he was paying top dollar, arranged for the installation of the best window gate in the store. That done, he found a telephone booth and placed a long-delayed call to his parents' home. He was grateful when Jeffers answered on the first ring, thus avoiding his family and the avalanche of questions they would surely have. He just wanted to be sure no announcement had been made regarding the ambassadorship. There was no message on his beeper, and Jeffers assured him there was no word, yet. Daniel was about to ring off when Althea got on the line—and started something churning in his gut.

"Daniel!"

"Althea!"

"Darling, you don't have to say another word. I heard about the accident from your dad. He said he was sure you would call, so I've been waiting by the phone, all morning. Are those poor little girls all right?" Althea's interest rang hollow, her voice curt and cautious to his ear.

"Well, yes, they are, sort of. Mandy was admitted for assorted broken ribs and won't be feeling good for a few months, but that's the worst. Katherine insisted on waiting until Mandy's parents arrived before she would allow me to drive her home."

"Oh. Of course."

But then, his own explanations sounded wanting. "She'd just walked away from a car accident, quite bruised, hysterical... I couldn't force her back to Long Island, could I?"

"No, Daniel, of course not. It seems like you did the right thing. How is she now?"

"When I left her, she seemed much better. She's a concert pianist, did you know that? She has a booking this week that she insists she's going to keep, barring the weather, so she must be okay."

"I'm happy to hear that because I wouldn't want anything to interfere with your flight tomorrow. To Paris, remember?"

"Is tomorrow Monday, already?" Daniel asked, dismayed.

"Yes, darling. Did you forget?"

"No, of course not," Daniel lied, perspiration breaking out on his forehead. "But, well, look, Althea, I've been thinking, about the engagement...maybe we should wait awhile." He could feel the instant charge, the tension that leaped across the wire.

"Wait?" Althea's voice was thin ice.

Dear lord, give me strength. "We have to talk...about things."

"About what...things?"

"I...things...well..." Daniel tried, but he couldn't find the words.

"Darling, are you getting cold feet? Is the famous, unflappable international lawyer getting cold feet? How adorable."

But Althea's voice was anything but affectionate. It made him stumble over his words. "I just thought that maybe I'd rushed us. I mean, my father did sort of pull the rug out from under me...us. I thought maybe you'd felt coerced, maybe you'd want more time to think."

"Think about what?"

"Marriage. It's a big step, marriage."

"Daniel, I've thought about it. Lots. It's been over a year since we started talking about this!"

"That long?" he asked lamely.

"That long."

"I didn't realize." When had it all become so complicated? But he strove to be honorable, he meant to be honorable. "Still, look, Althea, I've got to say it... I'm just not sure. If you don't, well... I'd like to put our engagement on hold. There's too much going on, you know that better than anyone. I have to...think. Our engagement...the way it happened, sloppy, not how I'd planned. Look, how about I call you when I get to Paris and we talk about this some more?"

"Daniel!"

He could hear the annoyance in Althea's voice—not hurt, not disappointment, only annoyance. It made him feel a little less guilty when the coward in him won out. "Look, Althea, I've got to go. I'm at a pay phone and there's a line waiting."

He hung up quickly and felt only relief. Glancing up at the blue cloudless sky, he struggled not to feel guilty at the way his feet hurried him on, heading back toward Katherine's apartment. Trying to figure a way to have it all—and Katherine. With Katherine. Because he suddenly knew that *without* Katherine it would be ashes in his mouth. Within a few short hours, she had filled the empty spot in his heart and magnified his vision so that everything filtered through her small form.

He struggled, too, not to fall over foot-high snow drifts. The cold biting at his ears and nose, his gloveless hands nearly frostbitten—the ridiculous effort it took to walk one lousy block! Still, Daniel wondered if he'd been away in Europe too long. The sun blazing on the silver stones of the skyscrapers, the sheer exuberance of walking the familiar streets, he'd forgotten how exciting New York could be, even in a snowstorm. He'd forgotten the camaraderie of New Yorkers under siege, even if it was only about a foot or two of snow, the cranky happenstance that hid the city's good humor even under duress. If one knew where to look, *if* one loved New York. Then, there was no other city, it ruined you for life. You would visit London, pass through Rio, frequent Barcelona, but you would *always* return to New York.

And then there was Paris. Beautiful Paris and its endless obligations—to the ambassadorship, which he secretly knew was his, to his family, who had invested so much in him, and to his countrymen, who expected him to make history and take them with him.

And Katherine, waiting at the end of the block, up the dark staircase, behind the heavily-bolted door, in her huge, overpriced apartment. Pretty little Katherine, not nearly so beautiful as Althea, but with a charm all her own. Was he fooling himself to think he could make it all work? Were his glasses too rose-tinted? Unpolished, unsophisticated, knocking at the door to his glass house, her only weapon a pocket full of innocence, Katherine was ready to do battle with powers she hardly understood. Katherine—the best thing that could have happened to him at the worst of times!

When she opened the door he knew he was lost. She was right, the color of their skin knew no boundaries. He reached for her, and she did not refuse him. "I swore I wouldn't, but damn it, Katherine, I want you so much, I'm burning up."

The dismay in his heart was reflected on her face. "Say yes, Katherine, please say yes. I'm begging you. Give me—us—this one day."

There was no guile in her voice and her eyes were clear as she laced her hand with his. "All right, Daniel, yes."

He didn't know a moment's hesitation, the hard shell he had so carefully constructed around his heart shattered. Not trusting himself to speak, he slid his arms around her tiny waist, drew her to his chest and buried his face in her hair. His hands caressed as he breathed in her scent and some faint citrus perfume, probably her second indulgence after McDonald's. For one brief moment his doubts flared, and he raised his head, his expression almost somber.

If she had expected him to be more assured, Katherine was mistaken. She stared back, unflinching, more than willing to give him the assurance he was looking for. Then on tiptoe, she flung her arms around his neck and kissed him hard. She felt his smile against her mouth and reluctantly drew back.

"You are going to make love to me, aren't you? You haven't changed your mind, have you?" Katherine asked playfully.

"No, ma'am, not after that vote of confidence!"

She felt herself weaken as his mouth descended, his lips persuasive as they lightly brushed her own. Kiss after kiss, warm and sweet and coaxing, he made her dizzy with want.

He was surprisingly gentle after yesterday's punishing passion, and, trusting him, she curled into his body.

Daniel felt her shift, felt desire leap between them. Near-kisses suddenly weren't enough, not given her unmistakable response and eagerness to please. And she did please him. Hunger belied his outward calm. Cupping Katherine to his hard body in a swift, sleek motion, his tongue traced her lips. Her taste was nectar, pure sensation, every parry with her tongue a challenge to his self-control.

Gently, he pulled her down onto the couch, his mouth burning as he explored her long neck while his hand found the buttons of her blouse. Beneath the fabric, he could feel her taut nipples, hear her low intake of breath as he bared them. Full, round breasts—they were so beautiful, they filled his hands. His for the taking as he closed his eyes and pressed his mouth to their valley. He needed more, his restraint was wavering. Tenderly, his hands trembling, he removed her clothes, then his own. Then he slid down her legs and buried his face between her thighs, searching out the most intimate part of her. He knew he'd found it when she cried out his name.

"Katherine, Katherine," he whispered over and over as he rose to his knees. With one quick thrust, he buried himself inside her. Groaning against her mouth as he pushed deeper, he prayed she found her pleasure before he made a fool of himself. She was so hot, so wet, so nicely tight...

There were no virgins at her age, were there? He rose up, wanting to ask, but joined to her silky moistness, it was far too late. He felt his muscles pulsate and bring him, unwilling, to his climax.

They collapsed on her sofa, and when he could breathe again, Daniel drew a finger over Katherine's mouth. "Katherine, are you—were you—a virgin?"

Katherine blushed and turned away. "Me?"

"Nobody else here that I can see," he said gently, caressing her cheek.

Katherine sighed. "Do we have to talk about this now?"

His brow to her temple, Daniel smiled crookedly. "Yes, I think so, even if I'm buried up to the hilt in your lovely body and feeling like I'd like to start loving you, again. Yes, I do think this may be the time for us to talk."

"You want me to defend my virginity?"

"I didn't ask you to defend it, just explain it. Or rather, explain why you didn't mention it. Come on, Katherine, virgins are a rare breed!"

"Maybe," Katherine allowed, somewhat irritated. "But there is no explanation, so don't look for one. I just never wanted to make love with anyone before."

Daniel frowned. "But why me?"

Katherine's face puckered. "Why not?"

"Katherine!"

"Daniel!"

"I definitely sense evasion, here. I have a right to know. You thrust a responsibility on me that I'm pretty sure I wouldn't have accepted."

"Oh, really, Mr. Boylan! Thrust, indeed! Next time I want to go to bed with a lawyer, I'll think twice!" Indignant, she tried to rise, but Daniel wouldn't let her budge.

"Katherine, you're playing word games with a master. Loving you was the best—the best!—but to make love to a virgin— I'm your first, I go down on your dance card. I would have liked a say in the matter. Making love with an experienced woman is another ball game."

"Less liability?"

"If you like. Way more pleasure for you, if I'd known!"

"Hmm."

"Were you saving yourself for your future husband?"

Katherine rolled her eyes in disgust, and Daniel smiled. "I know precisely the kind of jerk I am, and I'm more than sorry. I won't insult you and say I got carried away. I wanted you, plain and simple—or maybe not so simple, the part about wanting you, I mean. Oh, hell, Katherine, I can't figure it out."

"Thanks a lot."

"No, honey, I don't mean you. I mean, on some level, well, I didn't precisely lose control, but—"

"I think we're talking about passion again."

"Are we?" he asked, honestly confused.

For a smart man, Daniel Boylan was awfully dumb, Katherine thought, with a smile. "Hasn't it gotten through to you yet that I happen to like you? Oh, never mind, Mr. Boylan, you'll figure it out one of these days. Come on, let's move into my bed. It's more comfortable than this prickly sofa."

Exhausted from the events of the last twenty-four hours, Katherine and Daniel fell back to sleep. When he woke, Daniel was confused until he saw Katherine's golden sheet of hair across the pillow and remembered. His cheek resting on her pale shoulder, his brown arm curled about her naked hips, Daniel found the contrast between black and white erotic. He could feel himself responding to it. But then, the texture of her soft skin against the hard knot of his bicep was erotic, too. He knew their color difference was part of the enchantment, but was just as sure that wasn't the whole story. He wondered if he loved her. If he did, maybe he had no choice, maybe it just was.

His hands roamed of their own volition, down the hollow of her spine, to stroke her softly, wake her slowly to the exquisite delicacy of his touch between her thighs. He grew excited watching her pink up with pleasure, and, when she would have turned, he stilled her with his expertise and sent her to higher levels of pure, explosive pleasure.

"Oh, so that's what makes the world spin." Katherine sighed.

Yes, that's exactly what makes the world spin, Daniel thought to himself as he slid into Katherine's warm, wet sheath while she was still muzzy with the afterglow of his lovemaking. Ah, yes, exactly, he swore, as he gave in to his passion and hurtled them both beyond the path of control.

They slept again.

Or rather, Katherine slept, while Daniel lay awake all that long Sunday night. Staring up at the ceiling, he thought about Althea, his reluctance to commit to her, their awkward engagement. He tried to figure out what to do, but to no avail. Gazing down at the sleeping woman beside him, knowing he should leave, he knew he would not. He had been touched by that obscure something that transcended words, but that once felt, resonated in the heart.

He had let everything fall to the wayside—Althea, his career, his fame, his power, his family's opinion. He was drifting in a fantasy, and that fantasy was Katherine. He and Katherine, lost somewhere between tomorrow and yesterday, were young now, their passion was fresh, allowing them to overcome the more obvious obstacles. But later, when their passion burned a little lower, then a lot lower...

So many ifs. He would have to deal with Althea, first thing, be totally honest. Perhaps he and Katherine should keep their relationship under wraps for a while, see if things worked out between them. Surely she would prefer to have a little time with him without the flash of a thousand cameras in her eyes. Then, if things soured... She was smart enough to know the pitfalls for an interracial couple, much less for the high-profile couple they would be. Where they chose to live, their professions, where they dined, even where they vacationed, everything would be dictated by their uniqueness. Forget about the disappointment and outrage of their families, yes, they would definitely lose a few friends over this one, once they went public.

And the black establishment would hate him for this. Rip him to shreds. Their brightest star, they would cry, had turned against his own. They would accuse him of betraying his race, lambast him for buying himself a white woman. What was wrong with Althea? they would want to know. She had it all—beauty, brains, an incredible career, and she was black. And they would be right.

Althea! She, too, would suffer for his choice. She'd be hounded by the press right alongside Katherine, compared to her white counterpart in every way imaginable. Everyone would want to know the dirty details of their romance, how

Althea had failed him, why he preferred Katherine. Any disgusting tidbit would be fair game. He would have to tell Althea that it was over between them as soon as possible, so she would not be caught unawares. He hadn't meant for this to happen, it just had.

Yes, this was going to be a scandal of epic proportions. The president might not ask him to remove his name from the list of potential ambassadors, he was a fair-minded man and had gone out of his way to pave the diplomatic path for Daniel. But when the scandal broke—and there was really no other word for it—the president would expect that courtesy. Oh yes, this was definitely going to cost Daniel the ambassadorship. If the president were feeling generous, he might offer Daniel an out-of-the-way post in Asia, but even if he did, Daniel didn't think there were too many jobs for concert pianists in Siberia.

He must have tossed once too often, because toward dawn, Katherine stirred.

"Hey." She smiled sleepily as she ran her hand across his belly. "Come back down here."

Daniel slid down to rest his head on Katherine's breast. She moved persuasively along his body, but he coiled around her and held her tight, as if her warmth could erase his sense of foreboding. "We've really done it, haven't we?"

Katherine sighed. "Oh, my, yes, I do believe we have. But must we talk about it now? I mean, if we're going to get hell for this, could we have a little bit more of heaven? Just to make it all worthwhile." She laughed softly.

"I don't deserve you," he whispered.

"Probably not." She smiled. "But since you've got me, what are you going to do about it?"

"Katherine!" he protested, when she moved her thigh provocatively. "There's nothing left. Aren't you exhausted?" But his body had its own ideas, and they coincided with hers.

Later, they showered together, something neither had ever

done with anyone else, and a mistake, Daniel complained weakly, when Katherine insisted on soaping him up. But remembering the time, he refused to allow things to go any further. He had a flight to catch at Kennedy Airport, and his secretary was meeting him at the gate, to hand him his passport and briefcase. Katherine had a rehearsal to attend that afternoon. And he still had to dig out his car.

"We have a lot to talk about, don't we?" he asked as they dressed, his words sounding uncomfortably familiar to his ears.

"I suppose so," Katherine said slowly.

"You betcha," he said, his voice muffled as he hunted for his shoes beneath the bed. Then, inching up to where Katherine perched on the edge of the bed, looking like a forlorn fairy, he pulled her down onto the rug, his playfulness surprising even himself. Holding her hands prisoner above her head, he kissed her with sloppy hilarity until she laughed.

"I promise, I promise, to call you the minute I get to Paris, and when I narrow down my schedule, we'll arrange for you to fly over. Let's face it, honey, there are things I have to take care of, people I have to talk to—lots of people—it's only fair. Responsibilities...you understand."

"Of course I do," she said, trying to sound brave.

"Hey, you ever been to Paris?"

"Nope."

"You'll love Paris," he whispered as he nibbled at her ear. "Everyone loves Paris, even the French."

Katherine turned away, but Daniel's lips traced the soft hollow of her neck, shivery kisses for every word he spoke. "I'm not going to forget you, Katherine, if that's what's worrying you."

"No, of course not." She smiled valiantly. "But how will you remember me?"

"As this brave, beautiful woman who literally stopped me in my tracks. A freight train couldn't have been more effective," he teased.

Katherine's eyes filled, but she was unable to speak. Instead, she tried to memorize the contours of his face, the way he looked at her, his invisible warmth. She knew the sacrifice he'd made by saying those words, but there were volumes he'd left unsaid. And though she believed that he believed his own words, she knew that when he got to France, they'd become vague promises made between the sheets of a long and wonderful night, not strong enough to withstand the wintery daylight of Paris.

"Look, sweetheart, I've got to go. I still have to dig out my car. I'll call you tonight, I promise. It's a Concorde, so the flight won't be too long. Stay near the phone. And don't you forget me." Then he was gone.

"I won't," Katherine whispered.

And forced herself to pull it together. She was a musician, and she had a rehearsal. Finding her shoes, she finished dressing and stuffed her huge leather tote bag with her belongings and the required sheet music. She was playing Chopin. What timing. The consummate romantic! Life played tricks like that all the time, and with a philosophical shrug, she bundled up against the cold and stepped into the frosty winter air.

Trudging through the snow, she hurried to join the small crowd at a bus stop on Broadway. The consensus was that the buses were running, but how long they'd have to wait was anyone's guess. Some of the streets had been plowed, but it would take days before the city dug itself out from so much snow. The bus surprised everyone by lumbering along twenty minutes later, and Katherine was soon inside, huddled against one of its windows, staring out at the winter wonderland of New York City.

She tried—an impossibility—not to think of Daniel, wonder where he was and if he was thinking of her, missing her, making plans to see her again. His love was in his eyes, in his touch, in every kiss he gave her, she didn't dispute that. What she did not believe was that events would not conspire against them.

As they did, far sooner than she could have predicted, beginning with her greeting to a cantankerous, elderly janitor who was paying lip service to the blizzard with a rusty old shovel at the steps of the darkened concert hall. Katherine had to plant herself in front of him before he deigned to acknowledge her presence. "Excuse me, mister, but do you work here? Do you know what's going on? Where is everybody?"

"Hey, lady, you notice there's been a snowstorm hereabouts?" The old man snorted.

"But there's supposed to be a rehearsal today!"

"Not today, dearie," he informed her with grim satisfaction.

"Oh, no!"

"Who was you gonna play for, I'd like to know? They ain't exactly breakin' down the doors, now are they?"

Glancing at the barred doors, Katherine guessed she must be in a worse fog than she knew, not to have thought of this and called ahead.

"But you'll be wantin' to get paid, anyhow, girlie, so stick to yer guns. Don't let 'em get away with anything. Snow ain't yer fault."

The old man rambled on while Katherine stood on the sidewalk, wondering what to do. She supposed she should go home and use the extra time to make up for all the practice she had lost this weekend. She wished Daniel were there, waiting for her. But then she definitely wouldn't get much practice done, she thought ruefully, at least, not at the piano. The thought made her smile. Oh, well. She glanced at her watch. He'd be at Kennedy by now, flying to Paris in a couple of hours, barring any delays.

Jumping into a taxi that miraculously happened to be passing by, she ordered the cabbie to take her to Kennedy Airport. A sign, she called its passing, falling back on the seat with tremendous satisfaction. Daniel would be absolutely astonished when he saw her, but at least she would be able to give him one last kiss before he left. She couldn't think of anything more romantic or any better way to tell him that she loved him.

The cabbie deposited her at International Departures in less than an hour, but when she saw how huge the terminal was, she wondered if she would be able to find Daniel before his flight left. Luck was with her. After she'd ridden the escalator up to the main plaza, the young woman at the information desk pointed her in the right direction, and she found the correct gate in minutes. Finding Daniel was going to be more of a chore, she sighed, when she saw how many people were hanging about. The snow storm had caused quite a backup. He could be anywhere, even in the VIP lounge. Come to think of it, that was probably where he was. Finding him was only going to be harder with that crowd of reporters milling about on the lower plaza. So inconsiderate, the way they just took over the floor, forcing everybody to circle past them. All those obnoxious television lights and flashing cameras. Must be some movie star. Must be—

Daniel!

And Althea, her hand tucked in his, a wide smile on her glossy lips as they stood in the center of the circle.

Katherine skirted the balcony, her heart beating wildly as she tried for a better vantage point. Drawing so close she was almost above them, she strained to hear what they were saying, to hear what news they were making, feeling sick, knowing it wasn't going to be good.

"Yes, I guess I did surprise Daniel," Althea was saying happily. "I just couldn't bear to be parted from him. The airline was very cooperative, too."

Katherine's legs threatened to buckle. Clutching at the handrail, she watched her future disappear in a blinding glare of halogen.

But bright lights became Althea Almott. "Yes, ladies and gentlemen, all the arrangements have been made. Daniel's family is flying to Paris on Friday, and we'll be married by special license over the weekend."

The reporters lapped it up. How could they not? Tomorrow's front page news, with glorious pictures to boot. Wonderful pictures, Katherine saw, as Althea wrapped her arms around Daniel's neck and gave him a big kiss. The reporters were in heaven. Supermodel and smart young diplomat, a Marilyn Monroe and Joe DiMaggio for the nineties. Althea was lapping it up, too, and who could blame her? Katherine thought, not unkindly. He'd made promises...

"When did he pop the question, Althea? Were you really surprised? With all due respect, Mr. Ambassador, just one more kiss for the record? And, excuse me, sir, but could you say where exactly you were, when the president called?"

My God, it's official! He'd been made ambassador!

"How romantic," an elderly lady standing next to Katherine whispered. "He's so handsome, and she's so beautiful. I've never seen a real live supermodel before."

Her hands in a death grip on the balcony rail, Katherine stared down at Althea and Daniel, trying to see them through the old woman's eyes. Yes, they did have everything, she realized as she watched Daniel force a smile for the reporters. Althea clung to him playfully, knowing that half the world would see them on the six o'clock news and the other half would read the news in their morning paper.

"Come on, Althea, give us a little bit more. They'll hold the plane for you," one reporter shouted. "So when are you two planning on having those babies you've been taking about?"

Althea's beautiful face took on a deliberate, contemplative study as the reporters waited for her answer, but the answer was in the long silent look she gave Daniel. Daniel's eyes grew wide with disbelief and the reporters went wild.

"Hey, Althea, you holding out on us?" someone shrieked. "You prego, baby? When are you due? Come on, Allie, is it a boy or a girl? Twins?" The place was suddenly a madhouse as reporters scrambled for their cell phones.

Katherine watched Daniel beckon frantically to the security guards as he edged them toward the gate. She saw him whisper to Althea, his brow puckered, a black scowl on his brown face. When he chanced to look up, he noticed the crowd ogling them from the balcony and glared.

And he almost found Katherine. He would have seen the horror in her eyes, if he hadn't turned abruptly away. But she, too, had backed away, a casualty to the god Mammon, who laughed loudly as she ran down the corridor.

Chapter Four

Arizona—Nine years later

"Now, Dylan, you be sure to listen to everything Wilma tells you, hear?"

His light-brown eyes glued to the television set, Katherine's son barely registered her warning.

Katherine sighed and Wilma shook her head. "That child never gives me trouble, no how, Kat, so why you worrying your head, now? Just go play your heart out and have a good time."

Katherine bit her lip, unconvinced.

"Katherine Harriman," the housekeeper said sternly. "It can't possibly be us you're worried about, can it?"

Katherine looked at her, her eyes clearly worried. "No, Wilma, I trust you implicitly, and you know it."

"Then it's gotta be the concert eating you up," Wilma decided, with a knowing look.

Katherine sighed. "Well, it is my first big-name concert.

Flying off like this to California, playing with Sir Harry Paul, it just seems so much, and it's so far away.''

"It's far, all right. Halfway round the world," Wilma snorted. "No phones, either, in Los Angeles. Just became part of the union.''

"Okay, okay." Katherine smiled unwillingly. "But remember, Dylan and I have never been separated.''

Wilma looked at the young boy, his eyes glued to the television. "Yeah, it sure does look like he's going to suffer. And if I'm not going deaf, girl, I think that's the car service honking outside.''

"You're right. Okay. Dylan," she called as she picked up her bags. "I'm leaving!''

This time her son seemed to hear because he scrambled to his feet and ran to give her a hug. "Okay, Mom. See ya. And don't forget to bring me home a present.''

Katherine smiled as she returned her son's hug. Her exquisite tawny-skinned son with glowing amber eyes and an oh-so-serious mien. "I'll remember. Something violent and nasty, right?''

"Oh, Mom, you know!" He sighed the long-suffering sigh of every eight-year-old boy who ever had to put up with a mother who abhorred action figures.

On her way to the airport, Katherine congratulated herself on having found a wonderful woman like Wilma to care for Dylan. To guard the son for whom she lived and breathed, for whom she'd picked up the pieces of her sorry life when she thought there was nothing to live for. And now, another miracle. As a concert pianist beginning to gather her own following, she'd just been booked to play Los Angeles, commanding her first decent fee in years. Enough to pay some very overdue bills and maybe give them all a proper Christmas. There was even some talk of a recording, and some talk was better than none.

The flight was trouble-free, the plane landed in Los Angeles and Katherine caught a shuttle bus to her motel. The balmy California weather worked its magic as they drove down the San Diego Freeway, and she began to relax. After checking in, she made a quick call to Phoenix to let Dylan and Wilma know that she'd arrived safely and to assure herself that Dylan was fine. He was fine, and he was also asleep, Wilma told her patiently, so they chatted and she arranged to call her son in the morning, before he left for school. After a shower, she decided to take a little catnap but was so tired that she slept right through to the next morning and had to hustle to make rehearsal on time.

She was playing for Sir Harry Paul, who some considered to be the greatest conductor living. He was also known for his kindness and his keen interest in developing talent. Best of all, he considered Katherine to be one of his greatest discoveries. Hearing her play with the Phoenix Symphony Orchestra had been accidental, but the next thing she knew, Sir Harry had flown back to Phoenix on a surprise visit to hear her play again. Just to be sure, he had said at the time. Convinced of her talent, he'd personally arranged her California booking.

So there she was, living out a dream as she walked into the Music Center of the Dorothy Chandler Pavilion, praying her knees didn't give way. Sir Harry embraced her and introduced her around. Sensing her nervousness, the other musicians took her under their wings, and she was made to feel immediately at home in the strange hall. After an intense four-hour rehearsal, she thought she could conquer the world, or at least the music world of Los Angeles. She was at her peak, her hands never stronger or more informed, and she knew in her gut that the concert would go well.

Later, back at the hotel, she felt justified in treating herself to the sauna, but not before a quick call home. Dylan picked up right away. "Hey, Ma, did you get me anything, yet?"

"Hello to you, too," Katherine admonished her son, but her eyes misted over. She missed him terribly.

They talked about school stuff—how soccer practice went, why Tommy Lee made him fall on purpose, why he didn't eat his bologna sandwich, how come his teacher gave so much homework, and why was Wilma giving him another shampoo when he'd just had one last week! Endless injustice, until Dylan remembered that his favorite TV show was on and he had to go. Wilma took the phone but not in time to save Katherine's ears from being shattered as it clattered to the floor.

"Sorry about that," Wilma apologized. "Greased Lightening just took a running leap over his sneakers. But I guess you can tell that everything's fine here. How about you?"

It was Wilma who had insisted that Katherine go to California, arguing that it was time for Katherine to take her place in the limelight if she was really serious about her music. She could deal with her stage fright later, but for now, would she please sign on the dotted line?

Katherine had signed.

And it was Wilma, too, who had dragged her to the Biltmore Fashion Park and up the escalator into Saks Fifth Avenue the day after her advance had been received. She persuaded Katherine to buy the black sequined gown she was going to wear that night, the one that...clung, to put it mildly.

"Fits you like a glove, honey," Wilma had announced triumphantly. "Everybody's going to be forgetting that they're supposed to be listening to Chopin, not watching your rump. Oh, and honey child, don't take your bows too low!"

"Wilma!" Katherine had been shocked by Wilma's blunt assessment of her natural endowments, but secretly inclined to agree. It had been ages since she'd bothered dressing up, so why not try for a little sexiness? What harm could it do? Besides, once she began to play it wouldn't matter, she forgot everything except her music, and so would the audience, she hoped.

A quick nap, a light dinner of toast and tea—because those were butterflies she was feeling—and on to the Music Center. Between her music and her gown, she intended to knock some socks off tonight. Sir Harry was pleased to see her arrive early, and by the way they were staring, her fellow musicians were pleased, too. Ignoring their stares, she strode to center stage to check her Steinway, only to be nearly blinded by the huge, glittering candelabras. Sir Harry promised they would be dimmed during the performance. Satisfied, she sat down to her warm-ups and waited for curtain time. Peering out at the audience just before show time, Katherine saw that every seat had been filled. She could hear the rustle of the sold-out audience as it settled down, unaware of the turmoil she was going through. Listening to the orchestra warm up calmed her, so that when she was announced, she was ready, her nervousness and her black sequined gown forgotten, everything fallen to the wayside with the intensity of the moment. Not even the hush of the audience, breathless in their admiration for the beautiful up-and-coming pianist, penetrated her concentration.

She performed perfectly. Her long, delicate hands played of their own volition. The music eclipsed Katherine. Two nocturnes by Chopin and a sonata by Beethoven and the audience went wild. They gave her a standing ovation. She took three bows and, clutching a bouquet of yellow roses, was whisked offstage. Sir Harry hugged her and dragged her back onstage for another bow, never mind that she was laughing and crying at the same time. Everyone wanted to applaud the newest star of classical music. Offstage once more, a hand to her heaving chest, she closed her eyes and tried to catch her breath.

"Funny, all those years ago, no one told me you were so good."

Katherine froze, her smile fading. Maybe if she held her breath, if she didn't move, didn't open her eyes…

"Say hello, Katherine. It's the polite thing to do."

Katherine's heart skipped a beat, maybe several, until she opened her eyes. The raucous energy of the backstage theater melted away. All she could do was stare. Daniel Sheridan Boylan—a little gray at the temples, some lines around his eyes, but big as life and just as bold. Stunning in his tux, handsome as ever, a half smile playing on his lips even as the brown eyes fastened on hers brimmed with fury.

"Daniel?" she whispered, clutching the yellow bouquet to hide her shaking hands.

"In the flesh."

The dazzling fire shooting from his golden eyes was no match for the scathing contempt she heard in his voice. It made her wince. Well, okay, so he wasn't going to be friendly, what did she expect? That didn't mean she should lose her wits. Daniel was no longer the same guy she'd known, but she wasn't the silly chit who'd let him get away with murder. A few polite words would get rid of him. Raising her chin, Katherine met him, head-on. "Well, what a surprise!"

"All around, I should think."

"It's been a while."

"Nine years."

"That long?"

"Almost exactly, actually."

Fine, Katherine, you're doing fine, she told herself. Just swallow slowly, keep talking, stay cool, and he'll never guess you're ready to fall on the floor in a heap of hysteria. "You're looking well. Um, so how've you been?"

"Fine."

Oh, lots of help there! For goodness sakes, what did he want her to say? Hey, Danny-boy, long time, no see? Missed you, big guy? "It's been a long time."

"You already said that, Katherine."

"Er...of course. Sorry." Take a deep breath, Katherine, be cool. But it wasn't easy. He was burning her at the stake with his blazing anger and more fool her, she couldn't tear her eyes away. He held her prisoner with his rage—sweet torture, for now that she saw him, she could measure just how much she had missed him all these years. And it was an enormous amount, but he'd never know. She cleared her throat and was cool. "Your, um, family? Deirdre, May and

Rudy? And little Kiesha, why, she must be all grown up by now.''

"You don't know?"

"You know I don't," she said quietly.

"You're right, I do," Daniel agreed, although he sounded anything but agreeable. "It's all I do know, though. That disappearing act you performed years back was very thorough. I don't think Deirdre will ever forgive you, her best friend gone without a word, but I'm sure you had a good reason. And so I tell her, every time she mentions you," he said mockingly. "I was a good defense attorney, in my youth."

"But you don't sound as if you really believe that I had a good reason,'' she said softly.

"You're right, I don't. Not when I remember the way I left you. But I don't tell her about that."

Daniel's words seared her, but she would die before she let him know. "Well, it was so long ago," she said cautiously, "that I can hardly remember. I'm surprised you do."

He looked at her, contempt filling his eyes. "You're right. It was nothing memorable."

Katherine paled at his cruelty, even if she knew he had every right to retaliate. "Have you come to congratulate me, Daniel, or is humiliation more what you had in mind?"

But Daniel didn't answer. The stage manager had come rushing up and in his excitement, he didn't even notice Daniel. "There you are, Miss Harriman! We've been looking all over for you."

Daniel stepped back into the shadows as the harassed stage manager took Katherine by the elbow and nudged her toward the stage. "The audience is shouting for you! It's incredible, I've never heard the like! They're actually calling out your name! Sir Harry insists that you do another encore."

Grateful for the interruption, she let him lead her away, careful not to look back as she swept onstage, black sequins lighting her way. Sir Harry bowed as she took her seat at the piano and the concert hall grew silent. She wondered what to play, then played a few signal notes for Sir Harry. Surprised, he looked at her, as if to ask, are you sure? then nodded his permission.

She played Schumann's "Traumeri," the only piece she knew that could match the anguish in her heart. She played it for Daniel, in lieu of the farewell they'd never had. And as often happened when she played, she soared beyond herself. The audience was so stunned by the purity of her performance, they forgot to applaud when she was done, the highest accolade an artist could ask for. She struggled to rise but was so drained by the complexity of the piece, that Sir Harry had to come forward and take her by the elbow. Unsteadily, she rose and managed to scrape together a bow. The applause was thunderous, and she was grateful.

Gathering her wits together, she tried to exit via the side stage door but was surrounded by a legion of well-wishers. The crowd would not be satisfied with anything less than pictures and autographs, and she accommodated them all. When she tried again for the stage door, she was again foiled. Sir Harry was hosting a private party and was stationed at the door, playing traffic guard, directing his guests to various cars and limousines. When he saw Katherine, his eyes rose to heaven.

"My dear child, you were wonderful, simply wonderful!" he sighed, shaking his grizzled head. "Words cannot express. Thank you for coming to California! Thank you for coming to play in my humble music hall! Thank you for playing "Traumeri!" Thank you, thank you, thank you!"

"Sir Harry, it was your generosity that made the evening a success. You and your orchestra honored me by inviting me to Los Angeles."

Sir Harry was pleased at her acknowledgement but refused to take the credit due Katherine. "My dear child, you play like an angel. "Traumeri," imagine! I can admit, now, that I was worried, but tonight I have learned that you are more gifted than I thought."

Katherine was thrilled by his praise. Sir Harry was a force in the music world, kind words from him could make a musician.

"And look who is here—Ambassador Boylan." He hailed Daniel as Daniel strode their way. "Mr. Ambassador, my old friend, what do you think? Have we found a new star in our galaxy?"

Daniel smiled, but it was cold and lashing. "Sir Harry, I have always known Miss Harriman was something special."

Sir Harry was astonished. "You two know each other?"

"We go back a bit. Katherine is an old family friend."

It gave him grim satisfaction to watch Katherine flush as she stumbled over an explanation. "We're not what you'd call close friends, Sir Harry…it's been years."

"Now, now, Miss Katherine," Sir Harry clucked tolerantly. "How many years could it possibly be? When you get to my age, you may start to count, but for you young people, time cannot possibly matter. Am I not right, Mr. Ambassador?"

"Time has a way of making its own statement," Daniel equivocated.

Sir Harry was confused, but shrugged it off. The night was too glorious to waste on cryptograms. "Ah, well, in any case, dear Katherine travels in exalted circles, if she can count the Ambassador to France among her friends!"

"Sir, it is I who am honored to be in the company of such stellar brilliance, yours as well as Miss Harriman's."

"Thank you, Mr. Ambassador. And, yes, Katherine was wonderful, wasn't she?" Sir Harry gushed. "Celestial! Divine. A natural wonder. And pardon my forwardness, but since you are such old friends, and since you have promised to attend my little soiree—another honor on this wondrous night—would it be possible for you to squire Katherine? She is unescorted this evening."

"What? No husband waiting in the wings?"

"No husband for our dear Katherine," Sir Harry smiled. "All is for art!"

Daniel took so long to answer that Katherine was sure he was going to refuse, but he merely bowed. "I would be honored."

"And who would not be honored to be escorted by the Ambassador to France?" Sir Harry beamed. "Now run along, Katherine and don't lose this opportunity to catch up on old times. I'm sure Ambassador Boylan's time is limited."

Katherine was glad the limousine was dark, it helped to hide her face. She sat straight and stiff, careful to look anywhere but at her old lover. She didn't notice, until it was too late, that he had reached for one of her stray curls, twirling it between his fingers.

"I sometimes wondered whether, if I saw you walking down a street, I might not recognize you. If you'd dyed your hair or something."

"Daniel, please, no scandal," Katherine begged softly, her eyes darting nervously toward the driver.

"A scandal would be the least of your problems!" The anguish of nine years surprising him with its intensity. All those years, he'd known he'd missed her, but until this moment he'd not known how much. Now, memories surfacing, the knowledge threatened to overwhelm him.

"Oh, Daniel," Katherine whispered, "it was for the best, I swear it! Let me get out. Forget you ever saw me."

"Forget I ever saw you?" he repeated, incredulous. "Now, that would be nice. Do you think this is my idea of fun?"

When he saw her hand edge toward the door handle, he grabbed her wrist and dragged her hard against him. "No way are you going anywhere, dear Katherine! Sir Harry did suggest we catch up on old times. All tarted up and provocative as ever," he whispered, his glance down her gown an insult, "how could I resist?"

He pushed her away. "Anyway, it's too late, my sweet. We're going to be on the front page of tomorrow's papers.

Or didn't you catch all those cameras flashing at the concert hall?''

Katherine's hand flew to her mouth, terrified at this unforeseen twist.

He laughed, but it was cold and short. "Come on, Katherine, think of it as a smart career move. Budding pianist captures interest of ambassador. There are worse things than making the front page of the newspapers with an ambassador on your arm! I don't know what they are, but I'm sure of it. Like maybe running away from the man you supposedly loved, disappearing from the face of the earth. What do you think about that, Katherine?'' His eyes were raging coals as he captured her chin. "Or do you still not remember?''

Anger seared through Katherine. What a fool she was to let him ride roughshod over her! How dare he try to ruin her night, the triumph she'd been working so hard for, all these years? "For goodness sake, Daniel,'' she said, grabbing hold of his wrist, "let me go! We spent two days together nine years ago! A lifetime, when you think about it!''

"Don't rate yourself so highly, lady,'' he snarled, his hand falling, "it's just the momentary shock.''

"Yes, well, I didn't think I'd ever see you again, either.''

"You mean, you *hoped* you'd never see me again!'' he snarled.

"Daniel, would you like me to explain?''

"Explain? Why? Would you tell me the truth?''

"I would try.''

"Oh, for chrissakes, Katherine, what kind of answer is that?''

But if Daniel wouldn't let her speak, curiously, he wouldn't let her out of his sight, either, the entire time they spent at Sir Harry's.

He stalked her.

She nibbled on lobster patties, sipped wine, and talked to all kinds of strangers, but everywhere she turned, there he was, so close by she could almost touch him. When she settled on the sofa, he stood behind her. During an interview with a music critic, he sat across from them. When she sought refuge on the terrace, mingling with Sir Harry's other guests, he propped his large frame against the glass door, silent but watchful. And when the party ended, well past 2:00 a.m., she found herself sharing his limousine again, when he offered in a most public way to drop her at her motel.

But she had to laugh when she couldn't unlock her motel door. Fingers that had just played the most intricate music ever written could now not turn a simple key. Disgusted by her fumbling, Daniel took the key from her cold hand and unlocked the door. Watching idly, she wondered if he remembered the last time he'd opened a door for her. If he did not, she certainly did! Smiling bleakly to herself, she walked into the room. Hearing the door close, she hoped against hope that he had left, but when she looked she wasn't surprised to find him standing in the doorway.

"If you're worried that I'm going to try something, I give you my word that I will not."

Katherine smiled weakly. "I never expected—"

"But I do have a few questions that need answers," he interrupted her, his patience at an end. "And I'm not leaving till I have them. That isn't too much to ask, is it, Katherine?"

"But I'm so tired, Daniel. Can't it wait until tomorrow?" His sarcasm was wounding, but that wasn't the worst. She knew she had to give him something, and she would, of course, but her primary concern was for her—their—son. Their love affair might be nine years dead, but Dylan, the result of their single blissful night, was very much alive, and she must protect him at all costs. Unfortunately, her mind was spinning when she had to be absolutely clearheaded. If Daniel found out about the existence of his child, and if he wanted the boy, his money and influence would be an unbeatable combination. Settling back on a chair, she shucked off her shoes and tried for an expression of unconcern. "Okay, Daniel, fire away. I haven't played twenty questions in years."

Unimpressed by her flippancy, Daniel's eyes registered his disapproval, but his voice, when he spoke, was precise and to the point. "I want to know why you didn't you wait for me, Katherine. That's all I really want to know."

"Oh, Daniel, wait for what?" she asked with heavy irony. "I was little miss nobody and you were bigger than life. When the dust settled, and I could think clearly, I knew which way the wind blew. Not a match made in heaven."

"I loved you!"

"Oh, no, there was never any mention of love! Maybe you thought you loved me, and maybe you really did." She shrugged. "But you didn't need me, and you were never going to. Talk about a one-sided relationship!"

"You said you loved me."

"Did I? Did I really?" He couldn't see how tightly Katherine clenched her hands and forced herself to go on. "Well, if you say so, maybe I did. But then, so did Althea! Remember Althea Almott, your once and future wife? You guys made the six o'clock news and were in all the next day's papers, including those nasty supermarket tabloids that nobody reads! I remember that part very well! How she was going to have a baby," Katherine reminded him bitterly. "How she was going to have a baby, Daniel, for God's sake!"

"And how long did it take you to pack your bags, after you read all those nasty papers?" he sneered.

"I left New York a few days later," she said, trying to salvage her dignity. "There was no point in staying."

"And do you always believe everything you read in the newspapers?" he demanded in a cold fury.

"What are you talking about?"

"Think about it! Use the brain that God gave you, Katherine, and think about it!"

Katherine searched her brain, trying to figure out what he was getting at. Her memories of him were pure and clear, but of the aftermath, nothing. Intentional, once she knew she was pregnant.

The silence was deafening, but Daniel waited her out.

"I don't believe you!" she breathed, as his meaning became clear.

"But didn't you follow my career?"

"I made a supreme effort not to! I never wanted to hear the name Boylan again!"

"I'm sure you didn't. But since I'm not in the habit of telling tales, I suggest you have a dilemma. My marriage to Althea Almott was so brief that her wedding band didn't even leave a mark on her pretty hand."

Katherine looked down at Daniel's long, dark fingers, a question on her lips that she didn't have the courage to ask.

But Daniel knew. "Yes, my dear, I did what every honorable man does when he's caught in the baby trap. But I knew the answer way before it was official."

"Are you saying that Althea Almott lied about being pregnant?" Katherine gasped.

"I guess I am," Daniel said quietly.

"I assumed she'd lost it, miscarried. But why? Why would she do such an awful thing and lie like that?"

"It couldn't be because she loved me?" Daniel asked sardonically.

Katherine blushed, and Daniel laughed, but it was sorrowful. "Yes, well, you're right about that, although I console myself with the notion that at the very least, she liked me a little. She certainly liked the notion of becoming an ambassador's wife, but you knew that. And then, her days in modeling were numbered. Even if she chose to lie about her age, the camera could not. Twenty-five just about does it, unless you're a supermodel like Althea, and even for a supermodel, thirty is a killing age in the trade."

"Poor Althea!"

"Oh, yes!" Daniel mocked, his voice thick with irony. "One woman rides me for the take, and another takes me for a ride."

"If you mean me, I did not!" Katherine denied hotly.

"What? You mean you didn't want to be an ambassador's wife, too?"

"You could only have one!" Katherine snapped.

"Ah, yes, but I thought to have a say in the matter!"

The room flooded with their angry silence, old memories surfacing to shimmer in the air, mingling with their hasty words.

"I made you a promise, remember?"

"Yes, you did, I remember, but you made a promise to Althea, too!"

"A promise you damned well knew I'd disavowed. You didn't trust me, Katherine."

"It had nothing to do with trust and everything to do with politics. You had no say in anything, the moment they announced your appointment as Ambassador to France. Or rather," she said briskly, "the moment you accepted the commission."

"What on earth are you talking about?"

"Oh, Daniel," Katherine sighed, "you were on your way up. Did you really want to be stopped?"

"It was my choice to make."

"No, you're wrong there. It wasn't. And it wasn't my choice, either. It was the choice of all those people waiting in the wings—your family, your friends, people you'd never even met and never would. People who had been waiting for years. Their hopes were pinned on you. People who had watched you grow up and helped groom you for the big moment. People who would never have their moment in the sun, but whose children might. People who were struggling and needed a reason to keep going. You were that reason! What we had—and Daniel, I swear to you it was wonderful and I do remember every blessed moment. But it was only a few days, and you had things to do. Big things. Bigger than us."

"So you were just a one-night stand?"

"I was worse—I was a *white* one-night stand. A white woman who had shared your bed for a single night and day, not nearly long enough to build a lifetime on, not even in the best of circumstances. And I couldn't be anything else. I would have been your downfall. And I didn't want you ever, somewhere down the line, to feel the onus of loving me.''

''I would never have thought loving you a hardship.''

''We were young. Eventually, it would have happened. It often does, you know.''

''You've certainly taught me that!''

''For which I'm sorry. But whatever was has passed. Come on, do you really look at me with regret?'' she asked, surprised that he was taking the high road.

''Yes, I do,'' he said heavily.

Katherine shrugged. ''Youthful longing. You have my sympathy, and that of a few million other people in this world. Welcome to the real world.''

''Do you accuse me of living in a dream world? Have I had so much?''

Katherine's thoughts flew to Dylan, her lonely struggles of the past decade, and the ones yet to come flashing past. None of which he would understand, sitting there so famous and wealthy...and safe. Her eyes turned to angry slits, but her voice was carefully modulated when she answered.

''I guess I do, to an extent,'' she nodded. ''There's something of the ivory tower in the life you've led, Daniel. Pampered by servants and secretaries, dining at the best tables, never needing to bother with the mundane, day-to-day business of living. I mean, when was the last time you dropped off your laundry or had to make out a rent check or came up short on the grocery line?''

''Well, thank you, Katherine, for telling me that I've wasted the last ten years.''

''I didn't say that! I know you've done great things, saved lives, even, and the world desperately needs people like you. We were talking about my life, remember?''

''I'm not sure what we're talking about. I feel like we're going round in circles, and I'm missing the point.''

Yes, Katherine thought, you're right, Mr. Ambassador, and the point you're missing is your son, Dylan.

But before he left, she had to ask. "Daniel, if you loved me so much, why didn't you ever come looking for me? You've had nine years to do so." She was sorry the minute the words were out of her mouth, when she saw his look of rage commingled with grief. "I only ask because I, too, sometimes wondered."

"Why should I have looked for you, Katherine? You're the one who left, remember? Tell me, what the hell did you think I thought, when I found you had left New York?"

Katherine had no answer. Was this the time to salvage her pride, tell him of his mother's visit the next day? How Mary Boylan had stormed into Katherine's apartment, alternately demanding, cajoling and finally weeping and pleading with Katherine to leave her son alone. Begging with a mother's tears for Katherine to let Daniel take his rightful place in history. Sobbing that if Katherine really loved him, she'd be willing to leave New York. Mary had been willing to pay, and Katherine finally agreed to let her. Only to flush Mary Boylan's check for ten thousand dollars down the toilet after she had left. It was obvious Daniel knew nothing about this. But it wouldn't accomplish anything to tell him, except perhaps to alienate him from his family. There was so much Daniel didn't know. No matter what he thought, he was well-protected, by everyone, even by her. She wondered if he'd thank them if he knew.

Misunderstanding Katherine's silence, Daniel smiled faintly and shuffled to his feet, feeling tired. What difference did it make, anyway, where Katherine had been, now that he knew why she had left him? He had promised to call, and he had. She simply hadn't loved him enough to wait. He thought she had understood, the day he'd left, and if she had only given him one more day, nine long years ago, she *would* have understood. Hadn't she felt in his touch how very much he'd loved her? Did she think he made love with such abandon to every woman he met? "I was so lonely," he whispered.

Katherine nodded but couldn't speak. Oh, yes, she knew.

He walked to the door and paused, his hand on the knob, searching for a way to leave and make sense of the decade they had lost. He watched as she, too, searched for closure.

"Maybe, in the morning..."

Katherine smiled faintly. Another morning. No problem. But she knew she would be gone within the hour.

Chapter Five

When he returned to Katherine's motel room the next day, Daniel was furious to find she had checked out the night before. This time Katherine's trail was easy to follow. He didn't even have to call the concert hall. A few dollars to the hotel clerk did wonders, and once back at his own hotel, he placed a few key telephone calls and informed his staff that he was extending his vacation. Then, very discreetly, he booked a flight for Phoenix, Arizona. A floppy felt hat and sunglasses did the rest. Early the next morning he was parked in front of Katherine's garden apartment.

Phoenix, Arizona. Who'd have guessed? But not a bad choice, when he thought about it. Lots of sun, a community with a strong interest in the arts, a great place for a pianist, actually. But she seemed to have holed up in some sort of community housing, if the bicycles and toys strewn across the lawn were any evidence. He wondered why, since she had said the night before that she had no husband.

Money was obviously an issue. Musicians didn't make a

whole lot, it was true. Then again, those people least likely to complain about her long hours of practice were people who made just as much noise—or whose kids did. And community housing could be a good source of students. Yes, a smart move.

He wondered what the charges were for vagrancy. He'd been lingering awhile in his rental car. He was reluctant to trot up to her door and ring her bell for fear she would refuse him entry. Finally, Katherine appeared. Long legs, hips swaying, a golden waterfall of hair, that tilt of her head. He watched as she climbed into a brown station wagon that had seen better days—about five years ago. She was in a hurry, too, because before he could reach her, she was speeding down the avenue. He had no choice but to follow wherever she was heading. To his surprise, she drove into the Arizona Center Mall parking lot and parked beneath a copse of palm trees. Pulling up beside her, he jumped out to block her path just as she was locking the door.

"Daniel!" Her hand to her chest, Katherine collapsed against her car.

"Who'd you think I was, the local mugger?" he scoffed.

"I didn't have time to think of anything, you scared the living daylights out of me! My goodness, wherever did you get that awful hat?" She grimaced.

Forgetting himself, Daniel smiled as he twirled the floppy hat in his hand. "And here I thought I was looking kind of cool." When he remembered his errand, his amusement vanished.

Seeing him frown, Katherine sighed. Maybe running out on him had been a bad idea, but she hadn't dreamed that he would follow her to Arizona. It was a pity because she and Dylan loved Arizona. It was the only home he'd known. But if she couldn't get rid of Daniel before he found out about their son, she'd have to move. She wondered how she would explain it to Dylan, but one look in Daniel's bitter eyes told her she would find a way. First, though, she would have to make sure he didn't follow her again. The eyes she turned on him were cool and steady. "Daniel, why are you here? We said everything that needed to be said in California."

"No, Katherine, we did not. We would have, if you weren't such a pro at running away. Think you could stand still long enough for us to finish a conversation?"

"Are you sure that all you want is conversation?" she snapped. She hated sounding vulgar, but she wanted to alienate him quickly. She had, judging by his look of disgust.

"Are you offering me something more than conversation, Katherine?" His eyes were assessing as he looked her up and down. "After all these years, you're still a mighty attractive woman. It wouldn't be hard to persuade me," he said, his eyes resting on her breasts, "if you stood still long enough to try."

Katherine looked away. "You flew down here, didn't you? Uninvited. How did you unearth me this time?"

"Were you trying to hide?"

Katherine turned back, her arms wide. "I'm here, aren't I? I can't be doing a very good job of hiding, can I, if you're here, too?"

"Then you're running away," Daniel said slowly.

"Look, exactly what do you want?" she asked, her mouth a tight line.

"Want? I don't want anything."

"Mr. Ambassador, you're doing a lot of running around for a man who doesn't want anything. Pretty dangerous for someone in your position, isn't it?"

Hoisting a backpack from the front seat, Katherine locked the car. Her high heels clicked on the cement as she crossed the parking lot, heading for the mall. Daniel matched her step for step. "I just flew a few hundred miles to talk to you, Katherine. Surely your shopping can wait."

Katherine laughed. "Daniel Boylan, some of us actually work in malls!"

"Are you serious? I don't believe you."

"Believe! And if I don't show up, I don't get paid," Katherine explained patiently. "It's not exactly a union shop. More like a burger joint. And I'm the head waitress."

"You're a waitress?" he repeated, horrified.

"I like to eat, so I work. It's called staying alive."

"But your hands," he said with a downward glance. "And with your background, your talent! And it's so exhausting."

"Hey, tell me something I don't know," she agreed with a sigh. "But you know how it is, music is a sometime thing." She laughed when she realized that he didn't have the faintest idea what she was talking about. "Watch out! I do believe the pampered diplomat is peeping out beneath that godawful hat! Look, Daniel, I needed a steady, low-key, decent-paying job. Something which didn't demand much, a job that let me fit in my music. At first, I gave private piano lessons, but the money wasn't enough. So then I taught music for a while for the symphony outreach program, but it started to overshadow my own work. Making up homework assignments takes time." She smiled wryly. "And so does grading tests, not to mention parent meetings, open-school night, class trips, etcetera, etcetera. I needed to simplify things but an office job would have been too...busy. Hey, I do all right. Waitresses make fairly good tips. I have what I need. It keeps me in hand lotion," she said with a grin.

She saw that he didn't believe her and felt a spurt of anger. Who was he to judge the life she led? If she hadn't had a child, darn right she wouldn't be here. Yes, her career would have flourished a whole lot faster; nobody knew that better than her. But she did have a child. And not once, not for a single solitary moment, had she ever regretted her choice, so to hell with Daniel Sheridan Boylan. Waitressing, music and Dylan were pieces of a puzzle she had fitted together, and a darned good job she'd done, too.

"If it's any consolation, I'm just filling in this morning for a sick friend. I usually work the midnight shift. Better tips!" she snapped. "And it leaves my days free to practice.'' And to be with Dylan, take him to school, attend his baseball games, help with his homework—be an active part of his life.

They had neared the mall entry when the security guard passed by on her scooter, did a complete circle and stopped in front of them. She took a long look at the tall black man hovering over Katherine. ''Everything all right, here, Kathy?''

''Of course, Ellie, thanks.'' Following Ellie's look at Daniel, Katherine gasped. ''Oh, Ellie, come on! This man's a friend of mine.''

Ellie was unapologetic. ''Just checking.'' She shrugged and, tipping her cap, sped away.

''I'm sorry about that, Daniel.''

''I guess they don't have many black folk hereabouts.''

''They certainly do!'' Katherine protested. ''That's why I was so surprised at Ellie's behavior.''

''Then I guess you don't have many black friends.''

No, only a son! Katherine wanted to shout. ''Look, Daniel, I can't stop to talk, now. I have to clock in so—''

''So I guess I'll do some shopping,'' he snapped back.

''No!''

Her protest was so loud that Daniel stared. ''Why not? Look, Katherine, we're going to finish our talk if I have to wait all day, understand that. You're right, I did not fly all this way just to have breakfast. So, you go on to work and I'll meet you when your shift is over. We'll go back to your place. I want some privacy.''

''No, not my place!'' Katherine said quickly. ''It's...er...being painted.''

''Okay,'' Daniel said, agreeably. ''Then we'll go to my hotel. Look, I have to be back in Paris tomorrow. This is the only free time I'll have for months. If you don't agree to see me tonight, I'm going right into your restaurant and telling your boss you've got the flu or something. Now, are we agreed or not?''

"Is this how you practice diplomacy?" Katherine growled, and Daniel smiled.

"Arm-bending is an integral part of every summit meeting, and I'm very good at it."

"I can see that!" Katherine snorted and flounced off, leaving Daniel to trail behind.

She was dismayed though, when Daniel entered the diner a few minutes later, an assortment of newspapers tucked beneath his arm. Armed with huge sunglasses and that absurd hat, he apparently felt safe sitting in a mall luncheonette in the middle of Phoenix, Arizona. She watched as he settled down in a corner booth overlooking the promenade and beckoned to her.

Shaking her head, Katherine walked over to his booth, giving Daniel ample time to notice that she'd changed into a singularly unattractive uniform of yellow and black checks. He winced inwardly at the dreadful orthopedic loafers she'd put on, the kind favored by people with bunions. And waitresses, he realized with chagrin. Her feet must kill her at night.

Glaring fiercely, Katherine handed Daniel a menu and scooted back to the counter for a coffee set up. Still a healthy specimen of woman after all these years, he thought ruefully, watching her hips swing as she walked away. When she returned with his coffee, he ordered the biggest breakfast he could, the lumberjack special. "And take your time bringing on the pie, sweetheart," he drawled. "I'm a slow eater."

Daniel sat quietly in his booth for two hours, and though the owner glanced at him from time to time, no one bothered him because business was slow. He lingered as long as he could, reading practically every line of his newspapers and surreptitiously watching Katherine. She worked hard, serving customers, filling salts and sugars, swiping tables, and mopping up the revolting mess a bratty toddler had made. My God, he wanted to shout, just yesterday, this woman was playing Schumann with the Los Angeles Philharmonic! He'd had to stifle the impulse to grab the mop from her hand and drag her from the diner.

And do what with her? he wondered. She was right to ask why he'd come after her, right to wonder what he wanted. For the first time since he'd boarded the plane the night before, he questioned the impulse that led him to this sleazy diner thousands of miles from the Champs-Elysèes. He didn't have a single answer save the stirring in his groin that he tried to ignore.

Although he would have liked to stay in the diner—he had so much to think about—eventually he had to leave. Striving for anonymity, he put on his shades and tugged his hat low, and began to relax and enjoy his newfound freedom. Roaming around the mall, peering into the store windows, he tried to remember the last time he'd wandered aimlessly. Katherine was right, he realized, as he watched some kids fool around, listened to the strange music coming from their boom box, checked out their clothes and absurd but artful haircuts. He did live in an ivory tower. He was so out of the loop that he felt like an extraterrestrial just landed.

Shopping away most of the afternoon, he was not in the least surprised to find all of what he'd purchased was for Katherine. When he tired of his little game, he returned to the diner for coffee and dessert. Dressed in street clothes, Katherine emerged from the employees' door just as he was finishing his apple pie. Quickly throwing some money on the table, he gathered up his shopping bags and left.

"Let's use mine," he decided, as she walked toward her car. "We can come back for yours later. My hotel isn't that far."

"Don't you trust me to follow you?"

"Why should I?" he asked coldly.

"Well, try."

Daniel gave her a long, hard look, then decided it wasn't worth the trouble to argue. She must know, anyway, that he would just follow her home if she didn't tail him. "All right, you follow me. But open your trunk, these packages are for you.''

"What? Oh, Daniel, what on earth?''

"Give me a break, Katherine," he said irritably. "I have absolutely no use for green leotards.'' Dropping the unwanted bags in her trunk, he got in his rental and started the engine. But only when he was sure she was ready to follow did he begin to drive. They parked at a posh motel and took the elevator up to his suite. He ordered room service while Katherine settled down, so jittery that he didn't even bother to ask her what she wanted. When he hung up the phone, though, he knew she'd been listening because she jumped.

"Do you have to act so skittish every time I look your way? What are you so nervous about? I'm not going to jump you. I thought I made that clear.''

It was true, she was nervous, but only because he was sharp. She was scared to death he'd trick her secrets from her. At all costs, he could not. She was lucky to have been able to dissuade him from visiting her home. Lucky, too, that Wilma had nothing planned for that night and could stay with Dylan. But now that Katherine was here, she was a little sorry not to be on her own turf. The luxury of the suite, of Daniel, looming large, made her feel at a disadvantage.

"Did you really shop all day?" she asked, stalling for time although she knew a showdown was near.

"It's been a long time, and I've never shopped for women's clothing before. I really got into it. Wait till you see what's in those bags," he said with a small smile. "I told all the salesladies you were small...sort of.''

Katherine blushed. "Why did you shop for me? Why not shop for yourself?''

"My manservant does all that. Anyway, it was fun to shop for you. There are some totally ridiculous outfits in your trunk.'' Another time, it would have been funny, but her lack of enthusiasm rankled. "Return them, if you want." He shrugged. "I really don't care.''

Katherine wanted to protest that it was really very thoughtful, but Daniel was already busy at the bar. Room service arrived just as he handed her a glass of wine. The aroma of hot food reminded her how hungry she was. She might work in a restaurant but she was very careful not to nibble for fear of gaining weight.

They ate silently, but steak was such a rare treat for her that Katherine was soon digging in unabashedly. "You'd think I hadn't eaten in three days." She smiled as she pushed back her chair, not a green pea left on her plate.

"Judging by your scrawny body, I might agree."

Katherine laughed. "Scrawny, my foot! I'm exactly my correct weight, which suits me just fine."

"You could use more meat on your bones."

Katherine shrugged. "Sorry if my figure displeases you."

"I didn't say it displeased me," Daniel said soberly. "Come, let's move over to the couch, it's more comfortable. It's time you gave me some answers, don't you think? And perhaps you have some questions for me?"

He reached for her hand, but Katherine ignored him. Having sensed the measuring looks he gave her during dinner, when he thought she wasn't looking, she wasn't sure how she would respond if he touched her. She found safety in an armchair, settling deep into the cushions while she watched his every move from beneath her lashes.

Daniel was careful to keep his distance, dropping his large frame onto a sofa, his long legs stretched out before him as he nursed the last of his wine. "I married her, you know."

"I know." Katherine knew exactly what he was talking about. It was as if they'd never left Los Angeles.

"Do you want to know why?"

"She was pregnant," she reminded him, her lips a stiff, polite smile.

"Yeah. Funny thing about that," Daniel mused, "but when she told me she'd lost the baby, I was disappointed."

"Did you want a child that badly?"

"Maybe. I guess. I don't know. Oh, I know you think I

married her because of what you saw on TV, because of the elaborate lie she constructed—in a very public way. But the truth was, the idea of a baby didn't sit all that badly with me. It was the way she did it that bothered me, the fact that she didn't trust me to do the right thing. Hell, everyone in proximity of a television heard her announcement that night! I myself heard about my impending fatherhood together with half the country! I was more than a little angry, as you might have guessed.''

"I noticed you were shocked. You didn't seem all that angry.''

"Althea knew I wouldn't make a public spectacle. But after we boarded the plane, I could hardly bear for her to touch me. We hardly spoke the entire trip. I didn't know what to say. I didn't know what to do. I live in the limelight, Katherine. If I'd announced to the world that I'd made the wrong woman pregnant, I would have been ruined.''

Well, you certainly did make the wrong woman pregnant, Katherine thought ruefully. Still, she could imagine the blow it had dealt his manhood, the way Althea took swift control of his future and his obligatory acquiescence. It wouldn't do to say, of course, but she actually did feel a stir of sympathy for him. After all, it was so long ago.

"I'm not looking for sympathy, if that's what you're thinking,'' Daniel said, his voice sharp when he saw the compassion in her eyes. "I simply want everything to be crystal-clear between us. I want you to understand that when Althea finished weaving her web, I was not the only one entangled. My family was, as well, and that made all the difference. She was thorough, was Althea. Even before she got to the airport, she had arranged for my parents to join us in Paris the following weekend. For our wedding, damn it, our wedding!''

"Well, why shouldn't she?'' Katherine asked gently. "You were engaged, after all.''

"No, we weren't, Katherine. I had called it off, remember? At least, I thought I had. For Pete's sake, do you really think I would have slept with you if I were engaged? I asked Althea for more time and she gave me about an hour.'' He laughed harshly.

"Call it whatever you like, Daniel, but you had proposed previously. I was there at the party! I heard! Althea could do whatever she wanted.''

Daniel sat up, his spine rigid with anger. "We were just dating! I never proposed! It was a conversation between Althea and my father! He was the one who brought up the subject! Then suddenly he was rushing off, telling everyone it was a done deal. That's what you heard!''

Ah, yes, his father! Katherine closed her eyes, reliving the memory of that awful night in the Boylan library. How his family had crowded around Daniel as *they* made the announcement of his engagement! Part of what he said was true, but still… "In the end, though, you were married.''

"In the end, I was…married,'' Daniel agreed, his voice a raw rasp. "Althea wanted badly to go to France as my wife, and I won't insult you by denying that I wanted to be ambassador. It was my whole life, up till that moment. Till I met you.'' He looked at her, his eyes filled with remorse. "And that's all I've ever wanted to say to you, these last nine years. It's all I ever wanted to tell you, in every fantasy I ever had about meeting you again. The pretty girl with golden hair and sparkling green eyes. It was you I wanted, all those years ago. But I was young and ambitious.''

Well, she, too, had been young, Katherine wanted to shout! And pregnant not long after! A chill ran through her, something akin to anger, but it quickly dissipated. If Daniel had been lost to circumstance long ago, she at least had Dylan, and a lot of sins could be forgiven for the gift that was her son. She wondered what Daniel valued most in *his* life. She sure hoped his career had been worth it.

"I've lived every day of the last nine years thinking about you, wondering where you were, if you were safe, what you were doing. If you were married…''

"Not even once," Katherine said, smiling slightly when she saw him glance at her left hand.

"Not even once."

The silence in the hotel suite was deafening until Daniel roused himself. Katherine watched as he turned to her. He hadn't lost any of that easy charismatic charm she'd found so seductive all those years ago. The craggy planes of his face had been confirmed by experience, and a thick air of authority was now a heavy mantle on his shoulders. If his hair was a little gray, his shoulders were still as broad, his body still in excellent shape. It would be impossible to meet him as a total stranger and not know that this was a man of substance.

He seemed pensive, lost in thought until he dropped his wild card. "And then of course, wonder of wonders, she wasn't pregnant. It was all a lie. The oldest one known to man, and I fell for it!"

Katherine covered her eyes, not knowing what to say.

"She was very persuasive, and I...I was very vulnerable. She knew about us, did I say?" he asked quietly, staring at Katherine's bowed head. "At least, that's what she told me later, in the heat of anger. I don't know how the devil she knew, she wouldn't ever tell me, but she used the race issue, of course, insisting that a multiracial marriage would be the ruin of me. She even flew in some bigwig black politicos to argue on her behalf. They were waiting at the embassy when we landed in Paris, ready to talk sense into me. A reality check, she called it. For chrissakes, Katherine, she even phoned the First Lady and got her to read me the riot act. She pulled out all the stops. Every time I think about it, I get sick to my stomach. My God, I was a blind fool."

Katherine jumped to her feet, unable to sit still at the vision that suddenly rose to mind. Mary Boylan, sitting in her living room the very next day, pleading with Katherine to leave New York and leave her son behind. Mary Boylan! Was her fine, elegant hand to be seen in this? Was it really *only* Althea working so quickly—too quickly, as Daniel had observed—or had Althea had help that Daniel never suspected.

"But you stood by and let it all happen!"

"Let it happen?" he repeated, quietly accusing. "Actually, I was in the embassy library, putting in frantic calls to New York City. To be told, every bloody time, that, 'sorry, sir, but that number has been disconnected'! Shouting to the transatlantic operator that, damn it, it wasn't possible! Dial again...dial again...dial again! For days. My God, Katherine, couldn't you have waited even one lousy week to hear from me?"

Katherine was incredulous. "Wait for what, Daniel? Your engagement was all over CNN! And lest we forget, there was that coveted ambassadorship! Good lord, you can't imagine how cheap and dirty I felt. Oh, I'm not blaming you. I know I went in with my eyes wide open, but in the light of day it didn't matter. I just wanted to crawl in the nearest hole and die. I definitely did not want to talk to you and listen while you made up some foul explanation of why we'd...done what we done...much less listen to some pathetic promise about the future when there was obviously not going to be any future!"

Daniel leaned forward, piercing the distance between them. "Katherine, you're not being fair. We had only known each other a short while. I knew I wanted to be with you, I told you so, but I needed time. Looking back, don't you think we needed time? What I did know was that I did not want to marry Althea."

"Liar!" Katherine cried, wrapping her arms about herself to hide their trembling. "Don't you remember what you said that night, in your mother's sewing room? *Oh, Katherine, if only you were black, or I was white, what a fine thing we would have!* Have you really forgotten the way you pushed me away and ran right into Althea Almott's politically correct black arms?"

"All right, I panicked. But if you want to be precise, then

you ought to remember that all that happened before we spent those days together.''

"Well, you know the old saw," she said, with a choked, desperate laugh. "Be careful what you wish for, you might get it." Searching the room, she found her bag, but before she could reach for it, Daniel had blocked her way.

"We're not finished," he growled. "I'm divorced now."

Katherine was aghast. "Do you mean to say that getting divorced counts for less than marrying outside your race?"

"Be careful, Katherine," Daniel advised her. "If I made a few mistakes, I'm sorry, but times have changed. The world is more sophisticated. We have the chance now that we didn't have nine years ago."

"Has it changed enough to let you marry me?"

"Why this leap to marriage?" Daniel frowned. "I want to see you, make a fresh start. It's a bit premature to talk of marriage. We haven't seen each other for years. How do you know that you would even want to marry me?"

Because I had your child, Katherine wanted to cry. And because she could not love a man more. But he didn't know that. And now Dylan was more important than either of them. They'd had their chance, now it was their son's. But she couldn't say that. If Daniel knew of the existence of his son, he would take Dylan away from her, as surely as the sun rose every morning. Men like Daniel didn't leave loose ends. And since he had no other children, it would underscore his claim. Katherine looked away, refusing to meet his eyes. "I was only talking hypothetically. It's risky business, this marriage stuff, for a prominent man like yourself."

"There's an element of risk for anyone, but I won't deny there's added pressure for someone who lives in the public eye. I tried to keep my divorce low-key, but who wouldn't? I also don't want to be a damned statistic, twice divorced. It's true that I know a lot more about sex than I do about love," he conceded. "But what about you, Katherine? How much do you know about love? You ran away, you know you did, at the first sign of trouble. You didn't exactly fight for us, either.''

"No, I didn't," Katherine admitted, "and you didn't issue any denials of your impending marriage in any newspaper I read—not the next day, the next month, or the next year. So don't go blaming me, Mr. Boylan.''

"I don't blame you!" Daniel ground out, rubbing his brow. "I blame us both. But we're not children anymore. You've changed, I can see that, and so have I, but not so much that I don't remember what we had. I think you do, too. Can't you give us another chance?''

"A chance for what? A transcontinental love affair? Surely you can find somebody more glamorous...and willing! I don't do one-night stands, anymore, Daniel. You were the first and the last!''

"That's a rotten thing to say! I've been thinking about you for nine goddamn long years, and I want you as much now as I did then. I think it's a little more than sex! Don't tell me you feel nothing!''

His arms a cage she stumbled into unwilling, Daniel swooped down and challenged Katherine with a punishing kiss. Her mind would have liked to protest his angry urgency, but it didn't seem to hold sway over her body. Her senses whirled as she felt his tongue savage her mouth, demanding a response, and she hated how she savored every moment.

He felt it, too, in the heat of her body, the way she arched into him, the way her breasts seemed to swell beneath his touch. "You see, I'm right!" he whispered, tracing the delicate contour of her jaw with his finger. "You do feel something. Tell me what you want, Katherine. Anything. I'd give you anything.''

But Katherine could barely talk. To even raise her head was an effort, so devastating was his impact. Her cheek against the starchy cloth of his shirt, she could feel his heart pounding and knew it matched her own.

"We were good together, once, remember?" his voice

was a husky plea as his lips brushed her forehead. "It can be like that again."

Katherine froze at the magnitude of her desire. Another minute and he would have her on his sheets. Pushing him aside with a violence that surprised them both, she scoured the room for her belongings. "I have to go."

"Damn it, Katherine, why are you doing this?" Daniel scowled. "How many boats are we going to miss?"

Grabbing her bag, Katherine practically ran to the door. "Don't you have a plane to catch, Mr. Ambassador?"

"Is that how it is? Another disappearing act?"

"Mr. Boylan, you have my address. You may send me flowers every day, if you like. Perhaps you should have done that nine years ago. But you didn't. And no, Daniel, I don't really care to hear why you didn't try to find me after your divorce. It won't change a thing. Besides, I think you're wrong. You're far too prominent to date an ordinary waitress—especially a white waitress from the midwest. I think my skin color would have mattered less ten years ago than it would matter now! The press would have a field day, and so would just about everybody else. Just imagine the news crew waiting patiently outside the luncheonette—in the middle of a mall, for goodness sake!—the reporter biding his time till I got off duty so he could ask me a few questions. Like, when exactly, Miss Harriman, did you meet Ambassador Boylan? Or, how friendly are you and the ambassador? And, does Ambassador Boylan's ex-wife know about you two? Does the president? And how about that famous rag that nobody reads but that somehow has a circulation of four million?" Katherine shuddered. "I won't get vulgar, but they will, Daniel, they will! A man in your position has no time to...play. And that's putting it politely! The only negotiation you're allowed is at a conference table, certainly not in your personal life. You have no personal life. But I do, and I can't let it get mixed up with yours."

Hardening herself to the shock in Daniel's eyes, she hacked away at the feeble moorings of their love. "I'm sorry

Daniel, I'm just not rich enough or famous enough or gutsy enough to survive a love affair with you. So where exactly does that leave us?''

Daniel said nothing but Katherine managed a tight smile as she opened the hotel door.

"Quite what I thought, too," she whispered, her voice fading as she gently closed the door, leaving Daniel to stand in the twilight of hushed stillness, wondering where it all went wrong.

Chapter Six

Daniel didn't send flowers to Katherine when he arrived at the embassy, not that day, nor the next. And now, one year later, Katherine haunted him as he hurried down the hall to answer her call. He passed urns lavishly filled with roses and thought how Katherine had been holding yellow roses the night of her concert. Funny how the mind chose to remember such trivialities. Flowers were such soft womanly things. The chambers of his life were furnished with tooled leather, expensive brandy and Cuban cigars. No creamy lace softened its hard edges, no stockings hung to dry in his bathroom, no flowery perfume scented his bedroom. When he lifted the phone, his hand was shaking.

"Ambassador Boylan speaking." His deep voice had a harsh rasp.

"One moment, sir," the switchboard operator said.

"Irma, this is a private call. Switch to my private line, please."

"Certainly, sir."

An eternity of clicks later, Irma was gone, and the light, breathy voice of Katherine Harriman came through from thousands of miles away.

"Daniel?" Katherine was aching to spill over into tears, but she held them back with a bravado she did not feel. "Daniel, is this really you?"

"Yes, Katherine, it's me," he said slowly.

"Daniel, I'm so sorry to bother you…"

It was all too much for her, too big and there was so little time. She cried while he held on, waiting patiently until she could speak. But when she could it was a garbled mess. "My baby, he's so sick, and they're not sure why. He looks terrible. He's lost so much weight; he's got all those tubes in him he's…"

"Katherine, calm down!" Daniel commanded, trying to stem her hysteria. "What baby? I didn't know. It doesn't matter, I'm glad you called. What's the problem? Who is sick? Speak slowly. And louder. I can hardly hear you."

Her voice was so small, he could almost feel her collapse into herself. "Didn't you get my letter?"

"I'm sorry, Katherine, no, not until this evening."

"Oh. I wondered why you didn't call. I figured you were still mad at me."

"Then you must be desperate if you're calling me."

"Yes, yes…desperate."

"Katherine, I'm not angry, not anymore, so you can talk to me. Trust me. I'll help you any way I can, you know that. What is the problem?"

"My son. My son." There, it was out, she'd said it. She waited for him to speak and spoke instead to his silence. "They say they're doing everything they can, everything, but they, the doctors, they can't figure it out. They tell me what it could be, but not what it is. Yesterday, Dylan, that's my son, he fell into a coma!" She sobbed from halfway around the world. "They told me about a specialist in New York. She studies blood disorders. Daniel, you know I wouldn't ask, I swear I would never ask, not for myself, but he's so young—Dylan—I mean, and this doctor, she's so expensive. I'm sorry, but you're the only one I know rich enough to help me. Oh, Daniel, help me, help him, help my baby!''

"Katherine, calm down! Of course I'll help. Just calm down and tell me what you need. What hospital is your son in?''

Katherine named a hospital in Arizona. "Forgive me, Daniel, please forgive me,'' she sobbed.

"Katherine, there's nothing to forgive. You must know I'll stand by you. I'm glad you trusted me enough to call. You don't have to apologize for anything.''

"Yes, I do. I must!''

"Katherine, babies get sick all the time, their parents get all bent out of shape, and then the babies get better and the parents wonder what all the fuss was about. He does seem very ill, from what you say, but— Look, let me call the hospital and get a better picture of the problem. I'll arrange everything from here. You don't sound in any shape to do this. Let me speak to...'' Daniel forced himself to say it. "Let me speak to your husband. We'll work it out between us.''

"Oh, there is no father.''

He was surprised. "Oh. Oh well, of course,'' he apologized quickly. "I didn't mean to pry. It doesn't matter.''

Daniel could hear nothing but the low keening of Katherine's sobs until he heard her try to catch her breath. "Daniel, my son, my baby, he's not really a baby. Well, he's my baby, but... I know I should have told you, but... Bravery's not my strong point. You told me so yourself.''

"Look, Katherine, this really isn't any of my business,'' he said gently. "I'd help you under any circumstances.''

Thousands of miles away, Katherine heard the pity in his voice and knew that he still didn't understand. He would not be so kind.

"Daniel! My son, Dylan, is nine years old! For God's sake, do your math!''

The silence was prolonged, it stretched ten long years. Katherine could almost feel him thinking, calculating, and hear his harsh intake of breath as he stepped down from his ivory tower. She was listening so hard, she almost missed his next words.

"I'll be on the next flight out," he said quietly.

"Daniel!"

But the receiver was dead.

He was on the first Concorde out of Paris the next day, a private jet waiting when he landed in the States to fly him from New York to Arizona. He was at the hospital within thirty minutes of landing in Phoenix. Plenty of time to wipe the sweat from his brow but not long enough to quell his nausea.

The irony of celebrating life's crises with Katherine at hospitals was not lost on Daniel as he passed through the brass revolving doors. The woman who opened the door to his son's private room wasn't Katherine. She was a tall, older woman, very dark-skinned, silver-haired, dressed in a sturdy blue cotton dress. Unsmiling, she stepped aside. Ordering his bodyguards to remain outside, he entered the quiet room.

"Don't you even want to ask my name?" Daniel asked, disturbed by her laxity.

"I know your name, Mr. Ambassador Daniel Sheridan Boylan. I've known it forever. About time you showed up," she said fiercely.

Daniel glared back at the feisty old woman. "I didn't know."

"Well, now you know. I'm Wilma Batterson, Katherine's housekeeper and Dylan's baby-sitter, but mostly a family friend. Maybe their only friend, I'm thinking," she added pointedly.

"Not anymore," he swore softly.

There was derision in the look she sent him and a challenge in her voice. "Well, we'll just have to see about that, won't we? Fine feathers don't make fine birds, I always say."

"I'll bet you say a great many things, Miss Batterson," Daniel said smiling faintly.

"Only everything that's on my mind. Katherine and I go back a long ways. We have no secrets, that much I can tell you!" Then she proceeded to tell him more. "I must have told her at least a thousand times that she needed a man by her side—she needed the boy's father by her side. A boy needs his father, I say. But Katherine always said no. But it was just a matter of time, wasn't it? Long overdue, too. Seeing as how you're here, I reckon she finally listened to me. I'll go find her and let her know you're here."

Well, there was one less explanation he'd have to make, Daniel thought grimly, as he placed his overnight bag on a chair. He stood quietly, not daring to step toward the bed where a small boy lay, an IV taped to his thin brown arm. There were so many wires and machines buzzing that it was apparent the child was in coma.

His child.

Daniel didn't bother to hide his distress as he looked down at his son for the first time. He didn't know where to begin sorting out his feelings as, tenderly, he covered Dylan's small hand with his own. Caramel-brown—yellow-brown, now—and so frail, the toll of whatever disease his young body was fighting. The boy's features—Daniel couldn't be sure of course—but they looked too beautiful to be his, more like Katherine's, a lot like Katherine's. Well, he supposed the child ought to look like his mother. But the fingers beneath his were long like his own.

"Dylan," he whispered and heard his voice crack in the sterile, white void of the hospital. Dylan, he prayed, the boy's palm pressed to his lips as he claimed his son with his tears. Dylan, live and I will never leave you, I swear it.

Wilma found him that way when she returned. "Go see to your woman," she ordered him tersely. "Katherine is waiting for you in the visitors' room."

Daniel raised his head slowly, his amber eyes bleak, Dylan's hand still cradled in his. "Why didn't she tell me?"

Wilma looked at him with all the contempt she could muster. She had witnessed too many of Katherine's faltering steps to survive and make a life for her son, had herself been a large part of that uncertain history and had no use for self-pity. "There's an old expression, Mr. Ambassador," she said coldly. "You pays your money and you makes your choice. Yeah, I thought you'd have heard it. She's down the hall in the visitors' room, my Katherine. And don't you be giving her no grief, you hear? We take turns," she said when she saw him hesitate to leave. "He's never alone, my poor baby, except for wherever he's at, now," she added softly.

Daniel stepped out into the bright corridor, the sickening-sweet hospital smell turning his stomach. With the help of a passing orderly's direction, he strode down the long hall to the visitors' room. It was empty except for Katherine, curled up sleeping on an unforgiving plastic couch. Kneeling beside her, he nudged her shoulder and she jumped. When she saw who it was, she would have turned away, but Daniel caught her up in his arms. Too weak to fight, Katherine began to cry, wracking sobs that left her a muddled heap against his wet shirt, but he didn't care about anything except holding her once again.

They didn't try to talk. They just sat quietly. Anyone who walked in left quickly, not daring to intrude on their grief. Wilma came in at one point, stared at them curiously, then left without a word.

The next time Wilma appeared it was to say that Dr. Gabriel was examining Dylan but would like to talk to them when he was finished. Her voice was soft when she spoke to Katherine. "Honey, you look dreadful. You need a good, strong cup of tea. I'll go get us some."

Daniel noticed that Wilma didn't offer to get him anything, and any other time he would have laughed at the snub. But Wilma was right, Katherine looked awful. Her face was colorless, her hair looked greasy, and her vivid green eyes had become dark hollows of worry. She'd lost weight she could ill afford to lose. Watching her smooth down a crumpled dress that no longer fit, he realized what a featherweight she had been on his lap.

Katherine felt weak, her legs supporting her on sheer will-power, as she scrambled to her feet. Brushing away tears that still threatened to spill over, she stood motionless in the middle of the room.

"Have you seen him?" she asked dully, sparing them both the nonsense of a greeting.

Daniel didn't answer, just rubbed his neck, dashed a hand across his tired eyes, cracked his knuckles—and he never cracked his knuckles!—until he realized how nervous all his jerking movements must seem. Spanning the short space that separated them in three steps, he loomed over Katherine, his voice when he spoke a hard, cold blade. "Talk fast, Katherine, talk real fast. As if your life depended on it."

"Does it?"

"I'm pretty angry."

Katherine closed her eyes against the pressure of his hands as they slid about her neck. "Would it help to say I'm sorry?"

"Lady, you couldn't begin to apologize, the way you've played around with my life."

Cupping her chin, he searched her face, his grip on her neck imperceptibly tightening as she opened her eyes. "Daniel, you aren't entirely blameless, you know. You made choices, too."

"You kept my son from me!"

Katherine had never seen Daniel so angry, and the sight was terrifying. Though she knew he wouldn't hurt her, not physically, he was a master juggler of words. He would use them well. Unless she could make him listen to her first.

"He's a fine-looking boy, our son," she whispered, gripping his wrists. "Tall and dark, like you. He'll be a big man like you, too, a handsome man, a son to be proud of. He has hazel eyes, a legacy from me, I guess. Beautiful hazel eyes," she said softly, "with the thickest black lashes.

Wilma is always teasing him about his pretty-boy looks, telling him how the girls will be knocking down the door.''

Katherine refused to turn away, not even in the face of his unforgiving scrutiny. "Daniel, you didn't want me!" She sighed, exhaustion fighting with her need to stay awake. "You had so many chances to change your mind, to try to find me, but you never did. Over and over you chose your career, and every time you did, you rejected me. And when you rejected me, you rejected your son," she whispered.

"And you never needed me?" he demanded, shaking with rage. "While I was out saving the world, was I so useless to my own family?"

"Oh, we needed you, all right. You have no idea how many times I dialed the embassy. But I always hung up because there was no reason not to. I reminded myself it was what you wanted."

"How the bloody hell did you know what I wanted?"

Her lips a thin, white line, Katherine stood her ground, even in her exhausted and disheveled state. "I asked, remember? That night in the sewing room, the most humiliating night of my life! But it was your moment of truth, wasn't it, Daniel? Anything that happened after that was…just sex, only I didn't know it then. It was afterward, when I had time to think…''

"How dare you!"

"Oh, Daniel, I don't mean to denigrate what we had. They were wonderful days, and I treasure the memory. But you left with a smile, and not much else, certainly no serious commitment. Didn't it ever occur to you that you could have made me pregnant? On the contrary, you were married the following weekend! And I *was* pregnant, even if I didn't find out for another month. I thought it was nerves, at first, more fool me. And when I decided not to abort, I knew full well what my future would be, and that you wouldn't be part of it. That's why I always hung up on the embassy— the few times I called, in moments of weakness. But this…this time it was a matter of life and death.''

"I curse you for that decision!" he swore, dropping his hands before he succumbed to the temptation to throttle her.

But Katherine wasn't afraid. She followed him with her sad eyes and her sorrowful voice. "Daniel, take responsibility for your decision, why don't you? You chose power over love. Why don't you admit it?"

Daniel hauled her up so they were nose to nose. "All right, I admit it! Happy? No one held a gun to my head. And when I walked down the aisle with Althea Almott, I knew where I was headed. But I didn't know I had left my seed in your belly. Damn it, Katherine, it would have made a difference!"

"Not to me!" Katherine cried. "You couldn't have him without having me! And you didn't want me!"

"Oh, lady, I wanted you so much I could cry with shame."

"So you should have!" she retorted, "because it became my shame, when I became pregnant. Then life became bigger than just us, I had responsibilities to a child. It had to mean something, getting pregnant like that, the first time."

Daniel hesitated, wanting to say more, but, as if on cue, Wilma had appeared. Holding two hot cups, she gave one to Katherine as she glanced around the waiting room, then handed one to Daniel. "Yeah, well, as long as I don't see any blood."

"Thanks, Wilma, but I never leave traces."

Wilma snorted and said nothing, but only because Dr. Gabriel was walking toward them. Holding out his hand to Daniel, his smile was tentative. "Good day, sir. Glad to finally meet you. I'm Dr. Gabriel and I'm in charge of your son's care. Mrs. Harriman explained that you were travelling in Asia and almost impossible to contact. I'm sure these ladies are glad you're back, but I guess you know that."

Nobody bothered to correct the doctor on the name, although Daniel distinctly heard Wilma mutter something as they shook hands. If the women had managed to keep his identity a secret, it seemed a wise idea, now, for Dylan's sake. The boy's safety was going to be a major issue the moment news of his existence got out. Katherine's, too. An issue Daniel was going to have to deal with very soon. The two bodyguards standing sentinel outside would not be enough. And he had formed some very distinct ideas about how, on the long plane ride over. A few favors called in and some well-placed phone calls would do the trick. For now, the doctor was center stage.

The small group listened to what he had to say, which wasn't much. No change, no progress, and he snapped up Daniel's offer to fly in a specialist. When Dr. Gabriel heard the name, he was disbelieving. Dr. Sloan was too famous and important, she wouldn't come. When Daniel told him it was a done deal, that the famous Dr. Sloan was arriving on a private jet first thing in the morning, Dr. Gabriel was astounded, Katherine started to cry, and Wilma actually smiled.

The small group took themselves back to Dylan's room, Dr. Gabriel lingering to answer Daniel's questions while Katherine sat like a wraith, holding her child's hand. When the doctor left, Wilma asserted her authority.

"Take that woman home!" she ordered Daniel, "and don't bring her back till she's fed! And a nap would be nice, too," she said, glaring at Katherine. "That is one exhausted lady, Mr. Ambassador, so you take good care of her!"

Daniel nodded, accepting Wilma's trust. Katherine was beyond arguing, and they drove to her home in silence. She was a motionless figure huddled in the passenger seat, her head leaning against the window. Daniel practically carried her up the stairs when they arrived at her house.

"Coffee?" she mumbled automatically, as they entered, it was only out of politeness. Once Katherine left the living room, she never reappeared. Daniel decided to give her time alone. On his own, he looked around.

Shabby genteel, they called this in Europe. Not even. A frayed sofa, two nasty-looking armchairs, a flea-market coffee table that had seen too many wet soda cans. Even the knickknacks were sparing. But the window was filled with plants that gave the room life, a baby grand of some value stood in a corner waiting for Katherine, the few scattered toys... It hit him like a brick, this was Dylan's home. Somewhere was his son's room, filled with all sorts of treasures that Daniel had never helped him gather, the rites of passage in the boy's young life.

Feeling old beyond his years, he walked the few steps to the closed door behind which Dylan's most valued possessions were stored. Opening the door slowly, he used the hall light to peer into the dark room. He could see that Katherine had given Dylan the master bedroom and taken the smaller one for herself. Spying a small lamp on the night table, he crossed the room and switched it on. It revealed mostly shadows and allowed him to ease his way slowly into the world of a nine-year-old boy.

A very neat boy, Daniel couldn't help noticing—or a compulsive mother, more than likely—because Dylan's bed was carefully made and the room in immaculate order. All of Katherine's extra money must go to the boy, Daniel figured, judging by the expensive equipment that filled every nook and cranny. A tropical fish tank gave the room a blue cast, and the microscope sitting next to it was state of the art. A name-brand computer occupied center stage, along with a printer and a scanner! Hanging around the room were those bigger-than-life posters no kid could live without, many of them of African-Americans, Daniel realized in surprise. The books that filled the shelves included biographies of African-American heroes, too. And if he wasn't mistaken, that was a really good reproduction of an African ceremonial mask. It seemed Katherine made sure the boy took pride in his race.

Daniel sat on Dylan's bed and drank in everything he could, trying to get a handle on his unknown son. It was a few minutes before he noticed a picture on the shelf, a group of young boys in silky soccer uniforms. With blazing red shorts and socks and red-and-black jerseys there would be no mistaking them on the field. Daniel smiled. The Red Zebras, said the plaque in the picture. Daniel picked out his son in an instant. The tall, lanky kid with a build promising to be like his own. The kid with his mother's shy, awkward grin. Tawny-skinned, the result of mixed parentage, but blessed with tight black curls. Anyone with eyes could see he was a damned fine-looking boy, almost beautiful, as Katherine had said, and he would grow to be a handsome young man. In the not-too-distant future, Daniel realized with a painful wrench. The boy was nine now. He would be going off to college in less time than that. Tears filled his eyes with the weight of his loss, and he hugged the picture to his chest. "Forgive me," he whispered into the blank silence and bent his head in sorrow. Then he placed the picture exactly where he'd found it and went in search of Dylan's mother.

He found Katherine in the immaculate kitchen, staring sightlessly at the cup she was holding. A chipped cup, his critical eyes noticed. He couldn't help noticing, too, how bare the kitchen was, no cumbersome food machines taking up valuable space on the spare counter, no dishwasher in sight, the pots in the dishrack battered. They must live on the edge of poverty, what little she had going to Dylan, he guessed, remembering all the equipment in his son's room. Lifting the cup from Katherine's hands, he placed it in the sink. Wordlessly, he led her to the bathroom and turned on the shower. Just as wordlessly, he left.

When she showed up in the kitchen twenty minutes later, Katherine was wrapped in a threadbare robe. Daniel bet she had those thick socks on her feet because she didn't own any slippers. She smelled wonderfully of soap, her tired face was shiny from a good scrub, and her hair was freshly shampooed. She sat obediently when he motioned to the table where he had placed a steaming bowl of soup. Canned stuff, but at least it was hot. Sweet tea and buttered toast completed the meal, hardly an appetizer for Daniel, but he figured it was all Katherine would be able to manage.

When she was done, her head nodding with fatigue, Daniel took Katherine by the hand and led her to her tiny bedroom. Too weak to protest, she let herself be tucked into the narrow bed. "Sleep, now. We'll talk later."

She slept a long time, giving him plenty of time to think, to make decisions that were surprisingly easy, and to make the phone calls that would bring everything together. Then he gave himself a well-deserved catnap on her lumpy couch.

Katherine woke the next morning to the smell of freshly brewed coffee and the enticing smell of frying bacon.

And burning toast!

Stretching, she smiled. Dylan must be giving Wilma a really hard time to make her burn the toast. He probably couldn't find his sneakers again.

Her memory returned with a jolt.

Wilma never burned the toast, and Dylan wasn't looking for his sneakers! Throwing off the blankets, Katherine threw her legs over the side of the bed, not realizing until it was too late that Daniel was leaning on the door, taking in his fill.

"Very nice." He smiled, admiring her bare legs. "But then I always liked your body. I'm glad to see you've kept in shape." Not put off by the flannel nonsense she wore, he stared hard at her high, round breasts and let his eyes travel down to linger on her thighs.

Katherine was unamused by his blatant scrutiny. "Poor timing and poor taste, Daniel," she grumbled, trying to ignore his interest while she searched for her robe.

"Really, Katherine," he said lightly. "I was stating a fact, not trying to seduce you. I wouldn't, not now. I'm a grown man, perfectly able to control myself, usually..." Perversity made him linger when he saw how it annoyed her. He wasn't feeling in charity with her, anyway, even if he sympathized with her plight.

Unable to find her robe, Katherine had to cross to the bathroom in her thin nightgown, blushing like a rose.

Though it was buttoned to the neck, she felt naked, the way he watched her every step.

"Bastard," she muttered and knew it was a mistake the moment the words were out. Daniel grabbed her arm, his eyes a glittering haze of lust.

"So I am," he agreed, swearing crudely as he tunnelled his fingers into her hair and tipped her head back to meet the hard, insistent line of his lips. She tried to fight him, thrashing about until she realized it was only making things worse, that it would take more than a night of sleep to give her back her strength. But Daniel was generous. His mouth softened on hers the instant she relaxed.

"An aperitif," he promised, amused by her displeasure as he placed her back on her feet. "But for now—coffee's on!" Katherine glared at his back as he closed the bedroom door, furious at the small laugh he left hanging in the air.

Twenty minutes later, showered and dressed, she found him in the kitchen, hovering over a freshly brewed pot of coffee. "I must get back to the hospital. I've been gone too long."

He poured two mugs and thrust one in her hand. "I had Wilma's permission to let you sleep forever. But I made some calls a few minutes ago, and one of them was to the hospital. It's status quo. Now you've been updated, please sit down and eat. We'll leave as soon as you have breakfast, or Wilma will have my head."

She found herself eyeing a tower of buttered toast. One for me, ten for you, she thought mutinously. But five minutes later, when he placed a dish of scrambled eggs directly in front of her, she realized how hungry she was.

They hardly spoke, but when she finally pushed away her plate, Daniel seemed satisfied. "Now, may we go? Wilma needs to be relieved, too. And there's your doctor friend coming."

He eyed her as he munched his fifth piece of toast. "She won't need our help. Anyway, she's been there an hour already," Daniel told her, glancing at the clock. "Why are you surprised? I'm a bloody ambassador. It helps to get things done.''

The long, suspicious look she gave him, as he watched her over his coffee, almost made him laugh. ''Try to trust me a little, Katherine. I mean to make things up to you and the boy.''

Her lips pursed in disapproval made him laugh, and she left in a huff to gather up her belongings. When she returned, Daniel looked her over and thought the sleep and the hot food had done wonders for her. Not that they entirely removed the worry from her eyes or the circles from beneath them, but she was brighter, more awake, calmer. Was it too much to hope that his presence had helped?

They drove in silence to the hospital—just the way they'd left it—and went straight to Dylan's room. The specialist was there, delivered just as Daniel had promised, sitting by Dylan's bedside as she studied her new patient's chart and conferred softly with Dr. Gabriel. Dylan was inert as ever and Daniel read the disappointment in Katherine's eyes. She had expected a miracle. Well, there was still time.

Dr. Sloan rose to greet them, shaking hands with Daniel as if they were long-lost friends, Katherine noticed irritably. Dr. Sloan was upbeat, and her optimism was a comfort. What exactly the doctor said, though, Katherine hardly heard, content to let Daniel take charge. Daniel was right, he had the power, and people responded to it. Judging by the veneration in Wilma's tired, bloodshot eyes, she was seduced by it, too.

In the end, what with all the blood tests Dr. Sloan ran, Daniel's emphatic assurance that there was no sickle-cell anemia in his family history and Katherine's certainty that she hadn't taken any drugs while she was pregnant, it was decided that a virus might be the culprit. They didn't always show up on the tests, though, so it was a shot in the dark until the lab work came through. Dylan had all the symptoms, the doctor said, and Dr. Gabriel agreed that treating him for a virus certainly couldn't hurt. Time would tell. At least the boy wasn't getting any worse! But Dr. Sloan had brought a black bag full of medicines to try, some so new they weren't on the market yet. She looked at Katherine for permission. When Katherine nodded, the doctors left to confer and determine the course of treatment.

At which point, Daniel turned to Wilma and ordered her to take some of her own advice. When Wilma refused to go home, Daniel walked up to her and used his more than six feet to scare her into obedience. "You are to go home and sleep, old lady!"

Wilma almost blew a gasket. "Who you talking to, little big man? Your mama let you speak to her like that?"

"She'd box my ears if I did." Placing his hands firmly on Wilma's shoulders he bent his head, going eye-to-eye. "Come on, Wilma," he said softly. "We have to share the burden, and we need you, but not in the shape you're in. And I definitely need you in decent condition by tomorrow."

"Why's that?" she demanded.

"That's a carrot dangling in front of you, Wilma. Now, please do as I ask. No arguments. I asked the information desk to allow my limo to wait out front. It should be here by now," he said, glancing at his watch.

Unsure, Wilma looked at Katherine, but Katherine hadn't heard a word. She was busy bathing Dylan's face and hands, combing his hair gently, murmuring sweet nothings, just in case he could hear. Wilma left, vowing to return at three.

Katherine and Daniel never left Dylan's side. Ever efficient, Daniel had arranged for a decent lunch to be delivered from a local restaurant, knowing that hospital food could be pretty bad. Together, he and Katherine watched as Dr. Sloan returned again and again, watched as nurses came to set up the IV with the new medication, watched as they monitored Dylan's vitals, drew blood, took Dylan's temperature, recorded his pulse. With every procedure, Daniel saw Katherine draw a little more into herself, saw her shoulders droop and her face grow paler. There was nothing he could do.

Dylan lay on his bed, motionless, and only his awakening would count for anything.

True to her word, Wilma returned after lunch, looking a thousand times better. She took Katherine's place at Dylan's bedside and with a glare Daniel thought should be bottled, she ordered them out of the room.

With his hand at the small of her back, he steered Katherine from the room. "I've ordered a late dinner to be sent up around nine," he told Wilma. "Which is about when we'll be back. If we're late, start without us."

"There is no need for us to be gone so long," Katherine said coldly. "A walk around the block will be sufficient."

"We have business to attend to."

Katherine's brow puckered. "What kind of business? Is the doctor—?"

Daniel refused to explain. "No, no, nothing like that. We're just going for a short ride." He hurried into the back of a limousine as his bodyguards took the front seats.

Though she tried to guess their destination, she'd never seen these streets before. She thought they were pretty close to Scottsdale, but pride forbade her to ask. She was pretty curious when they pulled up to a rambling old ranch house and Daniel asked her to wait while he climbed the rickety porch steps.

She watched him take the steps in two, his back ramrod straight, his body lean, almost athletic. He had certainly kept himself in shape. Even in a crowd, he would be compelling, an aura of calm and command sitting comfortably on his broad shoulders. She had lied when she'd said she hadn't followed his career. She knew in great detail that he was widely admired for his agile mind, that he was considered an expert negotiator at the summit table and that he had been personally responsible for a peace agreement between two longstanding enemies two years before, almost earning him the Nobel Peace Prize. It was only his personal life that he failed to negotiate properly, and Katherine was intrigued by the paradox. Watching him stoop to accommodate the tiny old woman who had answered the doorbell, she wondered what he was negotiating now.

"They were expecting us," he said, when he returned a moment later, "but I just wanted to make sure. Sometimes even I'm surprised when things go smoothly."

Katherine grabbed her handbag, glad to leave the car. "Who lives here?"

"I don't know them personally." She heard the hesitation in his voice. "They're a lovely old couple, most cooperative. Mr. Louis—he's the justice of the peace—is wheelchair bound."

Katherine would have stumbled but Daniel caught her just in time. "A what?" she shrieked.

"Hush, Katherine. There's no need to scare them. That old woman must be eighty-five if she's a day."

Katherine was indignant. "How can I be quiet when you pull up to the house of a justice of the peace at seven o'clock at night! Daniel Boylan, what are you up to? Tell me right now or I won't take another step."

Daniel's heart wrenched at the sight she made, petulant and angry, her small pink mouth a stubborn line he ached to kiss. Soon he would. "We're getting married, Miss Harriman."

Katherine had to open and close her mouth, she was so shocked, but Daniel jumped in before she caught her breath. He dreaded her refusal and hoped his strained nerves didn't snap before he convinced her marriage was the right thing to do. Warring countries were one thing, but negotiating with a headstrong woman was a whole other ball game.

He trod carefully.

"Katherine, we must marry. If my having a…love child, shall we say?…is a cause for scandal, then the best thing I can think to do is marry the woman and legitimize the boy. Unless, of course, you have a better plan?"

Caught off guard, Katherine couldn't think much less speak, but one thing she knew was that she had never wanted things to happen this way! Daniel could see that in her face, and he sympathized.

"Sweetheart, if I could change the circumstances I would. I know you don't love me. Too much water under that rickety old bridge. But couldn't we come to an understanding for the boy's sake? He's got to be protected and so do you. Those gentlemen in the car are no joke. You'll be vulnerable, too, and marriage is the only sure way I can think of to protect you both."

Confused, Katherine looked away, biting her lips to keep from crying. Daniel would have held her, he wanted to, badly, but she was so jittery, he kept his distance. He didn't dare do anything that would make her bolt. If the boy didn't get better...Lord knew Daniel was doing everything in his power to make that happen, but if Dylan did die, well, Katherine would never marry Daniel. Hadn't she told him so last year? And he wanted to marry Katherine Harriman more than anything else in the world. He'd had a long time to think about it. He would give up the ambassadorship, if need be. He would use any argument to get her to the altar. "Dylan couldn't have a better life than the one I'm about to give him."

Katherine bristled, her green eyes finally showing some life, and Daniel hoped it was a sign that she was coming around. "He's had a fine life up till now! I've taught him to be anything—but first to be himself."

"I would never dispute your love for the boy. I was only referring to the *things* I could give him. To be blunt, things that money can buy. And some things they can't, like legitimacy. He'll need help figuring out who he is. All kids do, no matter their skin color. I can offer him that! Maybe I can't love him the way you do, but I'd like to try, Katherine. Won't you at least let me try?"

"But how can you be so sure he'll...?"

Daniel understood what she couldn't bring herself to say. "Sweetheart, I'm not sure whether Dylan will live or not, either, and I won't tell you otherwise. But I'm making sure he has a fighting chance. The rest is in God's hands. And right now, God is an eminent endocrinologist from New York City.''

Despite her fears, Katherine felt a slight easing in her belly. He was trying, she knew it, and she could not be more grateful. But she was very uncomfortable with the notion of marriage. She wouldn't have him thinking he was being emotionally blackmailed. And it wasn't settled in her mind that the things that had been important to him years ago, were not still important to him now. ''Your career, your family…''

Daniel looked her straight in the eyes. ''I'm not asking anyone's permission, if that's what you're wondering. Not this time around. I don't care what anyone thinks. I care about my son.''

''And suppose I don't want to get married?''

''Are you telling me that you're involved with someone else?'' He frowned. ''I never thought about that.''

''No, of course not,'' she snapped.

''No, of course not to which?'' Daniel echoed her gently. ''That you have no boyfriend lurking in the wings, or that I was rude not to think about the possibility?''

''Both, if you must know!'' Katherine snapped, and Daniel smiled.

''I can be overbearing at times, can't I? But you must know you're a beautiful woman, a bit straightlaced, but tolerably gorgeous,'' he teased. ''Well, if there is no boyfriend, then what's the problem? You've gone down a mighty long list.'' His brows rose as a new thought came to him. ''Is my skin suddenly too dark for you?''

Katherine took a long, wide swing with her pocketbook, but lucky for Daniel, he caught her bag midway to marking his cheek.

''Daniel, you can be so crude for a diplomat. Have I ever behaved as if the color of your skin mattered?''

''No, you're right, you haven't. I apologize. The color of my heart is the same as yours. My brain must be addled to think such a thing. But be kind, I've never asked anyone to marry me before.''

"And you haven't yet!" she added caustically.

"Are you waiting?" he asked, a wicked gleam in his eyes.

"Actually, I was wondering why I should agree. Should you bother to ask me, I mean!''

"Marry me, Katherine! I'm begging you! Do it for the boy, if for no other reason. Give him a father, his real father! If things don't work out, I'll give you a divorce a few years down the line. You have my word. But married even briefly, we'll be able to give Dylan legal status. Let's get it out in the open—us, our child, our marriage. Let's have no secrets from the world, no secrets to hide from Dylan. No secrets for him to hide, when he becomes a man. He doesn't know about me, does he?" Daniel asked, and Katherine had the grace to blush.

"It was too dangerous. He studied you in school, on United Nations Day or something, but that's all.''

Reduced to a book report! Daniel smiled to himself. "You do understand that, married or not, when the press gets wind of his existence, you and Dylan will be sitting targets for every weirdo out there. He'll have to be taught how to protect himself. I can do that.''

"It would make a splash, wouldn't it?''

"It will! A veritable tidal wave," Daniel agreed with a lopsided smile. "But I'll be there to run interference. I'm very good at that. It's what I do for a living. And I swear to you, Katherine, that I will do it even if you don't marry me!''

They heard a screen slam shut and turned around.

"Hey, young feller," they heard a high-pitched scratchy voice call. "Y'all aimin' to get hitched? It's nearly dinner time, and I got to get pa's meal goin'.''

"Our moment of truth, Katherine.''

"Oh, this is coercion!" she wailed. "I can't, I can't. Oh, I don't know what to do!''

He leaned forward and lowered his voice, but its urgency

was unmistakable. "Damn it, Katherine, think of the boy!" His hand firmly at the small of her back, he propelled her toward the house, feeling her resistance in his fingertips. Sliding his arm around her waist, he hoped the preacher and his wife didn't notice that he was practically carrying his bride.

The ceremony took two minutes. Things often go smoothly for those who have the clout and the money to make things happen. Daniel had both. As he filled out the marriage lines, his black curls gleaming in the dull lamplight of Mr. Louis's musty study, Katherine studied the man she had married, tried to guess at the power and prestige he wielded, the money that backed him. Until word of their marriage got out. Daniel would be despised for marrying white, scorned by his peers, who would never fully understand what Daniel was doing. She sure hoped *he* did. He said that he did, but he had so much to lose, far more than her. She had Dylan. Well, at least she was giving Daniel his son, but she wondered if it would be enough for someone who shook hands with kings.

"Hey, lady, I didn't think you could get any whiter." Daniel grinned when they returned to the car. "You aren't going to faint on me are you, Mrs. Boylan?"

Katherine ducked into the limo and wondered, as Daniel climbed into the seat beside her, why he suddenly seemed so big, and she suddenly felt so small. And resentful. And why not? The one thing she had never wanted to happen had just happened, a marriage of convenience, without love. For ten years she had worked hard to avoid just such a situation, and now, with the stroke of a pen, it was done.

They drove back to the hospital, both too preoccupied to speak, and when Daniel pulled up to the main entrance, Katherine dashed from the car. He watched as she mounted the steps, leaving him to follow, and he didn't try to stop her.

Wilma shook her head when he slipped into the room. "No change," she murmured with a sad sigh.

"Oh, some," Daniel said obliquely, peering over Katherine's shoulder to look at Dylan.

The doctors had come and gone. The dinner he had ordered had arrived from a nearby restaurant, so, silently, he passed around sandwiches and cups of hot soup. Over their meal, he told Wilma that he and Katherine were married.

Wilma didn't bat an eyelash. "About time," was all she said and asked him to pass her a pickle. Resigning himself to lifelong penance carefully doled out by his wife's best friend, Daniel passed the entire container.

It was the longest night of their lives. Praying, waiting, praying, waiting. But around four in morning they were rewarded. Or rather, Daniel was. The women were sound asleep, making the best of their uncomfortable chairs while Daniel stood guard at the bedside, holding his son's hand.

He felt just the slightest pressure, the faintest move, a feather tickling his fist.

Daniel looked down at Dylan and thought he detected the flutter of Dylan's lashes. Then the child was still, as if it had never happened. But Daniel knew at that moment that God was going to spare his son. He looked over at Katherine and Wilma, but decided not to wake them. There would be no purpose, the boy was quiet now. But soon. Soon.

The next sign of movement came around six a.m., as the women were stirring. When he told them to come look, Katherine rushed to the bed and took Dylan's hand, waiting for her own sign, while Wilma quietly wept.

The famous doctor from New York City smiled when she walked in. "Something tells me you have good news," she said when Daniel could not stop shaking her hand.

Dylan opened his eyes around three that afternoon, looked around vaguely, called out for his mommy, and promptly went back to sleep. But it was sleep, Dr. Sloan assured them. He was out of the coma, the crisis was over, she promised Katherine. Now came the hard part.

Chapter Seven

Daniel was standing by the window in Katherine's garden apartment, pushing aside the thin curtains when the pizza van drove up. He had to laugh when some of the reporters camped out on the lawn tried to buy up the pies. The deliveryman managed to skirt the small crowd and make it to Katherine's front door.

"Dylan, pizza's here," he called, and Katherine came out of the kitchen, wiping her hands on a dishtowel.

"We didn't order any pizza," she told him with a puzzled frown.

"Well, Dylan said he would practically die for a slice," Daniel said, letting the curtain fall with a sheepish smile, "and I told him that since he almost did, his wish was granted."

"Daniel, you didn't say that!"

"He thought it was pretty funny, didn't you, champ?"

The nine-year-old boy ensconced on the living-room couch, surrounded by every new GameBoy game that Daniel could find at the mall, the VCR, TV and cable remote conveniently balanced within reaching distance, grinned crookedly. "Hey, come on, Mom! I can't eat this baby food anymore," he complained, pointing to the untouched plate of mashed potatoes on the coffee table. "That stuff is making me sick."

"The kid needs some real food, Katherine. Soul food. If pizza isn't soul food, I don't know what is."

"No, sir, you sure don't," Wilma retorted, passing by with a basket of clean laundry. "Been living in that fancy mansion of yours too long. But don't you worry none, baby." She smiled beatifically at Dylan. "We'll be getting to that in a day or so. Fried chicken and greens, just the way you like them. And if a certain someone is a really good boy and stops complaining about his medicine," she winked at her beloved Dylan, "I just might take it into my mind to make a certain someone his favorite cake!"

Dylan's eyes lit up. "A butter cake?"

"A butter cake!"

"You promise?" Dylan and Daniel both asked in unison.

"I promise!" Wilma swore solemnly. "Now, you go enjoy that pizza. Why, I might even join you, if you ask me nicely. Smells mighty good to this old lady!"

Daniel groaned.

Katherine watched their byplay, knowing that Daniel and Wilma were going to spend their lives goading each other, and relishing every minute of it. She knew it as sure as she knew that pizza and fried chicken were probably exactly what Dylan needed to get his strength back. Why hadn't she thought of it?

She had to admit, as she watched Daniel tip the delivery boy, that his strong shoulders had been everything she'd needed or wanted this past month. Even as she watched, he was ordering a half-dozen pies for all the newscasters and bodyguards settled out on the lawn. He had been fabulous, camping out in the living room ever since Dylan had returned home a week ago, massaging and exercising Dylan's frail body back to health, humoring his sulks away, reading aloud, playing (and secretly enjoying, she thought) interminable games of Nintendo.

"Two large pies with everything, hold the anchovies, Master Dylan?" she heard him tease his son. His son. She still hadn't got used to it.

"Yes! Come on, Mom! Hurry up before it gets cold."

Katherine smiled. "That pizza does smell good."

Gathering around Dylan, they gorged themselves until Wilma stood up and announced it was time to return to her laundry. But when Katherine rose, Daniel took her hand. She looked at him, confused. He had been very careful not to touch her since they'd brought Dylan home.

"It's time for the three of us to have a little talk," he said pointedly, and Katherine knew immediately what he was talking about. The plea in her eyes said no, but Daniel held firm. If Katherine wanted to keep things low-key, he could understand that, but Dylan was so much better that Daniel was sure the boy could handle the news of their marriage. Dylan needed time to adjust to the situation, and if there was one thing that Dylan had, it was time. Daniel, on the other hand, could be called back to Paris at any moment.

Not that Daniel hadn't phoned the president immediately following his marriage and told him the whole sad story. The president had been all that was gracious, and had refused Daniel's resignation.

"So there's life in you, yet," he'd laughed loudly while Daniel fumed at the other end of the line. "Oh, come on, Daniel," the president said, reading Daniel's silence correctly. "You know you've got a reputation for being—how shall I put it?—a stick in the mud?"

Daniel wasn't so lighthearted. The president might think this was the funniest thing since Adam and Eve, but Daniel wanted everything laid out on the table. "You don't think this will put some backs up, sir?"

The president was philosophical. "Well, hell's bells, I do suppose it will, and then some!" He chuckled. "What of it?

Don't think you can carry it off, Dan, after ten years behind the wheel?''

"Sure I can. But what exactly am I trying to accomplish here?''

"Why, proving that America is the land of full-blooded men who know how to do the honorable thing—when they have to!'' He laughed. "Hey, is she pretty, this Katherine of yours?''

"Beautiful,'' Daniel growled.

"And the boy? Tell me that he looks like her, I'm begging you.''

"Quite a bit,'' Daniel admitted ruefully, "except for his dark skin.''

"Well, at least you know he's yours,'' the president teased. "Are they going to look good on the front pages? That's the question.''

"Definitely better than me,'' Daniel said, smothering his annoyance, but the president knew his man.

"Come on, Romeo, I'm just asking. Since it's not an election year, the goddamn press is going to gobble them up.''

"They're already parked on our doorstep.''

"Ah, most excellent! Most excellent! Look,'' the president said, "if the press wants to have a field day on this one, I say let 'em. How are we going to stop them, anyway? Yeah, go with it, Dan, cooperate, I say. A few pictures won't hurt, either. Yeah, better to flaunt it, before they misread your cues. And don't forget to mention my name. Hell's bells, it'll all die down, anyhow, sooner or later. The nine-day-wonder syndrome, you know. Personally, Dan, I think this is the best thing that's happened all year, to both of us. Yeah, I'll have the missus put in a good word for you at her press conference next week. You know, the woman's angle. Trust me, Danny, some good publicity, a little romance, the public will love it.'' And then he ordered Daniel back to Paris as soon as possible, with his newfound family in tow.

Daniel had already announced his marriage and the existence of his son at a brief press conference. Dylan might be the only person in America who didn't know what was up. Even now Daniel could feel the boy's eyes boring into him as he took hold of Katherine's hand. The child had been so ill the last few weeks, he hadn't noticed anything, hadn't even questioned Daniel's presence, and they had hoped he assumed that Daniel was some sort of nurse. The way things were, it would be a good guess. But last night, he had seen the speculation in Dylan's eyes when Daniel had jumped up to help Katherine serve dinner. The boy was a real smart number. He definitely knew something was up. A cool hand, too, the way he sipped his soda, quietly watching them. If nothing else, Dylan's air of quiet patience and his inscrutable demeanor betrayed him as Daniel's blood. Privately, Daniel was delighted. He had faced down many a statesman, but it was possible he had finally met his match. Damned if the kid didn't have the makings of a good lawyer, or maybe even...

Daniel laughed. Startled, Dylan and Katherine both looked at him, two pairs of almond-shaped eyes peering at him from heart-shaped faces that belonged to one another. That now belonged to him, he thought, with a fierce surge of pride.

"Dylan, do you know who I am?"

Dylan tolerated the dumb question. Adults talked like that. "You're Daniel Boylan. That's what you said."

"Yes, I did, but I didn't tell you my job, that's what I mean."

"You're not a nurse?"

"No, son, I'm not."

"A therapist?"

"No, and I won't play games with you. I'm an ambassador."

"Of what?"

Daniel smiled. "Of the United States. I'm the American Ambassador to France."

It was very silent in the living room while Dylan mulled that over. "Is it far?"

"A few thousand miles."

"Can you drive there?"

"No, you have to fly, or take a ship. It's across the ocean."

"Mr. Boylan is a very famous man," Katherine smiled weakly.

"He's an ambassador, Mom!"

"I know, I know."

"Hey, you two," Daniel growled in mock annoyance. "It's not the worst thing in the world."

Daniel started to explain, but Dylan was nobody's fool. "Are you my father?" he demanded, his hazel eyes fastened on the brown hand that held his mother's.

Daniel tried to answer but his throat was so tight he couldn't speak. Katherine was as white as a sheet and as helpless. They both nodded as if on cue and waited for Dylan to explode.

What Daniel knew about children he could put on an index card, so he was surprised at Dylan's calm reception. But then, Dylan was a Boylan, in spirit, as well as in form. Daniel thought he could detect a hint of excitement in the boy's eyes. "How did you guess?" he asked when he could swallow.

"Aw, it wasn't really much of a guess," the child said magnanimously, but the self-satisfaction in his voice betrayed him. "Mama's never brought a man home before. Boy, you sure are black!"

"You noticed?" Daniel said wryly. "Does it bother you?"

Dylan looked down at his light tawny arms and gave the question serious consideration. "I don't know."

"I appreciate your honesty."

"Mom says my skin color is a blessing. Do you think so?"

"I do. Do you want to talk about it?"

"Nope."

"Another time, then. I think maybe we should, when you're ready."

"Maybe," Dylan shrugged.

"There's a little something more you should know."

But Katherine stopped him. As Dylan's mother, it was her duty, as well as her right, to break the news. "Dylan, I know this may come as a shock to you, but, well, Mr. Boylan and I, while you were sick in the hospital, we, well, we were married," she finally managed to whisper.

Now they had his attention.

"No kidding?" Dylan sat up interested in the conversation. This could definitely have an effect on his life! But keen interest quickly slid into peevish indignation. "But hey, how come you didn't wait for me? Did Wilma go to the wedding? Oh, man, you could've waited!"

"Hey, kid, you were a pretty sick soldier there, and we had no choice." Daniel could see that Dylan didn't believe him and hurried to explain. "Look, it's one of those things about being..." Daniel was surprised to feel his face grow hot, "about being, er, well known. When things get into the newspapers, sometimes they get it wrong. We—your mother and I—we wanted them to get it right."

"Are you famous? Really famous?" Dylan was thrilled.

"In certain circles, yes."

"Then how come I never saw a picture of you in the poster store?"

Daniel looked over at Katherine and smiled ruefully. "I am famous, I assure you." And you will be, too, as soon as we come out of hiding. But Daniel didn't say that, it was too early, and he didn't want to alarm the boy. Or Katherine. He wondered if she understood how it would be. If she understood the implications of the guards that stood outside her door, even now.

The look Dylan sent him was doubtful, but he dismissed the unimportant detail with the obdurate eyes of a nine-year-old. "How come my mom doesn't have a ring? You can't be married if you don't have a ring!"

Daniel admired the rules the young boy lived by. "We

didn't have time,'' he explained solemnly. ''As I said, we were married rather quickly.''

Dylan glanced at his mother for verification, but she didn't look too happy. He swung his eyes back to the dark-skinned man with the serious face. Maybe he had always wanted a father, but geez, looking at this guy, maybe it wasn't such a good idea, after all.

''You know, I've been taking good care of my mom for a long time,'' he said thoughtfully. ''I don't think I need any help, thanks. As soon as I'm old enough, I plan to get a job. Then Mom can play her piano all day and not complain about her feet.''

Katherine clapped a hand to her mouth, and Dylan was disgusted. ''Aw, c'mon, Mom, you know you do.''

Daniel tried not to smile. ''I was hoping you would give me a chance to get to know you.''

Dylan frowned. ''Why'd you wait so long, if you're my father?''

Unused to the bluntness of children, Daniel felt a momentary flash of annoyance. Still, he would have answered except that Dylan's question woke Katherine up.

''It was my fault, darling. You must believe that. Until your illness, Mr. Boylan—''

''Daniel!'' her new husband corrected her tersely.

''Daniel! Daniel—he didn't know anything about you.''

Dylan's eyes grew wide, glittering with excitement. ''You mean you got pregnant, like on TV, and had an unmarried baby?''

Katherine's eyes filled. She knew exactly what he meant. ''I didn't mean to. It just happened.''

''It didn't just happen,'' Daniel said coldly. ''It was just as much my fault. Dylan, understand me now. Your mother is not to blame.''

''But, Ma, you told me that my dad died in a car accident!''

Her hands twisted together as Katherine searched for words. But Dylan wasn't interested in that part of the story, he wasn't even upset. The celebrity aspects of the situation were fast creeping up on him. "Wow, that makes me illegitimate!" he announced gleefully.

"Not anymore, son," Daniel said sternly. "That's precisely why your mother and I were married." He was surprised to see that the loss of his illegitimate status seemed to annoy Dylan.

"Hey, what if I don't want you to be my father?"

"I think your mother does."

"What about me? Don't I get any say in this?"

Daniel stood up and began to pace the room, perturbed at the direction the conversation had taken. He wasn't going to yield on that last point and wanted Dylan to know it. He also realized that he was dealing with a child, and he had a strong hunch he was being tested. Dylan was turning out to be an interesting adversary, clever in the way he was using his wits to fend off Daniel's siege. Daniel felt oddly proud that Dylan wasn't taking this all lying down. Clearing his throat, Daniel looked at his handsome child.

"I've pulled some strings, the papers are already processed. You legally became my son as of midnight last Tuesday. I hope you will come to like the idea, but you must understand that once I knew of your existence, I could not ignore you. I may not be as famous as some of those gentlemen hanging in your room, but I am in a high-powered and very visible position. Unfortunately, it could be dangerous for you and your mother if you were not under my protection. Do you understand what the word *vulnerable* means, Dylan?"

"Mister, you sure talk funny, that's what I understand! And I also understand that my mom's not wearing a ring, that's more of what I understand!" Dylan said stubbornly, focusing on the one thing that could make this all clear to him.

Daniel sighed. "She will have one. You have my word."

"Are you going to live here?" Dylan demanded, switching gears with astonishing speed. "There's no room," he announced, crossing his thin arms with satisfaction.

Daniel looked around the room and tried to see it with Dylan's eyes.

Home.

Impoverished, depressing, frayed at every corner. And so much more than he, Daniel, owned. He looked Dylan straight in the eye. "My home is bigger," he said thoughtfully. "Perhaps you would consider coming to live with me in France?"

Dylan was awestruck. "What about my mother?"

"She may come, too," Daniel said with a faint smile. "In fact, I am hoping she will."

Dylan grew quiet, then sidled over to cuddle in his mother's lap and lay his head against her shoulder. The meaning of Daniel's invitation had begun to sink in. "We'll have to think about it."

Katherine drew him close, and together mother and son looked up at the stern brown face that towered over them. Daniel stared back at the two round faces that were now dearer to him than life. "Perhaps I should leave you two alone for a while. I'll take a run over to that mall where you work, Katherine. Where you used to work, I should say," he amended, rubbing at his five o'clock shadow. "I need to purchase some fresh razor blades and a few other odds and ends."

"Like a ring?" Dylan said fiercely.

The question took Daniel by surprise, but he bounced back quickly. "Well, I was going to go elsewhere for a ring."

"Oh yeah, right. Running out already! Look, Ma, see, he's running out already!"

"My, my, aren't we the little cynic!" Daniel quipped, unused to anybody casting aspersions on his honesty.

Katherine had to smile. It would be fireworks for a long while before these two made their peace.

"I know for a fact that they have jewelry stores!" Dylan threw back.

"I was going to go to Tiffany's, if you want to know the truth!"

"Never heard of it!"

"Your secret is safe with me!"

"It's probably one of those dime stores that sell those phony zircons."

Daniel's eyes turned to cold slits as he rose to his feet. "Perhaps, when you are fully recovered, you would like to accompany me to the jewelry store of your choice and choose your mother's wedding band?"

"And engagement ring! I saw it on television. Two rings!"

"And an engagement ring!" Daniel promised. "I can see that this is certainly going to set me back some."

"Can't you charge it?" Dylan said unsympathetically. "If you're an ambassador, you must have a couple hundred credit cards."

"At least one," Daniel admitted, his brow raised. "Katherine, you have done a delightful job of raising this child."

Katherine shrugged. "Television helped."

Daniel bent to kiss her cheek. "You are welcome to come with us, when Dylan is back on his feet, and you probably should. I have the most awful presentiment that without your restraining hand, you will become the owner of the largest, most ostentatious diamond in the Biltmore Fashion Park."

"Well, it never seemed to hurt Elizabeth Taylor." Katherine smiled.

Chapter Eight

The diamond that flew to France three weeks later with the newly formed Boylan family, could have been bigger, but not by much. It caught the eye of their flight attendant, but then, so did the whole family. Even Wilma, who had agreed to accompany them, having no deep roots to pull up, was suitably impressed with the way Daniel had arranged everything. He obtained their passports almost overnight and even hired a packing company to see to the transport of their belongings.

Katherine, on the other hand, had been annoyed by his heavy hand. She knew she was having a case of nerves, but she couldn't help herself. Everything he did irritated her, even if she knew he was making their transition as painless as he could. He could have consulted her more. He was making decisions alone that a family should make together.

"Are we really going to be a family or is this all lip service?" she demanded to know on the day they were leaving. He had promised Dylan a dog. She hated dogs.

"Lip service? Why would I do that?" Daniel was confused.

"To save face?" Katherine insisted.

"With whom, I'd like to know? My life is public domain."

"I understand that, and I can live with that," Katherine said irritably. "But in the smaller, more personal things you're going to have to acknowledge my presence. And Wilma's. And that of my son."

"Our son!"

"Fine! Our son!"

"Katherine!"

"Don't you Katherine me! You're avoiding the issue. I want to know if you understand. Your opinion is not the only one that counts around here!"

"All right," Daniel snapped, "I understand, but—"

"The dog you promised Dylan! You didn't ask me about it!"

"Did you want a dog, too?" Daniel shouted as she stormed out of the room.

The truth was, Daniel had no idea what Katherine was mad about. He put it down to nerves but he had no idea how to fix matters. They had no privacy in the tiny apartment, and because they were not sharing a bed, no intimate moment existed where they could make their peace. Daniel had promised not to force himself on Katherine, and she was taking him at his word, a fact he deeply regretted. Thus, Katherine and Daniel's first argument as a married couple went unfinished, simmered between them, and accompanied them down the ramp of the Concorde.

France was beautiful in late August, if a little hot and sultry. From the limousine that met them at the airport, the Americans unabashedly stared across the boulevard teeming with people seeking the cool shade of trees heavy with foliage. The sidewalk cafés were crowded with people of all ages resting their elbows on tiny bistro tables, sipping (Katherine imagined) aperitifs or coffee, obviously in no rush. She drank it all in from the safety of the limo and could not wait to join the crowds. She promised herself that she would come here with Dylan the very first chance they had. He would order ice cream, and she would have a Dubonnet. She wasn't sure she would like Dubonnet, but she was sure going to find out! And in September, when Paris cooled off, she and Wilma would try to find that flea market she had heard so much about. They would go to Notre Dame this very Sunday, and the Arc de Triomphe, oh, and of course, the Eiffel Tower, yes, and the Louvre, and…

Katherine sat back in the car and smiled. It was a good thing they were going to be in Paris awhile. She would need that much time and more to explore it. Looking over at Wilma and Dylan as they, too, stared awestruck out the window, Katherine knew their excitement was mutual.

"Is this not the best birthday present, Dylan? Moving halfway across the world?"

"Oh, Mom, you know it!"

Daniel's head shot up. September. But of course…

Watching Daniel, Katherine realized how insensitive she had been, neglecting to let him know Dylan's birthday was approaching. But there was nothing she could do about it now.

Wilma chuckled. "Does that mean I should return the present I've got stashed in my valise?"

"No!" Dylan cried, horror written on his face.

Daniel watched their byplay and listened as they discussed how they would celebrate. Mostly, his eyes never left Dylan, still frail with newfound health. Anyone with eyes could tell that once this kid got back on his feet, he would be a human dynamo!

The embassy staff was lined up to greet them when they arrived. They gave Katherine her first intimation of her future role, when they handed her a huge bouquet of roses. With Daniel's guiding hand on her elbow, she managed to smile her thanks. Her composure lasted as long as it took to see Deirdre and May Boylan standing in the entry foyer.

"Katherine!" they both shouted in unison. "We've been waiting for days."

"When we heard—Daniel called—we wanted our visit to be a surprise!"

"Oh, you poor baby, don't look so shocked! We're sisters, now!"

Katherine's new sisters swooped down on her with hugs while she shot daggers at her husband for not warning her. They almost ate Dylan alive. They couldn't keep their hands off their little nephew, and he ate up every moment of their attention. Why shouldn't he? she realized, watching from the sidelines. He'd never had an extended family before. And wasn't that a baby in the wings? She wondered, noting Deirdre's pregnant belly. Now he would have lots of cousins, aunts and uncles, even a grandma and grandpa! No, not grandparents, she realized as she heard May explain to Dylan.

"Your grandma and grandpa would have been so proud of you, young man, if they'd lived to see your beautiful face. Oh, but, Katherine, didn't you know? They died four years ago, in an avalanche in Switzerland. And the irony was, they weren't even skiing, just driving down the wrong road at the wrong time. Daniel, you should have told them!"

So, Mary Boylan, you will not be here to play out the cruel hand you dealt us all! Katherine sighed and slid an arm around her son as they followed their new family into the drawing room. Glancing past her shoulder, she saw Daniel, standing to one side, looking as if he wanted to tell her something.

"You go ahead, darling, I'll be right there," she whispered to Dylan. "Don't worry, Wilma will protect you." She smiled, seeing the uncertainty in his eyes. "I'll only be a minute."

She held back and waited until Daniel crossed the foyer. "You could have warned me they would be here!"

"They wanted it to be a surprise."

"So it was!"

"I'm sorry, but I didn't want to alarm you. And they weren't sure they were going to make it. I guess you noticed that Deirdre is pregnant. Henry didn't want her to come, but when her doctor gave the all clear, he couldn't argue."

Katherine wavered. "Well, I'm not so sure about this."

"They're here to help you make the transition. For a week, anyway, and then the worst will be over. Katherine, you can't do this alone, and I've got to go back to work. The stacks are sky-high, and I've got a conference in Bonn in two weeks. I just can't lend you the kind of nonstop support you'll need over the next few months. You'll need help, and they offered. Besides, they're family. There would have been talk if they hadn't been here to greet us. No, that's not why they came," he said quickly. "Believe me, they wanted to be here. But if it makes you feel any better, I made them both promise not to ask any questions."

"Oh, thank you, Daniel!" The relief that spread across Katherine's face made Daniel glad he'd thought of it.

"You're welcome. Now, let's go say hello to the Misses Mayhem and Madness and save Dylan from an excess of kisses. I can see it's going to be a long afternoon, and I don't want my son to get overtired."

Since Katherine had always been on excellent terms with her new sisters-in-law, the afternoon was not nearly at difficult as she'd expected.

"Katherine, aside from a little jet lag, you look wonderful, after all these years." May meant it, too, as she ever so discreetly examined her sister-in-law. No fashion statement, true, but that could easily be fixed. Was it a love match, even after all these years? The way they looked at each other, when they thought no one was watching. And the child—a child!—what on earth had been going on all those years ago?

"It's good to see you both again," Katherine admitted shyly. "Since I left New York, except for Wilma, I've had no other close friends."

"You did leave rather abruptly," May observed, but

dropped that when she saw Daniel step forward to lay a protective hand on Katherine's shoulder, a hand she didn't remove. How very interesting!

"But your music," Deirdre asked. "According to Daniel, you're on the verge of stardom."

Katherine smiled. "Daniel exaggerates. I am accomplished, nothing more."

But Wilma would have none of that. "The girl's being shy. Anybody who doubts it, read the reviews of the concerts she's given in Denver, New Mexico and Los Angeles."

"Wilma's right. I was there in Los Angeles last year." Daniel told them. "She was stunning."

Satisfied, Wilma insisted on taking Dylan upstairs for the daily nap she'd instituted the day he came out of the hospital. It was a measure of his exhaustion that he didn't protest when she led him from the room.

"He's gorgeous, Katherine!" Deirdre gushed. "A little of Daniel and a lot of you, thank goodness!"

"Those eyes!"

"That hair!"

"He'll be tall—"

"Girls, enough!" Daniel laughed as he rose to his feet. "Katherine and I are tired, too. If you don't mind, we're going to follow Wilma's example and take a short nap. You should be napping, too, Dee. And I've ordered dinner in our room, if you both don't mind, so don't look for us tonight."

May and Deirdre rose, concerned and apologetic. "I hate to say it, but Daniel's right," Deirdre smiled. "You do look bushed. You get a good night's sleep, Katherine, and so will I. We'll see you in the morning."

Deirdre tiptoed up to give Daniel a sisterly kiss and then Katherine. "'Night, sister!" she whispered, giving Katherine a warm hug. "We're so glad you're home!" And that was as near to referring to the past as Deirdre or May dared to get. They'd given their word.

Reassured by the warm reception Deirdre and May gave her, Katherine took the grand staircase with a lighter heart than she would have thought possible hours before. But her irritation with her new husband resurfaced the moment she entered her bedroom to find it was the master suite and that her luggage was standing in the corner.

"Fontaine apparently hasn't had time to empty all your valises," Daniel observed as he closed the door.

Katherine grew pink, but Daniel didn't notice. He had thrown off his jacket and tie, wanting only a hot shower. Seeing Katherine standing stiffly gave him pause. "Katherine, are you all right?"

She turned to him, her lips a thin, mutinous line. "You did it again."

"Excuse me?" In the middle of removing his shoes, Daniel stopped to look at her, baffled.

"You didn't ask me whether I wanted to share your bedroom."

Tired and impatient, Daniel tossed his shoes in a corner and started rummaging around in a dresser for clean underwear. "Oh, for chrissakes, Katherine, you're being ridiculous!"

Katherine clenched her fists, trying to remind herself that hitting an ambassador probably was not the most seemly thing to do. "Daniel Boylan, don't you dare undress in front of me!"

Daniel stopped midstream, his shirt dangling from his shoulders, a broad muscular expanse of chest, covered with crisp black hair, revealed. Embarrassed, Katherine turned away, but it gave Daniel the satisfaction of knowing she wasn't indifferent. It must be her nerves. She was just a newlywed, after all. He approached her slowly, but she moved away from the embrace he tried to give her.

"I...I don't want to... People will think—"

"People will think that we're married!"

"Only in name."

"Is that what you tell your conscience?"

"This is... This would be a lie."

"What kind of lie?" Daniel demanded, his brown eyes taking on a steely cast as he blocked her path.

She hated that he did that, that he stood so close she could be…tempted. He smelled so good, too, so male. "It would be a sort of public proclamation that we…we cared for each other…in ways that we both know we don't."

"We don't?" he repeated, his eyes carefully shielded.

"Yes." Katherine sighed with relief. "I'm glad you see my point."

But when she tried to move, he pinned her gently to the wall, one hand enveloping a soft, round breast. Stooping low, he began to nuzzle her neck while his large hand did such wonderful things to her breast that her legs began to quiver. "Actually, I don't see your point, but my God, you taste wonderful!" His tongue traced a light line across her mouth and stopped at a corner to nibble, while his hand played havoc with the rest of her body.

Startled, she looked up at him with frightened eyes. "Daniel? Daniel, please."

He raised his head, his lips a hairbreadth from hers. "Please yes or please no?" he asked, his voice gruff. "If you want me to stop, simply say so."

Katherine clamped her eyes shut, thinking hard. She didn't care how handsome he was, or how appealing, she would not like to take him—or any man—to her bed without some sign of affection. Unfortunately, it had been made clear to her back in Arizona, that the union they had made was a marriage of convenience until such time… Until what time? Oh, she felt so confused, and his mouth on her body was so wonderful and—

"Oh, stop, stop!" she begged. But her hoarse cries didn't match the way her body begged for more, and Daniel knew it. His hand traveled her length to stop at the juncture of her thighs, his palm covering her mound, savoring the heat that warmed his hand. Lord knew, he was burning up.

"Admit that you want me and put an end to this nonsense," he murmured, his tongue rimming her ear.

"It is not nonsense!" Katherine insisted, giving him a swift, hard push. Free of his hold, she ran to the other side of the room. A rush of pink stained her cheeks. "I will not be manhandled! This is nothing but lust!"

Leaning against the wall, his arms folded across his chest, Daniel looked her up and down, not bothering to hide his anger. "What's wrong with good old-fashioned lust? And for my own wife, for heaven's sake!"

"When there is nothing behind it? Plenty!"

"You keep telling me that there's nothing behind it. Is that the way it is for you?"

"This marriage was made to protect Dylan, remember?"

"I remember many things. Dylan is only one of them."

"Well, I don't want to give him any false impressions."

"There is nothing false about your response to me, my dear. There never was."

"I'm not talking about sex."

"And are we only talking about sex?" he asked coldly.

"Daniel, why are you twisting my words?"

"I thought I was being perfectly clear. About what I wanted, I mean."

"You...you promised me a divorce, when everything died down. You do remember, don't you?"

His eyes narrowed dangerously. "Is that what this is all about?"

He did remember! Katherine hung her head. Was such a promise not the same as admitting that he didn't love her? People didn't get married with their divorce papers in their back pocket, did they? What would it make her, then, to sleep with a man who didn't even pretend to love her, even if that man was legally her husband? Come to think of it, she was surprised that he hadn't made her sign a prenuptial agreement. That was probably only due to time constraints. A man like Daniel didn't overlook that sort of thing.

Daniel watched her face, every emotion mapped out for him to see. But her thoughts, the thoughts that lay behind her beautiful face were a mystery, and damn it, he wasn't a mind reader. The drivel she spouted, Jesus, just listening made him want to strangle her! And him with a hard-on straining.

"If we got too involved, now, it would be harder to separate, later on down the road."

More nonsense! "My, my, you're so ready for that divorce! Aren't you even going to give us a chance?"

"Of course I'll try, but just not...not in all ways."

"If sex is the one thing that works well with us, so far, don't you think we ought to build on it?" His lazy smile died as he watched her twist her hands till her knuckles were white.

"Fine," he said, pushing away from the wall, furious and hurt. "I don't really give a damn, anyway. God knows, I've never had to force a woman. Let me know when anything means anything to you," he sneered. "I won't touch you until you ask. Damn you, Katherine, you'll have to beg me before I ever touch you again!"

Moving to the door, his roar was heard all over the embassy. "Fontaine! Move madame's things into the adjacent suite. She has need of more privacy than I can give her!"

Over the next few days, the embassy was more like a castle in a state of siege than the honeymoon hotel everyone had been expecting. Although Daniel and Katherine were careful to smile at all the right moments and make appropriate small talk, they were careful never to touch, meet each other's eyes or be alone with each other. Beyond sharing time with Dylan or greeting the sudden and enormous influx of well-wishers that came calling, they went their separate ways. Everyone could feel the tension in the air, they just could not name its source.

Deirdre and May pretended not to notice. After a private discussion, they decided that the newlyweds were probably just going through a period of adjustment. As such, it would be best not to interfere. Since they only had a few days to stay, well, shopping was so much more rewarding. And showing off their adorable nephew, who most of Paris was dying to see. So they browsed the exclusive shops on Avenue Montaigne, treated Katherine to her first Dubonnet on the Champs-Elysées, had tea at Angelina and dinner at Maxim's. At every step, they insisted Wilma accompany them, even when she would have stayed at the embassy. When she complained of her feet, they bought her new shoes, of the heat—voilà—a hat! And though they both deeply regretted their promise not to pry, they kept their word, and didn't ask Katherine a single, solitary question, for which Katherine was grateful. Until the last day, just before they left for New York.

"Katherine," May called after her last-minute packing. "Can I have a word with you? I'm leaving in ten minutes."

"Of course, May. I'm sorry that everything has been so rushed," Katherine apologized. Not that anything about her perfectly groomed sister-in-law ever looked rushed, Katherine thought with a twinge of envy as she followed May into her bedroom. Even now she looked gorgeous, dressed in denims that were probably handmade, a cashmere sweater that could only be from Italy, and leather boots that looked as soft as butter. Idly, Katherine wondered how long it took May to dress in the morning, when her kids had to be rushed off to school. She probably had maids and nannies to do that sort of stuff, Katherine reminded herself. As she herself did, now!

Only one valise remained on her bed, the rest of May's luggage was piled high by the door. "Never mind that," she said, when she saw Katherine's worried look, "it will all get done. Fontaine is so efficient. I really just wanted to say goodbye and good luck. You'll need a lot of that, I suppose, but I think you're going to be fine. And you're a very classy lady on your own, Katherine. It will stand you in good stead. I just wanted to… Look, Katherine, I know that Daniel has asked the family not to press you, but…"

"You can't help not?" Katherine finished for her with a small smile.

"No, I can't," May agreed with a rueful shake of her head. "But honestly, I don't know how Daniel could ask us such a thing. After all, there is this adorable little boy roaming around who Daniel admits to fathering. It does beg questions."

"And you would love to have some answers?" Katherine laughed to cover her discomfort.

"Not necessarily, well, maybe not this very minute," May admitted. "It's just that something obviously happened ten years ago, and… For goodness sake, Katherine, why didn't you come to us for help? I would have helped you, we used to be friends. The whole family would have helped you."

No, not the whole family, Katherine sighed, a secret she would take to her grave. She kept her features composed as she searched for an answer that would satisfy the family. She knew that whatever she told May would be reported to the rest of the Boylans. "Poor May, I wish I could give you good answers, but I really can't. Your brother and I spent some time together. It was so brief, it can't even be called an affair. I was just a kid in a panic, once I found out I was pregnant. It was so long ago, I can't even remember what I was thinking."

"It wasn't all that long ago. And whatever you want to call it, or not, it happened with Daniel!"

"A moment of sublime weakness," Katherine said with amused wonder, looking back at her foolishness.

"But you're sitting here now!"

"Believe me, it's a surprise to me, too!"

"Look, Katherine, two things I know," May insisted. "One is that Daniel never would have left you in the lurch like that. Never! So the second thing I know is that you never told him you were pregnant! Is that the part no one is supposed to ask you about? Okay, fine, I'm not asking. But I see the way he looks at you—"

"How does he look at me?" Katherine asked sharply.

"Hard! His eyes are hard, and watchful, as if he's waiting for something."

"Oh, May." Katherine dismissed her gently with a small wave. "You're being melodramatic. We're newlyweds, that's all."

"No, Katherine, it's more complicated than that, I know it is—for Daniel, at least. You haven't known him the way I have. All this," her shrewd eyes swept the elegant room, "it hasn't made him happy, not really. I know it gave Daniel the things he thought he wanted, but I've always had the sense that something was missing. Nothing anyone would notice, except maybe an overly protective sister," she admitted ruefully. "But something was missing. Every now and then, he'd have this faraway look in his eyes. I'd see it. I'd ask him, but he always waved me away with a smile, tell me I was being silly. And then you turn up after ten long years—and with his son, no less! So you'll forgive me if I wonder whether you have something to do with this great weight he carries around! So brief that it wasn't even an affair? But Katherine, it was *something,* wasn't it?"

"Oh, May—"

"Was it love? Did you love him?" May asked quickly, not caring that she interrupted Katherine. "I would have liked someone to have loved Daniel, even briefly."

"Well, I can see you're not going to give me any answers," May said, frowning in the face of Katherine's silence. "I can't say I wasn't warned. But pardon me if I can't help wondering whether you're going to make life worse for him or better."

A deep pain cut through Katherine as the truth of what May said sank in. "Oh, May, I didn't know you cared so much about your brother. I always saw all of you as the Boylan dynasty at work, creating an ambassador. In a million years, I would never have taken on all of you."

"You should have tried."

"I didn't have the courage."

"You had the courage to have his child!"

"Yes." Katherine sighed. "And you would have taken him from me! The Boylan machine is well oiled."

"Never!"

"So you say!" Katherine cried. "But I couldn't be sure. Surely you wouldn't expect me to gamble with my son!"

"Perhaps not, but it doesn't matter anymore, does it?" May said harshly. "It's what comes next that counts, doesn't it? You, your son, and my brother with his sad eyes."

It came as no surprise to see Daniel standing in the doorway when Katherine followed the direction of May's eyes. "The car is waiting."

The way he stood there, his dark eyes narrow with suspicion, Katherine was sure he must have heard at least part of what they'd said. Unsure of what to do, she hesitated, but May smoothly filled the awkward void.

"Are you playing valet, this afternoon, brother mine?" She laughed. "Or have you come to gather up your wife and wish me well?" Closing her last valise with a snap, she strode past them both and hurried down the embassy hall. With one last hug for Dylan, who was waiting with Deirdre at the foot of the stairs, and Katherine's promise to return with Dylan to New York for the New Year holidays, the Boylan sisters were gone in a flurry of luggage and loud goodbyes. The silence that filled the embassy with their departure was deafening.

Daniel and Katherine found themselves alone at dinner for the first time in a long while. Left to themselves, they eyed each other across an expanse of crystal and china, and found they had nothing to say. Acute embarrassment was a powerful leveler.

"More wine?" Daniel asked.

"No, I think I've had enough, thank you."

"You don't mind if I do?"

"No, not at all." *Three glasses, but what the heck!*

"You don't think I've had too much?"

"I wasn't counting." *Maybe it would put you to sleep.*

"You're sure you won't join me?" *Maybe loosen you up.*

"As a matter of fact, I think I'll call it a night. You don't mind?" she asked sweetly.

"I don't mind." *God forbid I minded! Would it matter?*

Only Wilma knew how things really were in the light of day. Though she heard the couple's unspoken message not to interfere, she couldn't help feeling disgusted with both of them. She knew they were in love, deeply in love, just as she knew they were the two most stubborn, proud people she had ever met. It was hard going for a woman used to speaking her mind. Only once did she show her irritation, a few nights later, when she excused herself for an early evening—telling them bluntly that she found them too exhausting!

It was Madame Berenice Beaucart, Daniel's old friend, who inadvertently helped defuse the situation when she came calling toward the end of the week. She showed up an hour after Daniel and Dylan left for the Eiffel Tower, a trip Daniel had promised his son and had expressly not invited Katherine to share. Fontaine ushered Berenice into the blue salon, where afternoon callers were received by the family. When she politely inquired as to the well-being of the young couple, Fontaine was nothing but discreet, but before he left to inform his new mistress that she had a visitor, Berenice was made to understand that, yes, perhaps the loving couple did need a guiding hand...the wisdom of maturity...so invaluable. They were old acquaintances, he and Madame Beaucart. He did not think he exceeded his place and neither did she.

"*Alors!* Madame Boylan, finally we meet!" Madame Beaucart smiled broadly as Katherine entered the salon. "I have read so much about you." She grinned wickedly, brushing Katherine's cheek with a kiss, her Chanel filling the air.

"Um." Katherine hesitated, unsure of protocol. Who was this frail woman, leaning so heavily on that elaborate ebony cane? Was she friend or foe? But whom to ask? Daniel had spirited Dylan away for the afternoon.

But Fontaine was there, the soul of discretion. "Perhaps

Madame wishes a fire to be lit? There seems to be a slight chill in the air. And perhaps some tea would be nice?''

Katherine sent him a grateful look. "Yes, that does sound good, Fontaine. If Madame wishes, of course,'' she asked, turning to Madame Beaucart.

Berenice laughed. "*Mais oui,* Madame wishes,'' she said agreeably.

Katherine breathed a sigh of relief. "Oh, and Fontaine, perhaps you would ask Wilma to join us? Wilma is my oldest friend,'' she explained to Berenice. "She's staying with us, for the duration.''

For the duration? Berenice nodded but said nothing as she settled into a chair. Katherine took a seat nearby, in an old-fashioned lady's chair that was so unforgiving she found herself perched on the edge. Fontaine lit the promised fire, but when he left to see about their tea, Katherine wasn't sure how to go on.

"So Daniel has gone out?'' the elderly woman asked. "Left you to Fontaine, has he?''

"I guess.''

"Men! Imbeciles!'' she said brusquely, taking Katherine by surprise. "So undependable! But that Fontaine, your butler, that man is a saint! You may count on him for anything, Madame Boylan.''

"Oh, please, you must call me Katherine.''

Berenice bowed her head slightly. "*Merci, ma petite.* And you must call me Berenice. I am Berenice Beaucart, Daniel's oldest and best friend!''

With the niceties settled, Katherine didn't know where to go from there. The truth was, she was so overwhelmed by all the changes she had gone through, she seemed to have lost her focus. No chattering magpie to begin with, she knew how to hold her own in a conversation. At least she had known, until she'd arrived in Paris. But Deirdre, May and all those strange people who had come calling, speaking in a language she hadn't used since her college days. She seemed to have lost every social grace she'd ever been taught.

Even now, she was never so grateful as when Fontaine arrived, cautiously supervising the young maid who pushed the elaborate tea trolley laden with a huge silver samovar, a delicate service, tiny tea cakes and sandwiches, napkins, sugar cubes and a creamer. Katherine took one look at the massive service and blanched. Eyeing the tea trolley as though it was an enemy of the state, she smiled weakly and forced herself to concentrate on serving while Madame Beaucart's high-pitched, melodious voice rang through the air. Miraculously, she managed to serve Berenice her tea without spilling a drop. Two miracles performed; when Wilma joined them moments later, she was able to do it again.

They spent the next half hour discreetly assessing each other over paper-thin cucumber sandwiches, lemon-seed cake and oolong tea. Katherine hardly spoke, but the way Wilma and Berenice carried on, a regular love affair had commenced! Talking children and grandchildren, the best museums, how to get around Paris, what to see first—their endless myriad details threatened to put Katherine to sleep. But then, she might be extra tired because she had not been sleeping well since her argument with Daniel.

"*Mon Dieu!* That Daniel, to leave you alone like this!" Berenice said at one point, turning to Katherine. "I shall certainly have to speak my mind to him," she decided, waving aside Katherine's protest. "On the other hand, there are some things Daniel cannot do. Maybe, I am thinking, it is a good thing I have come here, *non?*" she murmured, glancing down at Katherine's brown shoes with a moue of distaste. "Not Italian." She sighed heavily.

Katherine followed her look and squirmed until she remembered how many piano lessons she'd had to give to buy those shoes. Madame Beaucart obviously knew nothing about cutting coupons.

"Berenice, I have a favor to ask." Wilma smiled, ignoring

Katherine's irritation. "Katherine, here, she needs help putting together a new wardrobe, and I am willing to bet some good old American dollars that you know the best stores."

"What happened to Daniel's sisters, hmm?"

"Oh, they were wonderful," Wilma promised, seeing Katherine's warning glance, "but they had so little time, we just barely skimmed the surface. It was more a getting-to-know-you kind of week. Katherine, here, she needs the real thing, a complete overhaul. And unless I'm mistaken," Wilma sweet-talked, admiring Berenice head to toe, "you're the very one to do it."

"You and I, Wilma, we are going to be good friends, yes?" Berenice approved, returning Wilma's careful smile with one of her own. "And you are right. *Les boutiques, les magasins,* I know all the best shops! The ones which are not advertised to the general public! *Oui,* I will simply have to take you ladies in hand." She sighed loudly. "It will be hard work, yes, but, Daniel would expect it of me. And *Monsieur l'Ambassadeur,* he will pay for it all! That is the best part, *non?*" she added gaily as Fontaine slid quietly into the room.

"Madame." He bowed, startling Katherine as he presented her with a silver salver. "These cards have just been left. I thought you might wish to see them, since the messenger insists on waiting."

Katherine took the cards, but the names meant nothing to her. "Madame Shallotte and Mademoiselle Shallotte?" she read aloud, fingering the gold-embossed calling cards.

Madame Beaucart leaned forward confidentially. "*Vraiment,* Katherine, you should feel honored that they have been left so quickly. These women are powers in French society. Not as powerful as me, of course, but a force, all the same. And Mam'selle Shallotte, she would make you a good friend, too. She is almost your own age. Fontaine, tell the messenger that Madame will be glad to return their call in a few days."

He turned to Katherine for affirmation, she nodded, knowing she was way out of her league. She knew she would be wise to be guided by Berenice, but unsure, she sent Wilma a worried look. Wilma was unaware of her turmoil. Serenely sipping tea like the Queen of England, she was completely captivated by her new friend. The way they were chattering over each other, Katherine wondered how they understood themselves. Eventually Berenice leveled her wise, twinkling eyes on Katherine. "Well, my dear, have you decided?"

Katherine smiled politely. "Decided?"

"Why, whether you like me, whether you are going to let me befriend you."

Katherine smiled weakly, but Berenice waved her unspoken protests aside. "No, no, my dear, spare me the, how do you Americans say, the chitchat? I know I am an old busybody, but I like you very much and I insist you will like me, too. I have plans for you, eh, Wilma?"

Wilma grinned, a willing co-conspirator. "She does need a whole lot of work, doesn't she?"

"Oh, yes, but the shopping will help enormously. For both of you, my friends."

"Suits me just fine," Wilma said bluntly. "It's been a long time since I treated myself to a pretty dress. You, too, Katherine."

"I daresay we could spare a few dollars to upgrade our wardrobe," Katherine said slowly.

"A few dollars? My heart!" cried Berenice, a hand to her bony chest. "Maybe a few thousand, little one."

Katherine gasped, but Madame Beaucart was unperturbed. "Katherine, you are the American ambassador's wife! You must look, how shall I put it, a certain way. Look the part, like in the cinema, no? All that pretty yellow hair, lovely, lovely, but it needs a good haircut to show it off. A fringe don't you think, Wilma? And two inches off the bottom, with a bit of feathering. Yes! Perfect! And your friend, no, *my* friend, Wilma, she must also remake, yes? But she understands that."

Wilma definitely did. "Katherine, you can't go around looking like you still shop at a country store. Why, honey, you're practically royalty! You're going to attend balls, fancy luncheons, give speeches—that's right, girl, give speeches!'' she laughed when she saw Katherine's face fall.

"Well, ladies, I guess I better let you know right now that I sold the crown jewels a long time ago," Katherine exclaimed, exasperated by their grand schemes. "So how are you two going to fund your fancy shopping spree? You were joking, weren't you, when you said Daniel should foot the bill?''

"*Mon Dieu!* Is that not what husbands are for?" Berenice asked, incredulous.

Wilma evidently agreed, the way she was nodding her head. Not Katherine. "I absolutely cannot ask him to do that,'' she said firmly.

Berenice looked at Katherine as if she had lost her mind. "*Quelle horreur!* We have no intention of asking him! Daniel is as rich as Croesus. Everybody knows about the Sheridan Trust Fund and the Boylan Brokerage House. Do not blush so, Katherine. You Americans with your acts of disclosure, do you really keep no secrets? A few evening gowns?" She shrugged. "My dear Katherine, Daniel will not even notice the bills. In my day we used to call it pin money. Anyway, he would never dream of refusing. Truly, he would be too angry—yes!—if you embarrassed him by asking his permission to shop! He is a very proud man and even to imply that he was…hmm, how do you Americans say…thrifty? No, no! It is not a nice word. It would make him very angry, I can promise you!''

"Oh, I don't think he could be any more angry than he is now!" The moment the words were out, Katherine wanted to die. She could not believe her big mouth, and the way both women were staring at her, suddenly on the alert, neither could they. But where Katherine was silent, Wilma was candid.

"I never did hold truck with married folk having separate bedrooms!" she announced roundly.

"No!" Berenice gasped, trying to hide a smile.

"The way I see it," Wilma confided to her new friend, "there's a childish game of hide-and-seek going on in this here overfurnished barn!"

"Oh, hush, Wilma," Katherine cried. "You have no idea what you're talking about!"

"Oh, I got the idea, all right, child," Wilma snorted. "It's called pride. And somebody hereabouts is heading for a mighty big fall!"

Katherine was speechless, but Berenice was thrilled. Finally, something to interest an old woman in the winter of her years. The last social season had been so boring, but now, with the arrival of the Boylans, so obviously star-crossed, what fun they would have. And Wilma! A treasure! So handsome, so honest! Yes. But she said none of this, her pale, bright eyes a picture of watery-blue innocence above the dainty Limoges cup clasped in her jeweled, arthritic hand. Someday, she made a mental note, someday, she really must remember to thank Daniel!

Reeling from Berenice and Wilma's combined onslaught, Katherine was almost thankful when, as if conjured, the man in question unexpectedly strolled in, looking far too attractive in khakis and a dark-blue sweater. Katherine turned away, suddenly shy.

"Daniel, finally!"

"Berenice, how nice to see you after all these months. Wilma."

Berenice returned his greeting, her brow an exaggerated wrinkle as he bent to kiss her cheek. "I have been sitting here this last hour enjoying tea with your new wife and missing you. It is in all the press about your beautiful young bride. I have been practically eating *Le Monde* for breakfast, but I simply could not stay away any longer. I had to meet Madame Katherine Boylan for myself. They were right, all the newspapers, she is very beautiful, but we knew that. And Wilma, she is a rose! But where is the child, most of all, the child! I have been waiting this hour to meet the child!"

"Yes, good question, where is Dylan?" Wilma echoed.

"Did my baby really go all the way to the top of the Eiffel Tower, like he said he would?"

"Dylan made it all the way." Daniel smiled. "And would have stayed there the rest of the afternoon. It was my stomach that insisted we descend a whole lot sooner than he liked."

"They asked me to go with them," Wilma told Berenice, missing Katherine's look of surprise, "but I told them that when I wanted to touch the clouds, I would let the good Lord know!"

"A wise decision."

"By the way, I dropped Dylan off at Noel's house, on the way home. My secretary's son," he explained to Berenice as Katherine silently handed him a cup of tea.

"Noel and Dylan seem to have begun a lasting friendship. You don't have any objection to that, do you, Katherine? My car is going to pick him shortly."

"No, I have no objections," she said into her own cup. So quiet, so polite.

Daniel was careful to temper his annoyance. "I've taken the liberty of assigning two of my best secret service men to accompany him whenever he leaves the embassy grounds. At least until we settle on his schooling. For you, as well."

Dismayed, Katherine raised her head but Berenice seconded Daniel's decision. "A wise precaution, Katherine. Terrorism, kidnappers, who can say? France is not so bad, but these days..." she left off with a Gallic shrug. "Who can say?"

"As a matter of fact, I brought them along on today's outing, to let them all get to know each other. A wise decision for Dylan." Daniel grinned. "But those poor guys definitely looked green around the collar when we got to the top of the Eiffel Tower. All nine hundred eighty-four feet of it!"

"You bad man, how could you?" Berenice scolded. "I am glad I was not there to witness their misery. Well, I will have to meet your young man another time. But I had Kath-

erine, did I not? I have come to the aid of your pretty wife.
Why, just look at the poor lamb,'' she explained to Daniel's
puzzled face. ''So downcast, so solemn. It must be she is
the duck out of the water, no? So very lonely, this big city
of ours, is it not, my old friend?'' she left off tartly.

Daniel hadn't thought about that. His anger at being
banned from Katherine's bed must have clouded his common sense. Berenice breezed past his embarrassment, pre-
ferring to turn the screw. ''We were just talking. She has
this very foolish idea—how she got it, this I do not know—
that you will not fund her. Imagine?''

Katherine was mortified at Berenice's brazen speech and
would have defended herself, but one look at Daniel's fierce
expression and her hands fell to her lap. Daniel struggled to
keep his temper. Since their argument, she had been so subdued, her prolonged silences were beginning to grate on him.
He could deal with anger, hell, he wouldn't have any problem with an outright battle royal. But this silent treatment,
it made him twitchy. It made him speak more brusquely than
he meant, when he asked, regarding the money, ''If not me,
who?''

Katherine blushed fiercely, and Berenice nodded. ''Quite
what I said, too. Good, we will not waste more words over
the so-inconsequential matter. Also, dear Katherine will need
friends to help her negotiate the social circle. Find her feet,
as you Americans say. Good advice will be of paramount
importance. Since you seem to be so busy of late doing
ambassadorial things, very important, to be sure,'' she added
in her pithy way, ''do at least take this moment to assure
the poor child that I will be most useful to her. She is unsure
of me, you comprehend.''

Daniel's smile was serious as he spoke. ''Berenice and I
go back ten years, Katherine. She was my mother hen when
I took on the embassy and she is the *only* person in Paris
you can trust completely. You and Wilma must allow your-
selves to be guided by her. French society can be very complicated.''

Katherine bristled. Berenice understood and secretly agreed with her new charge. Daniel should be the one to take his young bride under his wing! But apparently he would not, and a quick glance at Wilma confirmed that she too, was unhappy with the situation.

With a private sigh for her own sensible, long-departed husband, Berenice smiled. "Well, good then. Leave everything to me. You know, I think the press conference was a good idea, but what about Katherine's hosting a tea? For the women only, hmm? It might be in order, what do you think? Introduce Katherine to society ever so slowly. Wilma, too. After all, it is the women who rule the drawing rooms to which Katherine will need entrée. Sort of take the bull by the tail, hmm?"

"Horns," Daniel corrected Berenice absently, careful not to stare at his beautiful wife as she refilled his cup with unsteady hands. "And not a bad idea, that."

"And your family. It was so good they gave their blessing to your marriage. It was of paramount importance. You and she must appear as one, and the family Boylan must be standing right behind you, always, when you do. Those naughty girls—your lovely sisters—they are adored here in Paris and carry much weight! Indeed," she decided, "they must fly back to France for the ball. *Le Bal d'Automne,*" she explained to Katherine and Wilma.

"Oh, no! Not a ball!" Katherine cried, Sleeping Beauty awakening with a rude crash and very nearly dropping the sugar bowl. "Not a ball! I've never been, I don't know how—"

"But, yes!" Berenice laughed. "In about a month's time! It is tradition, for over a hundred years!"

"Well, you aren't going to hear a peep from me!" Wilma grinned. "I don't have any problem going to a ball, for goodness sake!"

"Good! One less problem." Having said that much, Berenice sipped her tea, her pinky in the air as she proceeded to hammer away at Daniel. "As for shopping, *Monsieur l'Ambassadeur,* shopping needs a woman's touch. You probably do not know the difference between aqua and turquoise, but then, you do seem to be color-blind.''

Katherine gasped, sure Daniel was going to go ballistic, and was surprised to see him throw back his head and laugh.

"Oh, Katherine,'' Berenice explained gently, ''there will be so many jokes, you'll see. The newspapers, the television and radio, they talk of nothing else but you and Daniel. An interracial couple in the embassy! Mon Dieu! You are the most fun Paris has had in a long time. But do not look so unhappy. I am only trying to...how do you say...thicken you up, no?

"Toughen you up,'' Daniel corrected her.

"As you say. But, this is all too kind of me, don't you agree?'' she asked her audience.

"But my son was so ill! Isn't that more in line with a tragedy?'' Katherine asked, appalled at the notion that her family was providing the latest entertainment for France.

"Honestly, my dear, they could care less about your son. Now, about Ambassador Daniel Sheridan Boylan's son, that is a different story, I am sorry to say! And that is the very point, is it not?—the love child you and Daniel created so many, many years ago. *Le Courier Nationale* did the most wonderful article the other day. *Magnifique!* But where did they get those awful pictures? It was your hair, we must see to your hair, Katherine, as soon as possible.''

Katherine jumped to her feet. How Berenice could talk of Dylan's near-death and her hair in the same breath was beyond her, but Berenice tut-tutted her down. ''My dear child, surely you did not think it was going to be all fun and games, as you Americans like to say? Being an ambassador's wife is enormously hard work. If you cannot yet read the French newspapers—Daniel, you must arrange for Katherine and Wilma to have French lessons, no?—you must trust me that you are walking a very fine line between scandal and respectability. But I was there for your husband, ten years ago, when he arrived in my country, and I am here now, for you and your son. There is something poetic about that, no? How our destinies are interwoven?''

Katherine looked as though she was ready to faint, and Madame Beaucart grew impatient. "Come, come, cherie, do stop fanning yourself. We shall face them all down, but you must be brave. The ball will be a large part of the solution. The ball to end all balls, and you on Daniel's arm, in the most gorgeous gown ever created, by my good friend, Madame Paulette, it goes without saying. Come November, the French will be far more curious about your clothes than your private life.''

Although Wilma took it all in stride, Katherine was too dumbstruck to answer. Madame Beaucart was adept at taking over people's lives, and from the way he said nothing, Daniel was used to her domineering ways. It came as no surprise that when Katherine looked to him for guidance, he backed his old friend.

"Berenice is right, Katherine. The Autumn Ball is the event of the season and I'm the host. But I should say *we* now, Katherine. You must look your best, and Madame Paulette is the only one to dress you. She will only do it on such short notice for Berenice. I advise you to take advantage of her offer.''

His advice was more of an order, to Katherine's ears. She wanted his advice handed to her, not thrown in her face.

Berenice also thought Daniel was being a little heavy-handed, but of a philosophical bent in her old age—and thankfully not his wife!—she was not unduly alarmed by his lack of sensitivity. After all, Daniel was nearing forty, if she were not mistaken. She had always thought he had taken on too much at an early age, so that now, hmm, there was, perhaps, a tiny bit of the old dog a little too set in his ways and slow to the ways of a wife, perhaps? And Katherine, the beautiful, green-eyed heroine, from what Berenice could gather, the poor girl had very little experience in matters of the heart. An unfortunate combination because, as any idiot could see, they were madly in love! Why, look how studiously they avoided eye contact and were so careful not to touch hands even over a silly teacup! Why, the air was positively static! Berenice almost rubbed her hands with glee.

"Of course she will take my advice! Everybody does!"

The matter would have to be settled later because just then a little boy ran into the salon clutching a plate of chocolate chip cookies. Giving Katherine a giant kiss, then hugging Wilma, he graciously offered one to Madame Beaucart.

L'enfant terrible, Berenice realized instantly, not really needing to see Katherine's wide smile at the sight of her little boy, the image of Daniel, a miniature ambassador. Tawny brown, his hair a short crop, and a look of devilment in his hazel eyes as he offered round his precious plate of cookies.

"Cook said I must share."

A smart little man, too, Berenice observed with amusement. Not one to waste time with tasteless cucumber wafers.

Dylan took an instant liking to Berenice. Introduced, they became friends quickly, not difficult when she hung on his every word. He spent the rest of the afternoon regaling his captive audience with the tale of his adventure at the Eiffel Tower, and, in the minutest detail, the life of the ferret, as told to him by his newest best friend, Noel. He was so enchanting that it was not very hard to coax Berenice to stay and share the family dinner. After dinner, she watched as Daniel challenged Dylan to a game of chess.

"But I don't know how to play," Dylan complained, at an age where losing was risky business.

"You will, if you allow your father to teach you," Berenice piped up. "He is very good. I should know. I taught him."

Katherine was not surprised to hear this. Daniel had never been one for parties, at least when she knew him, and she was sure his social obligations at the embassy were onerous. Chess would have answered his need for peace and privacy. Dylan's greedy joy at spending time with his father far outweighed the threat to his ego, and he agreed to learn the game. Berenice decided not to bear witness and called for her car. Secretly, Wilma was in accord. Let the newlyweds alone. Scrambling to her feet, she declared that she'd never had a better day, but an early bedtime would do her old bones some good. Katherine wanted to leave, also. She was uncomfortable around Daniel and his deep, disturbing eyes, but when Dylan insisted she stay and watch, she couldn't come up with a graceful exit. Daniel smiled to himself, he understood her quandary, but he liked having her around, even if she made him crazy.

That's how he figured he was in love. If Moses had climbed down from Sinai and hit him on the head with his tablets, Daniel could not have known more clearly that he was in love with his own wife! Looking across the room at her golden hair gleaming in the candlelight, looking so miserable that she begged a hug he dared not give, he couldn't have been more sure. How ironic that if he took one step near her, she would scream the house down!

As soon as Berenice and Wilma left, the Boylan men sat down before an elaborately carved ivory chess set that Daniel had picked up in a Nairobi bazaar. For Katherine, the only good part of the whole evening was watching Dylan's pleasure at spending time with his father. Daniel ate up the adulation; he couldn't seem to get enough of his son. So when Daniel announced, in the most offhanded way, that he'd had his staff compile a list of boarding schools that Dylan might like to attend, Katherine nearly spilled her coffee.

Boarding schools? Katherine's head came up only slightly faster than Dylan's. Daniel smiled and tried to reassure them both before all hell broke loose. It wasn't his idea, he promised them, a small lie, but forgivable, he believed, given the world climate. It was just that when he had brought up the matter of Dylan's schooling with his staff, days before, they were the ones who had pressed him to face reality—that Dylan would not be safe in a Parisian day school. He needed a school that had an estate-like setting, where a stranger was clearly and immediately visible. There was no better way to keep Dylan safe than to send him to the countryside, to a private school, one that maintained a serious security system. A system he would have to upgrade, even so, out of his own pocket.

But so soon? Katherine protested. Calmly, Daniel reminded her that the school term was well under way, and now that Dylan was a perfectly healthy boy, school was where a perfectly healthy boy belonged.

Judging from the mile-wide smile on Dylan's face, the healthy boy agreed. The truth was—although he'd never say so to his mother—having spent the last couple of months playing the invalid, he'd had enough of staying home, of bossy adults, and of no kids to play with except for Noel— Noel was a great guy, but he was a year younger. Dylan was more than ready to return to normal life. Daniel, fine-tuned to everyone but his wife, had sensed that a while ago, hence the list of schools. But he played it very cool.

Well, if Dylan were very sure…

It just so happened that Daniel had had his secretary do some investigating, and what do you know, one of the schools had an opening. Beautiful grounds, a nice bunch of kids, a great staff. An all-boys' school, though. Dylan didn't mind, did he, not having girls around? Good, although perhaps someday Dylan would change his mind and decide they *were* good for something!

And in the most offhanded way…

Did he mention the varsity-class soccer field and Olympic-size pool? Yes, I think they did say two computer *labs*, not two computers! No, silly, he could not start school tomorrow, they had to visit the place first, didn't they? Well, even if he didn't, his mother would surely want to! But of course, as soon as possible, it was entirely up to Dylan. After all, he'd just been through some very big changes. They would all understand if he wanted to wait on the decision, take another month to acclimate.

"Acclimate?" Dylan echoed.

"It means getting used to things, like your move here to Paris, living in this big old mansion, the French language. Like getting used to your mother and I being married. Getting used to *me*."

"Oh, sure, but I think I'm pretty used to everything. I don't think I need another month to, er, climate!" said Mr. Cool, feeling as though a special treat was threatening to slip through his fingers.

Daniel listened very carefully. He didn't want any mistakes here, he wanted to be absolutely sure that this decision was fully Dylan's, that it had Dylan's complete backing, even if he'd been guided toward it. Daniel hid his smile and hesitated, "I don't know. Maybe you need a little more time with us at home."

"Hey, I'm used to you, I'm used to you!" Dylan protested, sensing he was losing ground. He sent an S.O.S. to his mother, but Katherine was a fixed star in space, trying desperately to hide her misery. Daniel knew that he would have to deal with her privately, but, unable to deal with them both at once, he must give the boy precedence.

"You mean you've had enough of us?" he asked slowly, returning his attention to Dylan.

"Hey, I didn't say that! I just meant, oh, never mind." Confused, Dylan was unable to find the right words, although he knew exactly what he wanted. Away from his parents' mysterious gridlock and out from under Wilma's eagle eye! In that order. He wanted to be able to kick his soccer ball around on grass that wasn't part of a compound, hang out with friends that were his age and not government spies, or whatever those guys were who followed him around and wouldn't share their walkie-talkies. He'd even do his homework for the privilege. Well, maybe.

Daniel smiled. He understood Dylan's impatience. "Well, a boy does have to have friends and there don't seem to be many available around here. You were lucky to have Noel, now and then. Lucky that his school work didn't take up all his time."

"Yeah, you're right, Dad. I really should be in school with other kids," Dylan said carefully, hope renewed.

"Studying, of course," Daniel drawled.

"Oh, yeah, sure, Dad. Definitely."

Daniel raised a thick black brow but said nothing. Listening to Dylan play his ace in the hole, Daniel knew for sure that Dylan was his father's son.

"I mean," Dylan said, his hazel eyes going all wide and dewy, his voice soft and innocent, the poster child for youthful sincerity, "if you and Mom are so sure about this, I guess I can trust you guys."

Small mercies.

But judging by the look on Katherine's face, Daniel was running alone with this ball. She looked as if she would burst into tears any second. He'd better quit while he was ahead.

"Okay, son. We'll scope it out."

"Tomorrow?"

"All right. Tomorrow," he promised solemnly, not daring to look at Katherine as he scooped up all the chess pieces.

Later that evening, when Dylan had been tucked in bed, Daniel knocked on Katherine's bedroom door. But Katherine was either asleep or pretending not to hear his knock. In either case, her door was locked. He was sorry. He would have liked to talk to her, explain his motives and relieve her fears. Instead, he walked down the hall to his own room, hands curled in his pockets, his shoulders hunched.

The next morning, they made an early start because it was an hour's drive to the school. Dylan was excited and talked the whole way, but Daniel picked up on Katherine's mechanical responses. He would have liked to do something, but he didn't know what.

If only he knew how aware of him she was, of the heat of his hard, lean body, of how she had to force herself to concentrate on the scenery. Not so difficult, though, because Provence was beautiful and the weather balmy. The ride was almost a relief to Katherine. When they had lived in Phoenix and the desert was at their fingertips, she and Dylan often

rode out on their bikes to watch the sunset. She hadn't realized till now how she'd missed those long rides.

Madame Coffier, the director of L'Ecole du Lierre, graciously greeted them in her office, made much of Dylan and
personally escorted them around the buildings and grounds.
The school occupied the grounds of a fourteenth-century
monastery, the mullioned windows lending the premises a
decided air of elegance, even if the inner chambers were
newly paneled and the floors thickly carpeted. The science
department was housed in a building that looked medieval,
although their Bunsen burners were definitely twentieth cen-
tury. Daniel and Dylan insisted on seeing every nook and
cranny, and Madame Coffier was more than willing to take
the time. In close detail, they toured the math labs, the En-
glish department—those were iMacs in the corner, weren't
they?—the language department where one could study
eleven—count 'em, Dad, eleven!—languages, and two gym-
nasiums, including the Olympic-size pool.

Nearing the close of the tour, Daniel requested they visit
the dormitories so that Dylan could see where he would be
bunking, should he attend that school. Madame Coffier ac-
quiesced but not without warning them that boys would be
boys. She could not account for the untidiness of the rooms.
Looking around the dormitories, personally, Katherine
thought they were a little too neat. She took small comfort
in the sight of a few rooms that looked as if a hurricane had
swept through them, or at least, some real, live kids.

What Katherine also noticed, when they were invited to
lunch with the boys in the dining hall, was that Dylan would
have to be taken shopping. The clothes these kids wore...
She shook her head. Straight out of no magazine she'd ever
read! Dylan was about to enter the world of the super-rich,
whether she liked it or not. The new friends he was so anxious to make would be the children of other diplomats, business magnates, writers, artists—rich and famous people who
hung with other rich and famous people. Impeccably
groomed people with impeccable taste. People who skied at

Gstaad, had second or third homes in the Caymans and a pied-à-terre in New York City. All the things which had stalled her marriage to Daniel. All the things Daniel had and was. All the things she was not. My goodness, she thought with horror, Dylan wouldn't be begging for in-line skates this Christmas. He'd be asking for his own cell phone, a beeper and a credit card!

Well, at least the dining hall was noisy and smelled like a cafeteria, Katherine thought with relief, even if these children were eating ham and cheese croissants! Searching for Dylan, who had been scooped up by some older boys, was a challenge. The twenty or so tables were filled with boys of all nationalities, she was relieved to see. Not knowing what to expect, she'd been afraid that he'd be the only black kid on the block. She needn't have worried. It really was an international school, even if they were all filthy rich!

Then it hit her. Her son was the child of a very wealthy man. With her marriage to this Midas, she had taken Dylan from his humdrum middle-class roots and thrust him into a world of affluence that previously existed for him only in books and movies. Whence the simplicity of Phoenix? she mourned, feeling homesick as she looked around the dining hall.

Madame Coffier must have noticed her anxiety, even if she misunderstood it, because she pointed to a distant table. Katherine followed her finger. There was Dylan, his status as newcomer making him the star attraction. He was having a great time, if the grin on his face was any indication. Katherine watched him as he sat in the dining hall, surrounded by a dozen other young boys who would soon be his new family. Her coffee grew cold in her cup while hot tears burned her eyes. On the ride home, she had to bite her lips to keep from crying and spoiling Dylan's day.

But Daniel understood. She was grieving. Cautiously, he slid his arm around her shoulders, felt her stiffen, then relent. He was almost grateful. It felt good, damned good, giving her comfort the way a husband should. No matter what Katherine said, she needed him! A wife needed her husband! And damned if he didn't need her to need him.

There must be some way to breach their gap. Hell, it wasn't Dylan who needed to acclimate, he realized with a jolt, it was them. Poor Katherine, putting out the hard line, but barely hanging in there. And him, acting the fool, so busy lusting after his wife that he forgot about the things that should come before. Things they'd never shared. Things like dating, romance, candlelight dinners, silly gifts, long strolls in the park. Things like friendship.

Chapter Nine

They returned to the embassy to find Berenice Beaucart hunched over some fashion magazines she had brought for Katherine. She was waiting patiently in the salon, sipping a café crème that Fontaine had brought her.

"*Ah, vous êtes arrivés!* Where have you all been?" she smiled. "The three of you look as if it's been a very long day!"

Perched against her knee, Dylan began to describe to Berenice exactly what they had been doing. Katherine interrupted after a few minutes to remind him that dinner would soon be served and he ought to go wash.

As Berenice watched the boy go, Daniel's secretary rushed in. "Mr. Ambassador, have you forgotten the Lawrence dinner party to which you were to escort Madame Beaucart? The Greek Ambassador will be there, and you did promise to pick him up at seven. If you don't get ready, you are going to be late."

Daniel's face fell. "Damn! Katherine, I forgot to tell you."

As she listened to Daniel apologize, Berenice watched carefully. If she wasn't mistaken that was a green-eyed monster shadowing Katherine's downcast eyes. Privately, she thought it was no bad thing for the new bride to be a little jealous of her groom. Maybe then she would agree to spend some time with her husband instead of relegating him to a tired old lady who would rather be home in bed with a good book, or even a bad one. Berenice could not know that jealousy was a seed that didn't need watering, even as she explained matter-of-factly, "Daniel, Katherine knows that she is not ready to appear in public. She has nothing to wear, yet, though her gowns are on order. And besides, she can barely hold her head up."

Uncertain, Daniel looked at Katherine. "Perhaps Berenice is right, Katherine. You do look tired, and it has been a long day. I'll try to be home early."

Katherine was forced either to smile or look like a sulky child. "Sure, Daniel, you two go right ahead. Don't worry about me. I had planned to have a quiet night with Dylan, anyway." No need to say that she had hoped Daniel would join them. But still, the thought hung in the air. What a fool she was to be thinking all the long drive home that Daniel's strong arm clasped about her shoulders had meant anything.

"Katherine…" Daniel faltered as she smiled politely and wished them both a good-night. He knew he was watching the fragile thread of their afternoon's intimacy unravel.

Katherine arranged for dinner to be served in her room, and Wilma joined them there not long after they all had showered. It was cozy, sitting around in their pajamas, just like old times, Dylan declared, eating fried chicken and collard greens that Wilma had made, desperate for an old-fashioned American meal. Over greens and butter cake, Wilma cross-examined Dylan about L'Ecole du Lierre. Dylan could not stop talking about how awesome the school was, and as Katherine listened quietly, she realized there would not be much of a separation problem on his part. When he fell asleep in her bed, something he had not done since Phoenix, Katherine was glad.

"What are you going to do when he's gone?" asked Wilma softly, as Katherine stroked her son's head.

"What are *we* going to do, don't you mean?"

"I ain't no married lady, Kat," Wilma reminded her as she rolled their dinner trolley out the door.

"You think I really am?" Katherine countered.

"Yes, I think you really are," Wilma said sternly. "And you'd be a fool to let him slip away!"

Worn out by the day, Katherine envied Dylan's slumber. Her own wandering mind kept her wide awake. Snuggled beneath the covers, gazing at her sleeping son, she lost herself in the recent past, reliving everything that had happened in the last four months. Dylan's horrific illness, Daniel's reappearance in her life, their marriage and consequent move to Europe. She remembered Daniel's want of emotion, his lack of surprise at hearing her voice, when she had first called the embassy—a phone call that had taken her days to find the courage to make. Even to this day, she was pretty sure she would never have made it if Dylan hadn't gone into a coma.

She wondered, too, after everything that had passed, if Daniel had any regrets. If he had played back the montage of their reunion and realized there had been other options. He was used to making snap judgments, wasn't he? They were a part of his job, so, no, he couldn't cry havoc on that account. But that was then. Surely now, their enforced intimacy must be a trial he regretted, even if they had married for Dylan's sake, even if the divorce he'd promised down the line made his marriage less painful. Another divorce statistic added to the coffers of the national failing called marriage.

No matter how quietly they separated, the tabloids would dance for joy because they would sell lots of newspapers and make tons of money on the backs of the never-ending

Boylan saga. Then would come the cheap paperbacks, written by anyone who'd ever known them for more than fifteen seconds. Even a tacky made-for-TV movie perhaps. The endless, glorious interviews their old friends would give on the talk shows. Perhaps even Althea, holding a handkerchief, careful not to smudge her perfectly applied makeup, so pretty…

Katherine was sleeping and only stirred lightly when she heard Daniel tiptoe into the room. She had the wit to notice the clock, though it was about 3:00 a.m. but couldn't be sure, her sleep had been so fitful. She thought, too, that he had stroked her hair, caressed her cheek with his fingertips. Maybe he had also bent to kiss his sleeping son, she couldn't quite remember. If Daniel had been there, he was gone before she could rouse herself. When she woke, late the next morning, she was alone.

Showered and dressed, she went in search of Dylan. He must have been up for hours, tornado that he was. On her way to the breakfast room, she passed the front door and felt the keen desire to escape overwhelm her. After being out in the country yesterday, the embassy felt like an oppressive mausoleum. Perhaps a walk, only for an hour. Dylan was safe, Wilma was with him, and maybe a hundred members of the embassy staff that always seemed to be roaming around. Looking round the hall, empty for once, she realized there was no one to stop her. Slowly, she opened the embassy door and peered out onto Avenue Gabriel. There freedom lay, three quick steps.

Carefully obscured by the drapes of his office window, Daniel watched Katherine hurry down the street. Where on earth was she going? Didn't she know better than to venture out alone, unescorted? Yes, she did know better… She must be stealing time alone, disappearing into the city to escape for a few hours…to escape from him. Look how light her step was, the smile on her face. She never smiled for him. When Dylan was gone, would she make that long walk again, perhaps to steal away with a suitcase in her hand? He felt as if he'd seen an omen.

Dropping the curtain back into place, Daniel ordered his secretary to have a bodyguard follow Katherine. Then, intending to work, he sat back down at his desk, but his concentration was gone. What little satisfaction did it give him, mooning about Katherine? He might as well keep dreaming, though, the way she slipped away without him, her head held high, the sun a halo on her head. He yearned to follow her out into the dappled sunlight, take her hand, beg her to let him accompany her. He would be content to do just that. Except that she had made it painfully clear that she suffered his presence.

He went looking for his son, instead.

When Katherine returned at dusk, exhausted, grimy and elated, she never knew she had been followed for the entire day. Ironically, at one point, she had placed a call to the embassy, to let them know where she was and not to worry. Not a problem, Madame, Fontaine informed her. Everyone was gone for the day. *Le petit monsieur* had been taken for a drive with his papa, and Madame Wilma was out at *le matinée*.

So much for the idea of inviting Daniel to meet her for lunch.

Instead of dining with her husband, Katherine had walked along the Seine, chatting with the artists who came to display their work, browsing in dusty book bins and getting completely lost. She was thrilled to find a church almost every time she turned a corner, each one older than the history of her own country. She felt as though she'd walked a hundred miles before she found her way home.

Fontaine promised to serve her a hot meal as soon as she was ready. Only, did Madame wish to eat in the dining room, or did she prefer a tray in her room, as everyone was out for the evening?

"Everyone?" Katherine asked, surprised.

"*Oui, Madame. Monsieur L'Ambassadeur* said please to

inform you that he was joining some friends for dinner, since you had not yet returned from your outing. And Madame Batterson has joined Madame Beaucart for dinner.''

"That was the ambassador's entire message?"

"*Oui*, except that he gave young sir permission to spend the night with master Noel.''

Katherine made her way to her room feeling more alone than she had in years. After a hot shower, Katherine mulled over her options while eating a steaming bowl of soup a maid had brought. Daniel had his diplomatic duties, Dylan was soon going off to school, and even Wilma seemed to be carving out a life of her own. Berenice might want Katherine to become the social doyenne of Paris, but Daniel didn't seem to need her to do that, and besides, that was no sort of life for her. It was time to return to her music, and, in truth, it was what she really wanted.

Returning home at midnight, Daniel spied the flicker of light in a doorway and found Katherine asleep on a sofa in the library. The fire that had been lit to warm her was a low bank of embers. Stooping to study his sleeping wife, he drank in every inch of her. The blue silk of her pajamas did nothing to hide her curves. Tenderly he picked her up, hoping not to wake her, glad when she didn't stir. She was so light, it was nothing to carry her up to her bedroom, his nose buried in her hair, freshly shampooed and smelling of flowers. He laid her down gently and drew up the bedcovers. Then dismissing his conscience—she was his wife, after all—he removed his clothes and crawled into the bed, curling himself around her so that they slept in the spoon position. The way she eased back into his arms, blue silk so delicious against his bare skin, he felt as if they did this every night. He believed he could have had her then and there. She would have responded in her twilight sleep. He sighed, and she would be furious the next morning. He had to be satisfied exploring her soft curves, telling himself there was no law against fondling one's own wife.

Dear God, how long did he think he would last, living

like this? Living a sham marriage, sharing a house that was a construct of hell, pawing at Katherine like a lovelorn teenager. Disgusted, he rolled onto his back, slipping his arm beneath his head to stare at the ridiculous rococo ceiling. But, in her sleep, Katherine followed him. Using his shoulder for a pillow, she burrowed into his side, her soft breath tickling and teasing him cruelly. Her arm thrown across his chest, her long leg straddling his thigh. Daniel groaned with the excruciating pain of her nearness. For the first time since he'd taken up residence in the American embassy, the stout cherubs dancing on the ceiling failed to make Daniel laugh.

Not that his whole life hadn't been a sort of joke. Ten years ago, when Katherine had offered herself on a platter and he'd refused her—joke number one. And why not? He'd been young and proud, he was going places and a Caucasian wife would have been so politically incorrect it would have cost him his job, probably his career.

Joke number two: hadn't she, now that he thought about it, been guilty of her own form of racism? After all, she hadn't exactly broken down his door, when she found out she was pregnant. She could have, she should have! Was it because they were not the same color? Had Katherine not dared to cross the color line, either? Until—joke number three—she'd been forced to.

She had said she knew how he'd felt back then, how he had made it very clear that he had places to go, things to do and see. And so he had. He'd been a greedy son of a bitch in his own way. But maybe, just maybe, she'd read the message a little too loud and clear. Maybe she should have fought him—and fought for him—a little harder, especially once she found out she was pregnant, maybe given the manchild he'd been at the time a chance to grow up and shoulder his responsibilities. How could she have been so sure he would refuse her, that he wouldn't have preferred her and the baby over the ambassadorship, given the choice?

Hell, why was it all right for her to accuse him of not coming after her, when she hadn't followed him, either? In her own way, Katherine had allowed him to escape, helping to make them both miserable, and cheating him of his only child in the process. Her revenge had been sweet, even if she didn't know it: he had chosen well, and she had let him.

Daniel almost poked Katherine awake. He wanted to talk, hash out the past, ask her if she thought they had a future. But they didn't have that kind of marriage, and he wasn't used to such intimacy with a woman. Disgusted, he jumped out of bed, not caring if he woke her, although it didn't seem anything would wake the sleeping princess. Fool that he was, on top of everything else, there he was with the biggest erection in town, and she was sleeping the grand moment away! On a deep sigh, he closed the door. Where was this all going to end?

The day of the Autumn Ball dawned with the crisp promise of winter. Katherine saw it in the drifting leaves that would soon become falling snow, in the brisk wind that blew the leaves aimlessly down Avenue Gabriel. Passersby who hurried past the American Embassy that evening were unaware that its mistress watched them go about their business with something akin to envy. With Dylan gone, settled in at L'Ecole du Lierre and ecstatically happy, Katherine felt adrift. Daniel always seemed so busy she figured he was trying to avoid her, and Wilma was spending more and more time with the indomitable Berenice. The one thing that grounded her was her piano. Even now, with the ball only an hour away, she wasn't interested in dancing. If asked, she would have preferred to plop down in front of her piano and lose herself in a Sonata.

That was not going to happen. She forced herself back to earth, the folds of her gown frothing about at her ankles as she strode from the room. Dressed in a shimmering green-gold chiffon gown whose only trimming was her bare, sleek body, and with her hair pulled loosely into a topknot of curls, Katherine was dressed so beautifully that Daniel would fall in love again. Well, that's what Berenice had said. Katherine was not so sure. Oh, she knew Daniel wanted her, she wasn't insensible to that! His eyes were hungry, his desire palpable. But as to what he felt, that was as much a mystery to her as his inviting a few select friends over for pre-dinner drinks.

I mean, did anyone really have fifty close friends? she mused, as she left the haven of the library. Another fifty friends were scheduled to arrive for the pre-ball dinner! And another hundred couples were arriving around ten o'clock for the actual ball! Shaking her head, Katherine paused before a mirror to give herself one last look.

"Madame looks lovely, if I may be so bold." Fontaine quietly cleared his throat.

Katherine spun round, her gown whirling about so weightlessly that she felt elegant and beautiful. "Why, thank you, Fontaine. And while I have the chance, I want to thank you for the incredible job you have done. The rest of the staff, too. I have already spoken to the ambassador about extending an extra few days' holiday to all the staff. We thought Christmastime would be best. People like to go home for the holidays."

"That would be wonderful, Madame," Fontaine said with a low bow. "Very thoughtful, if I may say so."

"Common courtesy, only. But Fontaine, if you would be so kind," she asked, suddenly unsure. "Please tell me, do I enter alone or do you announce me? How does it work, this going-to-a-ball business?" she asked with a small laugh.

"Madame, why not allow me to notify the ambassador you are ready so that he may have the honor of escorting you in? A beautiful woman shines more on the arm of a gentleman in a tuxedo," he advised.

"Thank you, Fontaine," Katherine said gratefully. "And Fontaine," she called softly.

"Oui, Madame?"

"If you ever should have more suggestions, well, you know better than anyone that I'm not very good at this embassy stuff."

Fontaine bowed again and hid his gentle smile. "It would be my pleasure, Madame."

A moment later, Daniel followed his butler out into the hall. "Katherine, I—"

For a moment, all Daniel could do was stare. "Katherine! You look...stunning. Glorious."

So she did, too, from her delicate topknot down to her tiny gold slippers, and in between, the delicate gold strands of a thread necklace that lay across her ample breast. My God, wasn't she even wearing a brassiere? Was that legal? He would have to watch her very carefully, other men...

Katherine blushed as his gaze seemed to fasten there, enthralled. "Daniel," she teased, "adjust your eyes a little northerly, please."

Raising his eyes with reluctance, Daniel met her amusement with his own. "You always were a beautiful woman." Without warning, he bent to brush her lips with his. "I know, I know." He smiled as she pushed him away. "Watch out for the makeup. I've heard it a thousand times."

Abruptly, Katherine's bubble burst, but Daniel smiled. "I have two sisters, Katherine, remember?"

She felt stupid, because he was right, and she had thought the worst. "Okay, Mr. Boylan." Katherine smiled weakly. "Let's introduce me to your fifty nearest and dearest before I chicken out!" Her hand resting lightly on her husband's arm, the Boylans swept into the salon while Fontaine followed closely behind, privately glad he was long past his youth.

If eating too many buttery canapés and drinking too much champagne was any measure of success, then the evening was a triumph, Katherine later decided, when she had dragged herself up to her bedroom and collapsed on the bed. Her feet ached from too many waltzes, and her face was stiff from smiling, but the party had been a huge success. Her innate shyness, coupled with a proud bearing, had been very appealing to a society that had seen it all. Katherine had

conquered Paris in one short evening with just such a combination, making no apologies for her awkwardness, remind-
ing herself that a lack of social acumen did not equate with
a lack of social grace. If she did not know who was who,
or upon which rung of the social ladder someone sat, still,
she knew how to waltz—Berenice had seen to that—and
wasn't her card filled within minutes! If she didn't incline
her head at precisely the correct angle, so be it.

Everybody fell in love with her. Everybody wanted to
know why she had taken so long to appear in public and
gently chided her for not appearing sooner. The men winked
at Daniel and called him a lucky dog, teasing him for trying
to hide his pretty wife. Their more astute wives recognized
the female factor for its greater significance. Now that there
was a woman to occupy the house, maybe the embassy
would throw some really good parties! And though Daniel
started to get a little peeved at the way everyone was fawning around his wife, Katherine lapped it up like a cat with
cream.

If Katherine had her court, Wilma had developed her en-
tourage. Berenice Beaucart had convinced Wilma to try a
new hairdo, a short crop that allowed for a delicate band of
rhinestones to loop her silver curls, and she looked regal in
a complementary dove-gray satin gown. Berenice could not
have been more pleased with the success of her charges, nor
of Daniel's jealousy of Katherine.

"She is beautiful, *non?*" Berenice observed idly, strolling
by his side, late in the evening. Katherine was dancing
with the Russian Deputy Chief of Staff, and it was easy to
see that Daniel wasn't liking it, the way his eyes followed
Katherine around the ballroom.

"He's holding her too closely," he muttered.

"I think," Berenice said, secretly thrilled by his jealousy,
"that Katherine is going to set Paris by the storm."

"On its ears!" Daniel corrected her irritably.

"Ears! Feet!" Berenice laughed. "Whatever you wish!
But my Katherine is the belle of the ball, and your doors

will not stop to be knocking on for a long, long time, mon ami, nor your telephone, either!''

"Telephones don't knock, Berenice, they ring!"

"*Oui, oui!* And the parties, oh, my yes, the parties you are going to have to throw, now that she is queen of Paris. Why, Daniel, if I were you, I would be ordering up a few more tuxedos, refurbishing that box at the ballet, getting out my opera glasses."

"I get the idea," Daniel growled, a grim eye slanted on his wife. "I just never thought—"

"Men!" Berenice snorted, as she watched Katherine dance, her heart filled with fierce pride. "They never do!"

Knowing nothing of this conversation as she later undressed, the newly crowned queen tumbled with her earrings and thought only of her husband. It had been so romantic, the way Daniel had bowed over her hand, a wicked gleam in his eye as he begged his bride for their first waltz. She had liked the way he'd said that—his bride—and very much liked the romantic way he had held out his hand. The pleasure of being held by him had made her feel light-headed.

Around the ballroom they had waltzed, the musician in Katherine completely in tune with the music, the man in Daniel completely attuned to her body. The airy gauze of her gown had been an attractive foil to his silk tuxedo, her fair face an engaging contrast to his own dark, rough lines. The entire ballroom must have sensed the moment, because soon she and Daniel were alone on the dance floor. A hundred and fifty years before, the dancing of the waltz had been scandalous, now she knew why. She noticed when his gaze took on a darker, serious cast, when he had pulled her so close she could feel his hard thighs. It was sinful, there was nothing like it, and she would remember it all her life! Certainly Daniel would, judging by the look on his face when he escorted Katherine off the dance floor, holding her eyes, ignoring the enthusiastic applause of their audience.

These were the thoughts that pulled at Katherine, later that night, as she got ready for bed. Until Daniel came to say good-night and saw her standing by her mirror, fumbling with the clasp of her necklace.

"Allow me," he insisted with a crooked smile.

"I can manage," Katherine said, suddenly shy. But he brushed aside her hands.

"You were quite a success, tonight," he said, playing with the lock.

"It was fun, wasn't it?" Katherine agreed, her heart thumping as she tried to ignore the effect of his hands on her skin.

"Maybe for you," he smiled faintly, "but I'm not sure I enjoyed spending five hours watching half the men in Paris drool over my wife!"

"I'm sorry. I didn't realize—" Katherine blushed.

"I'm only teasing, sweetheart!"

But she couldn't be sure, she couldn't see his face, her head was bent while he grappled with the clasp. When the necklace finally came undone, it slipped from his fingers, leaving his lips license to follow where the tiny clasp had lain. Myriad emotions went through her as his warm breath tickled the nape of her neck.

"Look at us, Katherine, see how beautiful we are together."

Katherine was too mortified to look in the mirror, for when her necklace had come undone so had her gown. Before she could stop him, Daniel had tugged the green gauze down past her shoulders until it was a shimmering pool about her hips. Even now, she could feel his hands gliding up her bare midriff to capture her naked breasts, creamy, lush globes that filled his palms. Daniel was sure they were the most beautiful sight he'd ever seen. "Look at me!" he whispered, when Katherine tried to turn away. "I want to see your eyes when I touch you, and I want you to watch. I want you to know precisely who makes love to you."

His arms holding her hostage, Daniel skimmed the shell of her pink ear, tracing its delicate arc with his tongue. Her scent was a lure that threatened his sanity, her skin a perfumed confection. When he saw her eyes grow heavy, he softly nipped at her earlobe till her eyes fluttered. Satisfied, he trailed his fingers down her belly to slip beneath the puddle of chiffon and search out the swell of her hips. She was a golden prize in the low evening lamplight, and he whispered his love for every part of her he touched.

She was frightened, he felt her tremble, but she was curious, too, he could see, when he cupped her chin and searched her upturned face. He also read the confusion in her eyes, but still, she didn't turn away when he lowered his mouth and gently coaxed her lips apart. Over and over he kissed her, slow, vital kisses, until she was limp, her defenses shattered. His own armor, too, was gone he realized as he gazed down at the exquisite creature in his arms, surprised by his fierce sense of possession.

He would never let her go! The odd thought surfaced and stayed. He would never let her go!

Katherine shivered as Daniel carried her across the room and laid her gently on the bed. Through hooded eyes, she watched as he removed his jacket. Then his tie. Every button of his silk shirt slowly twisted till it, too, was lying abandoned on the rug, his wide chest bared for her inspection. That this handsome, hard body would soon cover hers seemed a very good idea. The sensation of his lips on hers, while his hands roamed her body had been a heady combination. He probably knew that, he must have felt her tremble, but she herself was deeply shocked by her response. Just watching him made her head spin. The magnitude of his hunger, as he knelt on the bed, the tenor of his hard body more than ready to join hers, was suddenly disquieting. Panicked, she made a half-hearted attempt to escape, but Daniel guessed her intent. Laughing, he grasped her ankles and slowly dragged her back across the bed.

"Leaving so soon, wife?" he teased, pinning her arms above her head as he boldly appraised her body.

"Why do you keep calling me that?" Katherine wailed, fighting the devilish things he was making her feel.

"What do you want me to call you?" he murmured, his

free hand feathering her breast. "Does the word *wife* remind you too much of your position in my life?"

"You mean my conjugal duties, don't you?"

His eyes twinkling, Daniel raised his head and smiled. "Well, I did hope there was more to the party than dancing." Laughing, he caught her up into his arms. "Why do you fight us, Katherine, why are we even talking? So many words, when all you have to do is kiss me. Don't play with me, sweet Katherine. The way you looked tonight, no man in the room could tear his eyes from you. Can I help it if my own wife excites me? You flaunted yourself before everyone but the one man who could do something about it. Except for our waltz. You allowed me a single waltz."

"I had obligations to meet," Katherine protested.

"Then allow me mine," Daniel whispered hoarsely and captured her lips. For a long, exquisite moment the bedroom was silent. Then, sliding his hands down past her hips, Daniel lifted her into his lap, draping her long limbs over his heavy thighs. Admiring the thin, blue network of veins just visible beneath her skin, he settled between her legs and loved the way she blushed when she felt him quiver. And then, surprising even himself, he slid his arms around her waist and buried his face in her hair, his hand cradling her head against his chest. Wondering if her soft body curled about his would make it easier to bear the bittersweet knowledge that, whatever he had had in the last decade, he had not had her.

"Katherine, please don't torture me this way, if you're not going to say yes," he whispered.

Fighting the persuasion of his body, Katherine barely had the strength to speak. "Is it so easy for you? Is that all you want to say?"

"Oh, I have all manner of things I want to say to you," he promised softly. "And all sorts of things I'd like to do to your delectable body, all sorts of games I'd like to play."

On a sigh, Katherine rubbed her face against his chest, smiling at how his furriness tickled her nose. She was tired of arguing. The man could talk circles round half the power brokers of the world, but he couldn't tell her he loved her. Seduce her, yes, Katherine lamented. Like now. He was very good in bed, he always had been, but she didn't want to be seduced, she wanted to be loved. That was how a marriage was supposed to be! The idea of his touching her intimately, the way he was doing now, without loving her, was so wounding that perhaps she'd rather do without. But she couldn't find the words, and when he lifted her gown, she gave him her body. Gently but inexorably, he eased her back on the bed and laid his cheek against her soft mound.

It wasn't fair, she thought vaguely as she drifted to paradise on the coattails of his desire. It wasn't fair how easily he could slide between her legs and take her. It definitely was not fair that he was the only man on earth she couldn't resist, that he knew it and took advantage of the fact. With a hard, long thrust, he crushed any thought of protest, made her match him with her own crazy, driving need. He gave her more pleasure in ten minutes among the smooth silk sheets of her barren bed than she had known in years. When she climaxed, he was only a moment behind. They floated back to earth, unable to tell where one began and the other left off.

His head was nestled between her breasts, one pink nipple winking at him when he heard her sigh of disgust. "How could you?"

He smiled and squeezed the soft buttocks still clasped in his hands. "You fought me all the way, didn't you, Mrs. Boylan?"

"Get off me, you big oaf!"

Daniel laughed as he rolled onto his side. "You calling the ambassador a big oaf? Can I quote you on that?"

"I hate you!"

But when Katherine tried to rise, he grabbed her forearm and pinned her to the bed, a curious, tight look on his face. "I don't doubt it. And you probably hate yourself most for letting me take you so easily. How trite, Katherine."

Katherine clenched her lips and refused to speak, but her rosy blush told him he was right. He bent his head till his lips were resting on hers, so that she could feel them as he spoke. "You let me take you because you and I, we are lovers in the truest sense of the word."

Then abruptly, he released her and rolled off the bed. "If it makes you feel any better," he said coldly, as he walked to the bathroom, "I wasn't intending to make love to you. Attribute it to the excitement of the ball."

Huddled under the blanket, she heard the shower gush, but soon he was making sounds of dressing. Then, the sharp tug of the blanket. Her eyes clenched tightly, she refused to look at him, not even when he kissed her lips. "Never hide yourself from me, my beautiful Katherine," she heard him say as his hand followed the line of her slender spine down to roam intimately over the swell of her soft bottom. "I will seek you out, no matter how many blankets you use. Or however many cities you try to hide in!" Then, sliding off the bed, silent as a wraith, he closed the door with a soft click that said more than any words he could have spoken.

Daniel was furious the next day, and Katherine knew it. She had never been so happy to see Berenice Beaucart, as when she arrived at two o'clock to escort Katherine to a celebratory brunch given by *les femmes Shallottes* in honor of Katherine's debut.

"A very pretty outfit," Berenice observed when they were settled in her limousine. Katherine smoothed down the skirt of her pink wool suit and nervously fingered her pearls.

"Why are you so jumpy this morning? Post-party jitters, *cherie?* Or not enough sleep?" Berenice teased. "I saw the way Daniel was watching you all night, not letting you out of his sight for a minute."

Katherine shrugged. "I slept well, thank you."

"*Alors!* Then that is too bad! Or are those pearls taking a good punishment for no reason."

Embarrassed, Katherine clasped her hands and forced

them to lie still in her lap. "I hate these embassy functions, that's all."

"Then why do you go?"

"I have to, don't I?"

"Do you?"

"You said so. And so did Daniel."

"Did he?"

Katherine frowned. "Well, I think he did."

"But you are not sure?"

"What are you trying to say?"

"Me? I am trying to say nothing. It is you who wish to say something, *non?*"

Katherine squirmed. What a segue. Still, she turned to Berenice with a slight nod. "I wanted to thank you, of course, for everything. You've been so kind since I arrived in Paris. Daniel was right. Without you, Wilma and I would be lost."

Berenice nodded but said nothing.

"But I have been thinking lately…" She saw Berenice's faint smile and blushed. "I was thinking that I take up too much of your time," Katherine said on a quick breath.

Berenice tried not to smile and spoil the look of incredulity she sent Katherine. "*Mon Dieu,* I have been thinking just so myself!"

"You have?" Katherine asked, astonished and relieved.

"*Mais oui!* After your huge success last night, I think perhaps the fledgling sparrow has flown the coop, *non?*"

"The nest," Katherine corrected her gently. "Chickens fly the coop, birds fly the nest."

"As I said. But it is high time, I have been thinking, for me to take a little vacation, *non?* Especially so, after I saw how you were so enchanting to everyone last night, and how you charmed everyone with that naughty waltz you and Daniel danced."

Katherine turned beet-red, and Berenice laughed. 'Well, you have got your feet watered!"

"Got my feet wet, do you mean?"

"As I said. *Enfant,* you are on your own for the next two months! I have this morning booked a flight to Monte Carlo. These old bones need a bit of warmth from time to time. Paris is too chilly, this time of year. Christmas in Monte Carlo will be just the thing."

"How wonderful for you," Katherine said, hoping her relief at Berenice's departure didn't show too much.

But Berenice was shrewd, and she covered Katherine's hand with her own for one brief moment. "Katherine, I only wanted to help you."

"And you have, Madame Beaucart," she returned softly.

"Yes, I have," Berenice agreed. "In most ways. But not in all."

Katherine prayed Berenice was not going to talk about Daniel.

"So what are you going to do about him?"

"I don't know." She sighed, not getting her wish.

"He wears his heart on his Armani sleeve."

Katherine slanted her a look. "Not that I noticed."

"Katherine!"

"I did not say he did not desire me, Madame! I was simply hoping for something more."

"Don't we all!" Berenice snorted.

"Was I hoping for too much, to ask for him to love me?"

"Perhaps you cannot see what is in front of your nose, *ma petite.*"

"Oh, you're wrong there. I know what he wants," Katherine said sadly. "But I had wanted so much more."

"You have everything you need. He is sick with love for you."

"Lust. Make that lust!"

"Silly girl, is that what you think?" Berenice asked, incredulous. "Do please use the brain God bestowed on you and look into his eyes, Katherine! Have mercy on the poor man!"

Katherine sat silently the rest of the way to the Shallottes, mulling over what Berenice had said. But Madame Beaucart had saved her bombshell for the ride home. "*Ma petite,* I forget to say! I am taking Wilma with me."

Puzzled, Katherine turned her head and asked Berenice what she was talking about.

"I told you. On my sojourn to Monaco. I have invited Wilma to accompany me, and she has agreed. With great alacrity!"

"Oh, no, Wilma can't go!" Katherine protested. "I need her too much!"

Berenice arched her brow in disbelief. "You have flown the chicken coop, remember? This afternoon was a test, *non?* To see if you could hold your own. You passed admirably, my dear. *Les femmes Shallottes,* they adore you, and so does everybody else. If need be, they will be glad to take you under their wing. You do not need me and you do not need Wilma. You know, no one has said you must attend all these little fetes. As a matter of fact, since you have resumed your piano playing, you have a built-in excuse to avoid them. If you are sincere in resuming your career, as I hope you are, I suggest you keep your social calendar to a minimum. Of course, that is up to you. And that is the last piece of advice I am going to give you—at least until I return from Monaco!" Berenice chuckled.

Katherine slumped back in her seat, a picture of absolute dejection. "Wilma is very excited?"

"*Mais oui,* and you will not prevent her leaving, will you, Katherine? You will not drop rain on her procession?"

Katherine smiled wanly. "Rain on her parade? Of course not, not if she really wants to go."

"And why would she not? She has done her share of the baby-sitting for the sweet Dylan, my dear. Truly, he has no more need of her, now that he is in school. And nor do you. Now, Wilma will baby-sit this old lady, but it will be much more fun. Besides, Daniel has told me that he was thinking of returning home to the United States for the Christmas holidays. He wishes to introduce you and the boy to his family. That is one trip you will have to make alone, I am thinking. Wilma will not like to be in the middle when you take on the Boylans, and I'm thinking it would not be fair to her, Katherine. Me, I am suspecting that Daniel does not know the whole of that story, *non?*''

Katherine almost fainted. How could Berenice know what went on ten years ago?

Berenice looked at her sorrowfully. "As I thought, *ma cherie*. I always did wonder if someone had interfered, so long ago, with the lives of you and the ambassador.''

"Berenice, please don't ask me for answers I can't give you!''

"Yes, of course, my dear. But I am an old woman and I have seen much. I don't need the details. What I have learned in my old age is that star-crossed lovers are often star-crossed because someone else decided it was for the best! A father, a mother...''

Katherine burst into tears.

"As I thought. I am so very sorry, Katherine. And will you never tell him?''

Unable to speak, Katherine shook her head violently.

"So very well protected, our fine young prince. But would he thank anyone, I am wondering? He is not a happy man. Since the day I met him, he is not a happy man. *Alors!* I am sorry, Katherine, but Wilma will not enjoy such an outing as this, as you must know. You have ghosts to confront and you can only do so by yourself. Monaco will be a lot more fun for her, *non?* I have promised to take her to the casinos.''

"But I need her.''

"Nonsense. You need your husband. Give us a few babies, and you can have her back. But not before.'' Berenice watched Katherine blush and patted her hand. "My darling girl, everything will be all right, you will see.''

Chapter Ten

But everything was not all right. By the time Wilma and Berenice left the following week, Daniel and Katherine had barely moved toward simple civility. The older women had discussed it endlessly, had worried whether the young couple were using them as crutches, and, in the end, decided that their trip was a very good idea. They hoped the couple only needed time alone and would mend fences while the ladies were gone. It was so unfortunate, but these days, what could one expect with the younger generations? So quick to temper, so impatient with the world and with each other.

Dylan was the kid caught in the middle. If he ever wondered why his parents seemed so jumpy, he wasn't home long enough to worry about it. Enrolled at L'Ecole du Lierre, he wasn't home a great deal anymore. He loved every minute of school and only missed his mother a little bit. He had become a star soccer player, and his tennis wasn't bad, either. As long as he kept his grades up, the school allowed him to play both sports. When he did stand still long enough, he attributed his parents' tension to the loss of his fabulous company. Why they would worry about him, he wasn't sure, but everyone knew how weird grown-ups were. His friends, occupying the same center of the universe, thought he was probably right. Still, when Dylan came home for a long three-day weekend and brought along half a dozen new friends, his visit was a breath of fresh air to the embattled parents. For seventy-two hours, the embassy was filled with the shrieks of healthy young boys, and even the press had a field day tracking the goings-on of the little prince.

As parents, Daniel and Katherine did their duty, cheering on Dylan's soccer games when they visited. Because he traveled so much, it was difficult for Daniel to make many school events, but he took as many red-eyes as he could and flew the Concorde whenever possible to streamline his time. Katherine understood that he was trying to be a good parent, and she was grateful for Dylan's sake. The boy positively worshipped his father. She knew full well Daniel could have paid the bills and been done. She recognized, also, that this thing called parenting was new to Daniel, while she'd had ten years' practice. She wanted to give him some pointers, to help make the going less rough, to tell him he didn't have to be perfect. He didn't always need a solution for Dylan, being available to his son was often enough. But things were so tense between her and Daniel that she kept her advice to herself.

Their truce was made more uneasy at a breakfast they shared one morning, when Daniel informed Katherine that they were returning to the States for the holidays, the arrangements were made, the embassy staff had been given vacation time, and his secretary had rearranged his schedule. Katherine should see to her packing, accordingly.

Katherine was furious. And scared. She had no one to confide in, not Wilma or Berenice, who were living the good life in Monte Carlo, and certainly not Daniel, who was adamant about going home. He wanted to introduce his son to his cousins, and he had given Deirdre and May his word that he would return for the holiday. And, no, Katherine could not stay behind. She was his wife and would act like it, at least in some ways!

The tension remained for days, until the Christmas party for all of Dylan's newfound friends. Daniel's staff drove themselves into a frenzy trying to please Katherine, who wanted Dylan to have a Christmas party of his own before they left for New York, one with a distinct American flavor. So on a Saturday afternoon, thirty-five pre-adolescents filled the ballroom, now transformed into a makeshift cowboy ranch, replete with cardboard cows, makeshift horses and a good deal of broken-down junk from the embassy attic. All the children came dressed as cowboys, wearing red bandannas and checkered shirts, spurs on their heels and ropes dangling from their belts. When asked very politely by the ranch foreman—Fontaine—to please hang their six shooters at le Bar Americain—yes, the one that was serving whiskey ice cream—none of them complained.

Daniel made it home in time to enjoy the last hour, just as he'd promised. When he walked into the now-unrecognizable ballroom and saw his son playing with the other kids, his heart almost burst with happiness. It was all Katherine's doing, he knew. His wife had created this family. Hovering over the table she'd arranged solely for the parents' use, he watched as she passed around cheese platters, sliced sponge cake and poured coffee. He marveled at the luck that made her his. Marriage to Katherine may have been part of the big picture, but his love for her had been his secret agenda. Now, he could stroll to her side and bestow a husbandly kiss on her cheek without reservation. He knew she would not publicly refuse him, and he stole that kiss just in time to hear her answer a question he himself had put to her recently.

"Well, music is more than a career, it's my life."

The mother who had asked understood. She felt that way about her writing. When she didn't write, she was a cranky terror. Why, her husband begged her to write every day!

Everyone laughed, although as someone pointed out, she was not an ambassador's wife.

"Well, that won't always be true," Daniel heard Katherine say.

The young mother sat up, scenting gossip in the air. "Do tell?" she asked, her coffee cup suspended.

Katherine frowned. "Ambassadors aren't lifelong appointees, are they? Look at me," she laughed. "I don't even know how long Daniel's tenure is!"

The young mother looked around the ballroom and grinned. "The accommodations aren't bad. I'd opt for a lifelong residency, if I were you."

"Too true! Forget about child support, Katherine, and go for the house," another mom suggested with a giggle.

Katherine smiled at Daniel. "Just how long is your appointment?"

So she was going to hold him to his promise. Daniel's heart dangled from the thinnest of threads, at the end of a line called divorce. "Bored already, darling?"

"Not likely!" she chuckled. "It's not every day your kid gets to throw a party at the American Embassy in Paris! But I was thinking the other day that there were more things to do in life than be an ambassador's wife. Or are you at the mercy of politics? Not a good bedfellow, I think." Everyone laughed when Katherine clapped a hand over her mouth, realizing too late what she had said.

Late that night, after Dylan had gone to sleep, and Katherine had crawled into bed, Daniel stopped by her bedroom.

"I just wanted to speak to you for a moment," he apologized, seeing how tired she looked. And how bewitching, barely covered by a frivolous nightgown. He tried not to look, but it was hard. Lavender silk on ivory skin was very sexy.

"It was a terrific party. You did a wonderful job. Dylan was thrilled."

"Yes, he was very happy, wasn't he?" she agreed, plucking at the bedcovers, wondering why Daniel was really there.

He hadn't been to her room since the night of the Autumn Ball. She had no idea where they stood.

"There was something I wanted to ask you about, something you said this afternoon at the party."

"Yes?"

"I've been hearing you practice piano again. You sound good, damned good." *You look damned good, too, and I wish you'd stop wriggling around like that!*

"Yes?"

"Um…yes."

"Thank you."

"You're welcome." What for? He had completely lost his train of thought.

"Oh, this is ridiculous, Katherine!" Daniel smiled as he balanced himself on the edge of her bed. "All I want to know is if you really mean to resume your career. How serious are you about returning to the public arena? Concerts and all, I mean."

"I'm pretty serious. Is there any reason not to be?" she asked, alarms going off.

"No, no," Daniel assured her quickly. "There's no reason. It's just that as an ambassador's wife, I thought there might be certain duties you'd wish to assume."

"I suppose I can manage a few." She chose her words carefully, not wishing to seem contentious. Lately, she'd been floundering, and she knew her music—or the lack thereof—was the reason. It had fallen by the wayside, in lieu of other priorities. Now that Dylan was settled and Wilma established, she hoped to reclaim her life. She needed to return to her piano, and she hoped he wasn't there to apply restrictions.

"I suppose that new music teacher you hired is everything his bill says he is?"

Katherine sat up, indignant. "Are you complaining about his fee? Is that what this is all about?"

"No, no," he assured her, shaking his head and trying hard not to watch as the strap of her violet gown slipped down her arm. "I'm just asking. Philippe was the one who brought it to my attention."

"Your local spy!"

"Katherine, he's my secretary, it's his job. I promised him that I would confirm the fee, that's all. It seemed a bit high to him, but if you say he's the best, I take your word for it. I trust you."

It was the damned piano teacher—the far too good-looking, very young, very French, very sexy, very white piano teacher—whom Daniel did not trust! Not since he had walked into the music room the other day and caught the son of a bitch with his arms around Daniel's wife! Teaching Katherine a hand exercise Daniel thought they only used in golf. Teaching Madame a *very* complicated finger technique, the guy had quickly explained. But damned if he hadn't gotten off that bench real fast, when he saw the look on Daniel's face. All unbeknownst to Katherine, of course. Because, innocent that she was, she had no idea the guy was putting the make on her.

But Daniel knew. That *mano-a-mano* thing passed between them, one, two, three, and the guy had immediately backed off.

This time.

Would the guy really keep his hands to himself, or did he plan to seduce Katherine when Daniel wasn't there to protect her? Granted the man's credentials were impeccable, but Katherine was temptation to any man and an absolute babe in the woods when it came to spotting that sort of thing. Damn, she couldn't even spot it in her own husband! Which was misery for Daniel. Just look how her breasts swayed so beautifully beneath that flimsy gown.

"There was something else you said this afternoon," he said, his voice neutral, his body anything but. "That bit about the ambassadorship not being a life tenure."

"Oh, that! It was only idle chatter. I was only wondering if you had other plans. If you ever thought about returning to the States, for instance. You're still pretty young, you know."

So she hadn't been discussing divorce! Daniel almost shouted with relief, but his reply was casual. "I thought that's what you meant, but I couldn't answer you in front of our guests. If the newspapers ever got wind of my leaving, or that I was even thinking about it, there would be hell to pay. It would disturb the global picture somewhat."

"Are you that important?" Katherine frowned.

"Hell, no!" Daniel smiled. "But the picture is."

"Oh." Sighing, Katherine shook her head. "It's so hard for me to understand. I was only wondering about the future."

"Do we have one? We spoke once of getting a divorce, if you remember?" He was cool, oh, so cool, but it hurt to hold his breath, waiting for her response.

"Is that why you're here? To ask me for a divorce?"

"You were the one who brought up our future!"

"I was only referring to yesterday's newspaper," Katherine said irritably. "There was an article in *Le Monde* quoting a speech you gave at an orphanage. Something about giving back to the community. It made me wonder what was on your mind, that's all."

It wasn't the assurance Daniel was looking for, but the only thing that would really reassure him was being invited into her bed. Since that wasn't going to happen, everything else was an also-ran, and he would have to settle. That didn't mean he'd have to like it.

"The papers are right for once. Lately, I've been thinking. What if I'm tired of the limelight? What if I want to retire from the diplomatic rat race, maybe to law or a judgeship? Would you object?" Would you care? He felt his heart race, waiting for her answer.

Katherine thought seriously, then shook her head. "Daniel, I don't know if you'll ever be free of the limelight. You're just too important. But a judgeship does sound good, or even teaching, perhaps. You don't want to do this the rest of your life, do you? I know for a fact that there are parts of this job you hate. I see how your staff cajoles you into attending certain functions.'' She laughed. ''Certainly there are enough gaps to fill back in America. You are a very valuable asset to the African-American community.''

Daniel sighed. ''African-American, Caribbean, South American, what about the white community—your community! Don't I have anything to offer them?''

''I hadn't thought about it.''

''That's because you're white and you don't have to think about it! Or maybe it's because I'm black? Is that it, Katherine? Is it because you have no intention of staying married to this very black man anyway?''

Furious, Katherine threw back the covers and scrambled to her knees. ''How dare you bring race into this bedroom! We've… I've let you…we've done things… And when you know there's never been anybody else! I've had your child! Doesn't Dylan get me beyond that Maginot color line of yours? Is my complexion always going to come between us?'' Swelling with indignation, Katherine was glad Daniel was sitting on the bed. It made it easier to slap him! As hard as she could!

Daniel never felt the sting of her slap; she tumbled straight into his arms when she lost her balance. All warm, slippery silk and some sort of divine flowery-smelling soap, she was a heaven-sent gift. He held her tight as he rolled them over to the middle of the bed, but not before he locked his lips to hers. By God, it was wonderful the way she bucked and squirmed beneath him, swatting his back like a kitten while she tried to kick him away.

Not for a minute did she relent and neither did he. She was a positive virago the way she tried to fight him off, and Daniel had never experienced anything so erotic. Her mouth was the only constant and he took advantage of the fact, kissing her long and deep, not daring even to come up for breath, not even when she clawed at his back.

Until, as suddenly as she began, Katherine stopped. Her

legs fell slack, and her arms fell wide as she gasped for air. His head balanced lightly on her heaving breasts, Daniel waited to see what she'd do next. She didn't move. When he dared to raise his head, her eyes were closed, her cheek was resting on the blanket. Sure of his prey, he lowered his mouth. His tongue roamed the delicacy of her soft, ivory breast, suckling her through the silk. A jutting, pink nipple blossomed, straining against the cloth, and he grasped it in his mouth, tugging it to attention with his teeth.

Katherine cried out, but he didn't stop. Not when he felt her body jutting into his, her arms wrapping about his head, pulling him into her arms. He did more, he was adept, his expert touch undeniable. Feeling her defenses weaken, his mouth grew more insistent. She groaned, hating how her body seemed to welcome him as he drew off her nightgown until it was just him and her body. What torment, his mouth brushing the pulse point of her throat while his hand spread across the moist juncture of her thighs. My heavens, sweet heavens! Katherine felt a delirium of delight sweep down to her toes. Dear lord, wouldn't he touch her? Please, there! And there! Oh, how did he know how to do all these wonderful things?

Katherine naked was a feast for his hungry eyes, and Daniel greedily explored every hollow of her frame, her willowy spine, the impress of her elegant shoulders. Shaking with want, he meant to be kind, but found it hard to be gentle. Katherine's lips, parted in surprise, were as much a seduction as her whole body. Not bothering to hide his need, he devoured her mouth, savoring every moment. And while he tantalized her with his mouth, his hand seared a path down her belly to search out her more private pleasure. It was a study in lust, he had no doubt, and the way she was writhing, she was with him all the way. The dormant sexuality of her body had been awakened, and she couldn't disguise her reaction. Not from him. Not here in this bed. On whatever other plane she chose to meet him, this one could not be denied.

As he slipped between her legs and penetrated her soft, moist heat, he could feel himself begin to pulsate. She was so ready and eager, Lord, a gift from the gods! She would kill him, the way she was carrying on. Then he smiled, and thought the craziest thought. Wasn't Katherine going to be the maddest woman in town, the way he was going to lay her down and take her tonight!

Chapter Eleven

May met them at Kennedy Airport when they returned to New York for the Christmas holidays. Thinking back, Katherine wondered whether it wasn't true that the key moments in her life hadn't been managed at airports. Or hospitals, she thought ruefully, as she dutifully hugged May. The rest of the family was waiting to greet them at the house where May and Rudy now lived. Including all his cousins, May told Dylan with a wink. But Dylan didn't care about his cousins. He was in love with his gorgeous, sweet-smelling aunt who was trotting around the terminal in the most amazing high heels, beckoning to the skycaps like a queen.

The drive to Long Island was faster than anyone had a right to hope for, and when they arrived at the Boylan mansion, Dylan was silenced by the palatial wealth of the estate. He didn't know they were that rich! But the worst was all these strangers, kissing and hugging him. His Uncle Rudy, whom he had met briefly in Paris, was laughing and slapping his father on the back. He'd never seen anybody else dare do that!

His cousin, Kiesha, thinking she was Queen of the Nile, the way she walked around ignoring him. Geez, but she was almost as beautiful as Aunt May! Those babies with names he couldn't remember that everyone kept throwing in his face, and his Aunt Deirdre—call me Auntie Dee—threatening to have another one right there in the living room, if he wasn't real nice to her. It looked like she might, too, cause her belly was so big. And who'd have thought, Uncle Henry was whiter than Mom!

They stayed two weeks and Dylan thought it was the best two weeks of his life, even better than when his dad married his mom because he didn't get any presents then, but boy, was he going home loaded! The best of the best, was that every once in a while someone would slip him a dollar, or a five, or a ten-spot! Then they'd whisper, don't tell anyone. He would whisper back, heck, no, he sure wouldn't, no sir, no ma'am, his lips were sealed. Why would he tell? He was already ahead about fifty dollars!

And opening all those presents under the biggest tree on Long Island, now that was important! A three-hour ordeal that nobody seemed to mind. At one point the adults suggested a coffee break, but everyone knew they were only joking, weren't they? When the gifts were done and the mess of wrapping and ribbons bagged, and everyone's presents put away, the menfolk took hold of the kids and decreed a massive, world-threatening, surrender or die snowball fight! No negotiating, they warned Daniel. Amidst giggling and shrieks—and the most mismatched snowsuits and gloves and hats and boots imaginable—the menfolk managed to get their kids outdoors.

The women rightly opted for coffee in the den. Massaging her belly, Deirdre plopped down on the sofa with a cup of tea and a box of Belgian chocolates. "You know, Katherine, I'm still wondering why you didn't want to contact us, after you knew you were pregnant. And, no May," she scorned,

when she saw the look her sister sent her, "I don't care if
Daniel doesn't want us to pry!"

Katherine sighed, but she knew she had put it off as long
as she could. This conversation was a long time coming. So
she would deal with it once, now, and never again! "What
was the point, Deirdre, when Daniel was married to Althea?
It would have been so awkward. Anyway, I was doing okay.
If I'd been destitute, maybe I would have phoned, but I never
was. I had a little savings and my mother helped me out—
as long as I didn't move too close by! She hated the idea of
becoming a grandmother. To this day she's never seen my
son. And then I got lucky. I found work right away in Chi-
cago. But one winter in Illinois was enough for me! That
was the year they had three blizzards! After Dylan was born,
I set out for warmer climates. Hot, sunny Phoenix fit the bill.
They have a desert right smack in the middle of the city. I
could teach music part-time and still be with my son. Not
having to answer to any boss, that was important. When I
finally found Wilma, she's one of the best things that ever
happened to me. She got me through the worst, and what I
do for her now is only a small repayment. She's beyond
that! She's my family!"

"Had enough, Deirdre?" May frowned. "Does the poor
girl really have to explain any more?"

Annoyed, Deirdre stared at May. "Dylan is our kin, May.
We have a right to ask questions. And you yourself used to
ask me what happened to Katherine Harriman. Too bad you
didn't ask the right person," Deirdre admonished her sister.
Turning to Katherine, she leaned forward confidentially.
"He never saw her again, after the divorce. I thought maybe
you'd like to know that, if you don't already."

Caught off guard, it took Katherine a moment to realize
that Deirdre was referring to Daniel and Althea Almott.

"Why, he won't even watch her on television. She does
commercials, you know, and she's awfully good. But if he's
in the room, well, he doesn't say anything, but he gets up
and leaves. Suddenly he's gone!" She snapped her fingers.

"And you never liked her, either, May," Deirdre observed dryly as she closely examined the box of chocolates.

May was defensive. "It's not that I hated her exactly. But it did annoy the hell out of me that she didn't love Daniel and didn't give two hoots that he didn't love her! Daniel and I had words about it at the time. And then it was a done deal! I was so angry, you can't imagine. I only went to the wedding because I didn't want to embarrass my brother. He'd just been made ambassador, remember. And besides, my mother would have killed me." May laughed. "I tell you, Katherine, as weddings go, it was the closest thing to a funeral! No, really! Nobody had a good time, least of all Daniel! I didn't know why, at the time, but I guess I know why, now. The way I saw it back then was, too bad, bro'! We didn't speak for years afterward! He'd moved to Paris, of course, and we were here, so it wasn't a big deal, but I really washed my hands of him, at that point. I was just so angry at the way he had turned into such a…stuffed shirt."

"That's putting it politely!"

"Deirdre, I'm trying to be polite because Daniel is Katherine's husband. Believe me, I could cuss, if I wanted."

"I do believe you did, at the time." Deirdre grinned. "But my, my, Katherine, I haven't heard my brother laugh so much in years. It's all due to you, sister-in-law. My goodness, I don't think I've seen him play in the snow since we were kids!"

"It's Dylan who pleases him. Having his son means everything to him."

Deirdre and May exchanged glances, then May shook her head at Katherine. "We see the way he looks at you."

"Positively lecherous! Dripping with desire!" Deirdre giggled. "Talk about a lovesick puppy," she teased. "Except he isn't a puppy any longer, is he, Katherine?"

Katherine blushed. How could she confide in them her estrangement from their brother, when they were so pleased? How to explain that Daniel didn't love her, that they were only together for Dylan's sake?

Thinking back to their arrival, when they were led to his old bedroom, Katherine remembered the way they'd both separately eyed the king-size bed as if it were a bed of nails. It would have been funny, except that it wasn't.

"I'll take the sofa," he had sighed.

But when he'd tried to get comfortable that evening, his long legs brushed the floor, and his head was at an awfully weird angle. Reluctantly, Katherine invited him to share the huge bed, and they slept together their entire stay, each careful to keep to his or her own side of the bed. If Daniel woke some mornings with his arm wrapped about Katherine's waist, or if Katherine found herself snuggled into his side at dawn, neither said a word. They greeted the new year with the Doylan clan, but they were both exhausted by January, and not from sleep deprivation.

Wilma and Berenice returned mid-January, too, their own trip a rousing success. Katherine picked them up at Orly Airport, deposited Berenice at her home, and continued on to the embassy with Wilma, who thought that Katherine looked too pale and had a faraway look in her eyes. It would be interesting to see how Daniel compared.

In the days that followed, Wilma decided that she couldn't figure what the heck was going on. There seemed to be a suspension of hostilities between the couple, but no easy affection existed that she could detect. That is what she told Berenice, when she finally had a moment to call her. After much soul-searching, the two women finally decided that drastic times called for…a honeymoon! Why, the newlyweds never had one, did they? It would be a belated wedding gift. As such, the couple could not refuse! Once it was decided, there was no stopping Berenice and Wilma.

And Berenice insisted that romance could only be served by a ride on the Simplon-Orient Express!

With the connivance of Daniel's secretary, Philippe, they secretly booked a compartment for two days, the time it would take to travel from Paris to Venice. They followed that up with a suite at the Hotel Cipriani on Giudecca Island.

One of the foremost hotels in the world, Berenice told Wilma. Their plans formulated, Philippe insisted they tell Daniel. Even if the couple could not leave till March, the month the Orient Express resumed service to avoid the February snow, it wasn't that far away at all, and Daniel would need time to clear his calendar. If they wished for an element of surprise, they might present it as a fait accompli.

So one afternoon, the ladies summoned Daniel to Berenice's mansion, a block from the exclusive Boulevard St-Germain. Dusting the light snow from his shoes, Daniel stepped into Berenice's famous red salon to see the two women settled like crows on a blood-red sofa. Ever the diplomat, he was always careful not to smile when he visited Berenice's home. She had always had a secret affinity for bright colors and in this room, where she often entertained, she had allowed herself free rein. Every inch of space was red, tons of gold trim adorned the red sofas and red drapes, even the walls were overlaid with red brocaded wallpaper. Red and gold and black were reflected in the figurines and knickknacks displayed on whatnot tables scattered about the chamber and in the glass-enclosed bookcase that lined one wall. There wasn't a person in all of France who would not give their soul to be invited to tea in the splendid salon.

"It has all has been arranged, Daniel. Two days on the Orient Express and two weeks in Venice," she told him proudly as he made himself comfortable.

Daniel smiled politely. "Are you leaving again, ladies? You just got back to Paris."

"You are the one going somewhere!" Wilma announced, quickly taking up the reins. "With Katherine! Berenice and I are sending you and your wife on a honeymoon!"

"A honeymoon?" Daniel chuckled, disbelieving.

"That's right, Mr. Ambassador, a honeymoon! Something you should have taken a long time ago! We only hope it's not too late."

"Wilma is right, Daniel. You and Katherine are in a very

sorry state. We are giving you this opportunity to mend the corrals.''

"Fences!''

"*Mais oui,* as I said. If you cannot figure out how to mend this one little fence, I do not know how you will go on with the rest of your life. Certainly, it will not be with Katherine, not at this velocity.''

Wilma nodded. "My goodness, Mr. Ambassador, for a diplomat, you sure are slow on the uptake!''

Berenice agreed. "It is all arranged, *cheri.* Your part is to get Katherine on the train by nine o'clock of a Thursday night. Naturally, you must keep it a surprise, or she may refuse to go, but surely you can manage that, *non?* Breakfast in Zurich, lunch at Innsbruck, tea in Verona! What could be more romantic? You may forget about the packing of clothes. Wilma and I have decided you won't need any! An overnight bag will be enough. Italy is quite warm this time of year. A few bathing suits will do, and that you can buy in the shops. Treat Katherine to a few new dresses, she will like that very much, especially if you do the choosing! But remember to be fussy,'' Berenice advised him. "Insist she try on many things, to show off her figure. She will think that you care.''

"But I do care!''

Berenice smiled. "You see to the pretty lingerie, and then she will believe you! I suggest you purchase them in advance. A few expensive silky things. Have them waiting at the hotel. She will be impressed!''

Wilma was more prosaic. "Daniel, Katherine is leading you by the apron strings,'' she declared. "You've got to take that girl in hand and drum some sense into her, or, mark my words, someone else is gonna do it!''

Daniel's thoughts flew to Katherine's music teacher, and Wilma saw him frown. "Ha! So there is someone waiting in the wings!'' she declared triumphantly.

Daniel denied it hotly.

"But she is—how do you say?—the healthy young woman, *non?*" Berenice quizzed him wickedly.

"Of course she is!" he said indignantly.

"Then you had better bustle, *non?*"

Daniel heaved a hopeless, heavy sigh. "You mean hustle, don't you, Berenice?"

"Daniel," she said softly, seeing how unhappy her friend was. "Katherine loves you!"

Daniel looked at her hopefully. "Do you think so?"

"Yes, Daniel, I do! She loves you," Berenice promised, and Daniel believed her.

Chapter Twelve

Daniel walked about with such a mysterious expression, Katherine found herself tiptoeing about the embassy. Although she knew their rift had upset him, she had soon had enough of his sour face. Coincidentally, the morning they were to leave, Katherine exploded. Daniel was off to work so late, Philippe had already stopped by twice to speak to him. For goodness sake, why was he dawdling over breakfast?

Wilma hid her smiles behind her napkin as Daniel pushed aside his chair, ignoring Katherine's irritation. Oh, by the way, he said as he was leaving, he was seeing an old friend off on holiday that evening, so she should not expect him for dinner. But, hmm, perhaps Katherine would like to come along? Daniel had been invited to ride along a couple of stops, well, it wasn't just any train. It was the Orient Express.

The Orient Express! Katherine gasped. The queen of all trains. The most elegant lady who ever rode the rails. If this was some sort of peace offering, maybe she should take it.

All right, she *would* like to join him, she wasn't all that busy. If that was what he really wished.

It was, Daniel promised solemnly.

By eight that evening, Katherine was dressed in a simple black sheath and sweater coat, sitting beside Daniel in an embassy car, on her way to the Gard de Nord. When they arrived at the station, Daniel hurried her aboard, hoping to avoid the press. As previously arranged, a steward immediately led them to the elegant Bar Car, where Daniel had also arranged for champagne to be chilling.

"Chateau Latour?" Katherine read, a bemused smile on her face as she was seated. "What did I do to deserve this?"

Daniel shrugged as he watched the waiter fill their crystal flutes. "I wish to spoil you tonight." When the waiter withdrew, he raised his glass. "To my beautiful wife," he saluted.

"Daniel," she asked, her suspicions suddenly aroused. "Is this little trip in the way of a truce?"

"It's whatever you wish it to be, Katherine. But for this one evening," he said, raising her hand to his lips, "I would like us not to argue."

Embarrassed, Katherine pulled her hand away and tucked it in her lap as she looked around the stunning carriage, arranged in the manner of a living room. Created in the Art Nouveau style, it was a sinuous blend of polished brass and gleaming wood. "But...but...where are your friends?" she asked. All the other occupants seemed to be strangers.

Daniel was pleased with her sudden case of nerves. It meant she wasn't indifferent. How unfortunate that she'd sensed so quickly that the other occupants of the Bar Car were not of their so-called party. "Oh, I'm sure they'll be joining us in a bit. I would hazard a guess that my friend and his wife are settling down in their compartment. I'm sure they'll join us just as soon as—"

"All aboard!" The cry of the stationmaster interrupted him.

"Oh, look, Daniel, the train is moving!" Katherine cried,

her nose pressed to the window as the platform lights began to blur. "Isn't this so incredibly exciting? I'm so glad we came."

"All aboard!" the stationmaster shouted again. "Next stop, Flughafen!"

Daniel grinned at her confusion. "Zurich," he explained.

"Zurich! Isn't that rather far for an evening's ride?"

"Perhaps. Or perhaps you will find it too short. One never knows. Come, Katherine," he urged, as the train began to pick up serious momentum. "Let us drink to...departures and arrivals!"

She stared at him for some moments, then shrugged her shoulders. Their waiter had returned, bearing the most elegant tray of hors d'oeuvres. It was much more pleasant to dine on chilled oyster and mushroom canapés than to bother with train schedules. Daniel would take care of all that. "Such service," she observed, as she eyed the pâté de foie gras. "I guess it pays to be an ambassador."

"As much as it pays to be his wife?"

"At times." She grinned as she sipped her wine.

"Which times?" Daniel teased.

"Hmm." Katherine thought for a moment, then smiled. "At Madame Paulette's, the dressmaker! Remember how quickly she made up my gown for the Autumn Ball? She did it for your sake, not mine. Berenice told me so!"

"Humph!" Daniel snorted, but she could see he was joking. "I was hoping for something more important."

"What could be more important than Madame Paulette?" Katherine teased. "Just ask her! Or didn't you like the way I looked, the night of the Autumn Ball?" But, suddenly remembering what happened after the ball, Katherine blushed. Daniel remembered, too, judging by his naughty expression.

"Yes, I liked very much how you looked that evening. I did get my money's worth, didn't I?"

"Hmm." She nibbled on a tiny spinach pastry, unsure of what to say. "Daniel, don't you think we should go and find your friends? There must be some sort of foul-up, don't you think?''

"Thank you so much!''

"Oh, I didn't mean it that way! I just meant... Well, they aren't here and you said...''

"I give up, Katherine. There is no friend. We're going on this little trip alone." He withdrew a heavy vellum envelope from his suit pocket and handed it to Katherine. "Here, read this. It explains everything." He watched as she withdrew a sheet from the envelope, her brow rising when she recognized the handwriting of her friends. Between them, Wilma and Berenice had scrawled out the story of her abduction, and Daniel knew the exact moment she got to the part about him being blameless—she was scowling! But when she got to the part about a honeymoon...

"Honeymoon?'' she shrieked.

"The food on the Orient is reputed to be excellent,'' he coaxed quietly.

Daniel watched the play of emotions on Katherine's face as she considered the letter from every angle. She looked furious, ready to pounce, and he felt his heart pounding, knowing their future depended on the outcome. His head down, his eyes closed, he awaited her verdict in silence. Slow moments passed before he heard the delicate tinkling of crystal and looked up to see her holding out her goblet.

"I am rather hungry,'' she said softly, and smiled as he refilled her glass.

The Star of the North, Katherine sighed, her breath taken away by some of the most beautiful marquetry ever created, when they'd moved to the world-renowned dining car. Although she'd read about it, never in her life did she think she'd be having dinner in this famous carriage.

They dined on steamed sea bass, caviar sour cream, crisped potatoes and sauteed broccoli. And when he saw how much Katherine enjoyed it, Daniel ordered a fresh bottle of Chateau Latour. They talked quietly, about the food, Dylan, Paris, prudently, they stayed on the safest subjects. By the time they finished their entree, they were so stuffed they opted not to have dessert. But magically it appeared anyway—glazed peaches and pink biscuits. And a bottle of brandy for the gentleman? the mâitre d' offered. After all that champagne, it was easy for Daniel to persuade Katherine to join him in a glass of Benedictine. He told himself it was perfectly all right to get one's wife a little tipsy.

Tipsy she was, and giggly. So much so that by the time they were out of Paris and well into the countryside, Katherine was having grave misgivings. "Daniel, I'm feeling a little bit dizzy. Do you think I've had too much to drink?" she asked, pushing her brandy aside.

"Nonsense," Daniel said, moving it back. "It must be the motion of the train."

"No more, Daniel! Are you trying to get me drunk?"

"Have I succeeded?"

"No!" She smiled, rising to her feet. "I just need a breath of fresh air." But she plopped back down, unable to walk. "You, sir," she said, pointing an accusing finger in his face, "you have gotten me sloshed!"

Daniel laughed and took Katherine's hand. "Come, wife," he said softly.

"Where are we going?"

"To a party," Daniel told her softly. His arm firmly around her waist, Daniel discreetly led her down a long narrow corridor until they came to an ornate door marked Reserved.

"Daniel, I don't think I feel like a party just now."

Daniel smiled down into her worried green eyes and reassured her. "Don't worry, it's a party for two, just you and me, my darling." Opening the door, he gently steered her inside the tiny compartment.

Lit softly by long-stemmed tulip lamps and embellished with more exquisite marquetry, the cabin was Edwardian elegance personified. A tiny table stood to one side and a plush love seat and armchair were grouped near the large picture window, dark now because it was way past midnight.

"How beautiful!"

"Good enough for that honeymoon we never had?" Daniel asked, as he locked the door. "I'm hoping it's not too late. A big mistake, not having a honeymoon, don't you think? Things might have gone differently, if we'd taken the time."

"I suppose…" Suddenly shy, Katherine wasn't too sure what she supposed. Daniel had distracted her by lighting a small candelabra and dimming all the other lights. The room was pitched into such dark shadow that she didn't dare move. The gentle sway of the luxurious compartment was her only clear sensation. But she didn't need to move, she didn't need to do a thing. Daniel was the master of ceremonies. Clearly, he had planned this evening to the last detail, the way he was moving about the room! She shivered as he made his way to her side, unsure of what to expect. Tenderly he traced the line of her cheekbone, then lowered his mouth to brush hers softly. Warm and moist, the tang of brandy still upon his lips, it was a delicious sensation that made no demands. Then he raised his head and took her arm with gentle authority.

"Come. Sit by my side, and let's watch the sky."

"But it's night. There's nothing to see!"

"Then you won't be distracted when I make love to you!" Daniel smiled as he drew her to the loveseat.

Curled up together, they watched the night pass by, seeing only a cast of bright stars. Daniel seemed in no hurry. He had one arm slung about her shoulder while a glass of brandy dangled from his other hand. Her head pressed to his chest, Katherine could hear his heart beat. Beneath her cheek, she could feel a hard, flat nipple pressed lightly to her skin, and to her nostrils came the warm male scent that belonged only to him. That was the way they sat, soothed by the rhythm of the railroad wheels as they whirled toward seduction. Every so often, Daniel would turn his head to press a lazy kiss to Katherine's hair. Or trail his fingers down her arm. Or stroke the sensitive, bare surface of her neck.

But by and large, they just sat and enjoyed each other's company, not even bothering to speak.

Only the change of pressure in Daniel's fingers told her when his interest took a new turn. Shifting slightly, he put aside his glass and, one by one, began to unfasten the buttons of her dress. He only needed to undo a few before he was able to slip his hand beneath the wool. Gently teasing her, his thumb examined the extent of her arousal, measuring the peaks of her upturned breasts. It was maddening, and she believed it was intentional, the way he played with her and nothing more. Even in the near-dark, Katherine could see the wanton gleam in his eyes when he found the clasp of her brassiere.

But the champagne took its toll. Not even the sweet torture he subjected her to could keep her eyes open. The slow wicked swirl of his fingers on her breast had a mesmerizing effect, and a warm, languid fog overtook her.

"Daniel, where's the bedroom?"

Daniel smiled when he saw what was happening. "I see that I was too smart for my own good!" Sliding his arms beneath her legs, he carried Katherine into the tiny bedroom that had just enough room for a closet and two narrow berths, upper and lower. He laid her down on the lower berth, which he'd hoped somehow to share, but judging by the way she burrowed into the blankets, it didn't matter where he slept that night. Removing her shoes, he returned to their tiny salon to share a glass of whiskey with the shadows of his past.

Katherine woke three hours later with a ravaging thirst. When she realized where she was, she climbed off the berth and went looking for water.

"Feeling better?" Daniel smiled when the door flew open and his disheveled wife stumbled into the room. "I didn't think I'd be seeing you this soon."

"Oh, my head! This is all your fault! I need a drink!" she groaned, giving him a black look.

"The hair of the dog, darling?"

"Very funny!" Katherine snapped, gulping down the iced water he thrust in her hand.

"Your toothbrush is in that little overnight bag in the corner. A nightie, too," he added, with a twinkle in his eye.

"Is that it? Is that all my luggage?" she asked, staring at the small bag. "A nightgown and toothbrush?"

"How much do you think you'll need?" he asked, a speculative look in his eyes.

"What, exactly, were you planning for me to wear...or not wear?" she demanded, her hands on her hips.

"Katherine, Katherine!" There was a trace of laughter in his voice but Katherine made herself immune.

"How long, exactly, were you planning for this...this kidnapping...to last?"

"Come on, Katherine! Kidnapping? Really!" he scorned. "One does not kidnap one's wife!"

"It seems to me that *one* has, no matter what *one* says!"

Daniel ignored Katherine's accusation as he handed her the bag. "Perhaps it would be a good idea to have a wash-up now? The bathroom is this way. Come, let me show you. It has all the amenities, only in miniature."

"Don't you dare come near me, Daniel Boylan!" she said when he would have taken her elbow.

"Oh, it's no problem, Mrs. Boylan," he said graciously. "I wouldn't want you to get lost...on our honeymoon."

"Our honeymoon? Well, you can just forget about that, I've changed my mind! I said stay where you are! I'm not going to get lost walking ten steps! But I am going to call the police! Are there police on this godforsaken train?"

"Gendarmes, I would hazard a guess. But what are you going to tell them, sweetheart?"

"That I've been kidnapped!"

"By your husband? Are you really going to tell them that?"

"Oh!"

As he opened the bathroom door, Daniel had to bite back his laughter at the way Katherine carefully inched past him.

He had her trapped before she was halfway past, his lunge
for her swift. Lifting her into the air, he shocked her with a
kiss that was unrepentant. Then as suddenly, he stood her
back on her feet and kissed the tip of her nose. "Make sure
the water doesn't scald you," he advised with a small smile,
as he closed the door.

Oh, that man! Katherine shivered as she stood staring at
the bathroom door. Just who did he think he was, manhan-
dling her that way? Kissing her like there was no tomorrow!
Kissing her like she had no say in the matter, picking her
up like a rag doll and...and...and...making her feel all
crazy! Why, just look at her now, she thought, peering in
the mirror. Her face was so flushed, she was redder than an
apple. She didn't know whether to splutter or wash. Well, if
she washed, maybe she would cool down.

"Ready for bed?" Daniel asked blandly, when she finally
reappeared, every button of her dainty bathrobe fastened.
"It's pretty late, don't you think, and I'm very tired. Most
everyone on the train has been asleep quite a while."

Katherine clasped her hands together, her knuckles white
as she stood as far from him as possible. "I...um...I did
just take a nap, you know, so I'm not all that tired."

"So you did. I forgot," he admitted agreeably.

"I think I'll just sit here by the window and watch
the...er..." They both looked past the window into the dark
night.

"Perhaps a magazine..." Katherine blundered on. "But
since you're so tired, please, feel free to go to bed."

"Oh, no, I wouldn't dream of leaving you to sit here
alone! I'll wait up with you."

I'll wait up with you.

Ominous words to Katherine's ears. She watched from the
corner of her eye as he picked up the book he'd been reading, the minutes dragging as he turned the pages. What had
she let herself get into, agreeing to remain on the train? She
should have left hours ago. Why hadn't she? That dreadful
champagne, that's why! He'd done it intentionally, gotten

her drunk—well, practically!—so she could hardly think straight! But why had he gone to all this trouble? Hadn't she made it clear from the onset that she wanted nothing from him, would only take what he gave for Dylan? Never mind that he was always kind to her, and patient, never raising his voice, generous...

"Bedtime, Katherine," she heard him call softly. Katherine sat up with a jolt, mortified to find that she had nodded off.

Horrified, she watched as Daniel rose and removed his robe. Barechested, he was wearing only pajama bottoms! Apparently, he had taken the opportunity to change while she dozed.

"Time for bed, Katherine." He offered her a forgiving smile when she just sat there staring, but he could hardly keep from laughing when he saw which way her eyes went, their worried look, the way she chewed her lips. It was a good thing she didn't play poker.

"There's a bed behind that door, and we are going to make use of it," he announced firmly.

Jumping to her feet, Katherine took refuge behind her chair, her lips suddenly dry. "Are you serious? Do you really think I'm going to go to bed with you?"

"Yes, I really do!" Daniel said, his mouthing twitching.

"Oh, I don't think so," she said proudly, her chin high. "I make my own choices! And besides, that bed is awfully small. It's not even a real bed, it's only a berth! This chair would suit me just fine."

"As God is my witness, Katherine, I will pick you up and sling you over my shoulder before you sit down in that chair again!"

"You just try it!" she dared him, her eyes angry slits of rebellion.

Thus challenged, Daniel flung aside the chair that Katherine was hiding behind. One look at the firm set of his jaw told her he wasn't joking. "Well, maybe I am a little tired, after all."

More regal than a queen, Katherine scooped up her trailing robe and marched into the tiny bedroom. The luxurious bedchamber of satin bedcovers and silk lampshades was small, and a man of Daniel's size seemed to fill the compartment. She was terrified to move for fear of bumping into him, and she dreaded that, the way he was wandering around half-naked. Flaunting himself, that's what! That hairy chest, the way his muscles bulged...

"Katherine, come to bed!"

Startled, Katherine jumped. "But, it's cold in here! Aren't you cold? I am!"

"No, I'm not a bit cold," Daniel said, drawing back the bedcovers. "If you would get into bed, you'd be much warmer."

Hmph!

"Perhaps you need help removing your robe? All those buttons..."

"I'll do it myself, thank you!" she grumbled, slapping away his hands.

Slowly, she began to unfasten her robe, first the top button, then the second. Daniel watched her every move, his eyes riveted on her hands as she worked her way down. If only she knew, his lips were dryer than hers. My gracious, he wondered, as he watched her robe fall to the floor, who was seducing whom? Wearing some useless lacy nightgown he could hardly wait to remove, she had no idea how beautiful she looked, her face flushed, her hair tumbling past her shoulders. Or how she made him feel. He swallowed, he was trembling like a kid on his first date. She could have him on his knees, if she only she knew!

"You forgot your slippers," he said hoarsely when she flopped down on the berth.

Raising her nightie as she removed some sort of rabbity-looking slippers, Daniel was beguiled by the sight of Katherine's long legs and the image that leaped to mind, those long legs wrapped about his waist. He almost made a begging fool of himself.

"Daniel, don't you think—"

"Katherine, I can hardly think!" he muttered as he watched her scoot to the far side of the berth. It was hard to keep his eye on the bigger picture when her tush was wriggling around in the air.

He didn't say a word as she burrowed beneath the thick blankets. Amused by her antics, Daniel dimmed the lights but instead of climbing into the berth, he drew up a chair. Reaching out to trace the outline of her hip, he felt her flinch and withdrew his hand.

"Katherine, honey, at least open your eyes. Please, sweetheart, pay attention. I want to talk to you."

No sound, but somehow he knew she was listening.

"Katherine, I…" he floundered. "This is incredible! I always seem to have the right words for everyone but you."

He knew by the way she didn't move that she was trying her best to ignore him, but determined, he pressed on. "I love you, Katherine," he said solemnly.

Katherine was paralyzed. She had waited so long for him to tell her he loved her, now that he had, she was at a loss for words.

"Do you hear what I'm saying?" Daniel said softly. "I love you! I always have. I've wanted to tell you so many times, these past months. I almost did, too, quite a few times, but I chickened out, every time!" he admitted bitterly. "I was afraid, terrified, that I would scare you off. That you would panic, back away…and leave me. Now look at me. I finally have you captive, and I become a supplicant!"

Katherine peeped her head from beneath the blankets. He could be many things, had been many things, he was a man of complex emotions, but what would he reveal to her tonight? How far would he go?

"I need you to be my wife, Katherine," he begged when he saw that he had her attention. "In every sense of the word. I want you to fuss over me, fight with me, attend dull, boring parties with me, try to keep warm with me in the freezing rain while we watch Dylan play soccer or football or baseball or whatever. I want to be your husband, with all the freedom that entails. If you stay, I need you to promise not to leave me. Ever! That definitely would be the worst, losing you again! I couldn't bear it if I did. I don't want you, otherwise. Smiles that don't reach your eyes, carefully chosen words with hidden meanings, or maybe none, I wouldn't know since I don't have the right to ask! Coming home every night wondering if you're there, it's been a nightmare. And these sparing gifts of your body—''

His earnestness won out. Katherine turned to him, her eyes hazy and unfocused. Gently he pushed her tangled yellow hair from her eyes. "Sweetheart, I can't live like this. I need to know that if I make love to you, I won't have to wait another year to be invited back to your bed! Damn it, I don't want to be invited! I want sovereignty over your body. I have to know that when we get to Italy, this really will be a honeymoon.''

Hearing her silence, Daniel turned away and bowed his head. "I see I've left you unmoved. Well, I've made a lot of mistakes, haven't I? All right, then, you can have your divorce, just as I promised. Take Dylan, no strings. I won't demand custody, just give me decent visitation rights. You've done a fine job with our son up to now, and I trust you will continue to do so. It has become unbearable for me to live with you under these conditions,'' he confessed, his voice thick with irony. "Fool that I am, I find that I'm in love with my wife! Deeply in love with my own wife.''

Katherine stole to her husband's side and draped herself over his big, square back, her breath tickling his neck.

God in heaven, what madness was this? Her breasts pillowed on his back, her scent enveloping and enervating, Daniel could hardly bear it. "Katherine, I do love you, I swear it! I have done so, forever!''

"A long time, *forever*.''

"A long time, yes…''

Sure that Daniel had already done so, Katherine forced herself to calculate all the strikes against them. Knowing that he, too, at some point in his life, had calculated precisely what he had given up not to love her and that it had been a great deal. Sliding into his lap, she wrapped her arms about his neck and pressed her forehead to his. "It must have been very difficult for you, thrust into the limelight so young, living in a fishbowl."

"I should have given it more thought," he said sadly. "But I was in such a rush. I was going to do great things."

"You had a heavy load to bear. I would have added to it."

"You would never have been a burden to me, Katherine, but I was too young and foolish to know it."

"Any choice you made back then would have felt like a burden, and life should not be a burden."

"It would not be, with you beside me," he swore softly.

"Oh, but wives are often lost in the translation," Katherine argued. "And as for the white wives of black husbands—*very famous black husbands,* at that—they don't win too many popularity contests, do they?" Katherine tried to smile but Daniel had no room for smiles.

"I know that there are things I will not consider if you will not consider remaining with me, no matter what."

"No matter what?" she mused. "Not for the fainthearted, is it, this business called life."

"There are definitely times when I would agree with you," Daniel smiled faintly. "You asked me once, and I would like to answer you now. There is nothing I would like better than to return to the States. I have been away from my country far too long. And I would like Dylan to be brought up in America, where he belongs. It's his country, it's where his roots are and his family. But I would go home only under certain circumstances."

Framing his face with her long musician's fingers, Katherine searched his eyes. "And what might those be?"

Her gaze was so intent, that Daniel couldn't speak for a moment. He didn't want to share another single night with her if she didn't love him back. He wanted license to her body, yes, but to her heart, too. "Katherine, I'm pure exhausted loving you. But without hope of gaining your affection, I have no sort of future, I don't even want my son. That's how much it would hurt, if you were not a part of the whole."

Katherine found his uncertainty touching. Shifting in his lap, she snuggled into his arms. Everything he'd taught her, she gave back to him in a single, shy kiss. "Do you think I ride the Orient Express with every man I meet?"

"Oh, Katherine," Daniel groaned, crushing her to his chest. "I love you so much!" Cupping her soft bottom, he balanced them against the sway of the train, his lips on hers, a lost soul come home.

Then he laid her on the narrow berth and followed her down. Splayed beneath him, her long legs cradling his thighs, she was a fantasy come true. He heard her whimper as he pressed his palm to her most private place. And her breasts, even through her nightgown, he could feel them burning. But it was her mouth that drew him, it always had. He had always loved to kiss her, he could kiss her forever. Over and over, he returned to her rosy mouth, his tongue teasing first the one corner, then the other, until she smiled and he could hurry past her parted lips. Kind and gentle and worshipful, and then he wasn't, but she didn't seem to mind. Her breasts swelled, dancing between their meshed bodies, their heat burning through the lace of her gown. He knew exactly how they would fill his hands.

Katherine also knew that one touch from this man set off fireworks she never seemed able to control. No matter what she said or tried to do, she was susceptible to him, some sort of biological phenomenon. She wasn't responsible. Pheromones or some such nonsense. Sad but true, she sighed happily. When his passion began to get the better of him, his body close to bursting, she wrestled past her lethargy. Just once she would like to be in charge. Abruptly she straddled him, pressing his shoulders into the mattress. "Lie still," she commanded.

Surprised, Daniel looked up and saw the determination in Katherine's eyes. "Go to, wife," he said, wickedly, spreading his arms wide in helpless abandon. "Have your wicked way."

"I do believe I will," she said sweetly, smiling at the sight of all those muscles that he had reined in, fair exchange for the pleasure she was about to give him. Running her fingers through the crisp mat of black curls that covered his chest, she scraped her nails over his flat, brown nipples. She followed the torment with her moist tongue, with soft swirls about his breast, then sudden, biting nips that threatened to unman him. Until she laved them again with gentle persistence.

When he would have raised his arms, she clamped her hands over his biceps. They both knew he could have taken her, but she trusted him, so he would let her play. No matter what the cost, he groaned, hard put to keep control when she was shimmying around like that.

Feeling naughty, Katherine slowly removed her nightgown while Daniel lay there in panting disorder. Stretching her arms high, her breasts became jutting pink crests. Close your eyes, will you? She laughed when she saw him try to resist her. Like a sleek cat, she lowered herself, matching him skin to skin, her mouth a wide smile as his torment became more than apparent. Oh, but it was so hard to keep her balance, she apologized, as she wriggled about, using his shoulders to balance her weight. How she did keep from falling? So sorry! But if he would only keep still... There! Good! Now she could—

With one swift motion, Daniel swung Katherine beneath him and thrust himself deep inside her. "Do we have a future, Katherine?" he demanded to know.

"Yes!" she cried as his hardness electrified her.

"Do you love me?"

"I love you!"

"Do you swear it?"

"I swear! Oh, please, make love to me, Daniel!"

"I want more children," he said fiercely, gritting his teeth against her plea. "Will you give me more sons?"

"And daughters?" Katherine laughed as he tumbled them between the sheets, buried to the hilt inside her.

"Especially daughters!" he said. Entwined, they lay there, till he stopped to take a deep breath and start all over again.

*   *   *   *   *

Wilma's Butter Cake

3 cups all-purpose flour
1 teaspoon salt
1 teaspoon baking powder
1/2 teaspoon baking soda
1 cup (2 sticks) butter or margarine, softened
2 cups granulated sugar
4 eggs
1 cup buttermilk
2 teaspoons vanilla
1/4 chopped pecans (optional)

For the butter sauce:
1/2 cup granulated sugar
1/8 cup water
1/4 cup (1/2 stick) butter or margarine
1-1/2 teaspoons vanilla

Grease a 12-cup (or 10-inch) tube or Bundt pan on bottom only. Set aside.

Put first nine ingredients in a large mixing bowl. Blend on low speed of electric mixer until combined. Beat for additional 3 minutes at medium speed.

Sprinkle chopped pecans into bottom of prepared pan, if desired. Pour batter into pan. Bake in a preheated, 325 degree oven 60 to 75 minutes, or until toothpick inserted in center comes out clean.

While cake is baking, prepare hot butter sauce: In small

saucepan, combine sugar, water and butter; heat until butter melts. Do not boil. Remove from heat; add vanilla. When cake is done, remove from oven and run a spatula or knife around edge and stem of pan. Prick cake (still in pan) with a fork. Pour hot butter sauce over the warm cake, letting it soak into cake. Cool cake completely before removing from pan. Turn cake onto serving platter.

Note: This cake is rich and moist and freezes nicely.

Hometown Heartbreakers:
These heart-stopping hunks are rugged,
ready and able to steal your heart!

Coming soon from

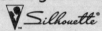

SPECIAL EDITION™

The return of her popular miniseries
from *USA TODAY* bestselling author

SUSAN MALLERY

The series continues with:
GOOD HUSBAND MATERIAL
SE #1501, on sale November 2002

Kari Asbury had burned him once…and left a scar that
Sheriff Gage Reynolds couldn't forget. Then Kari reappeared
in his life just as a shocking family secret was revealed! The
hunky lawman was helpless to control his feelings for the
gorgeous former model. But with his life changed forever,
could he truly commit to Kari?

Available at your favorite retail outlet.

Where love comes alive™

Visit Silhouette at www.eHarlequin.com   SSESM

eHARLEQUIN.com

community | membership
buy books | authors | online reads | magazine | learn to write

magazine

❤ —————————————————————— **quizzes**

Is he the one? What kind of lover are you? Visit the **Quizzes** area to find out!

❤ —————————————————————— **recipes for romance**

Get scrumptious meal ideas with our **Recipes for Romance**.

❤ —————————————————————— **romantic movies**

Peek at the **Romantic Movies** area to find Top 10 Flicks about First Love, ten Supersexy Movies, and more.

❤ —————————————————————— **royal romance**

Get the latest scoop on your favorite royals in **Royal Romance**.

❤ —————————————————————— **games**

Check out the **Games** pages to find a ton of interactive romantic fun!

❤ —————————————————————— **romantic travel**

In need of a romantic rendezvous? Visit the **Romantic Travel** section for articles and guides.

❤ —————————————————————— **lovescopes**

Are you two compatible? Click your way to the **Lovescopes** area to find out now!

Silhouette® —

where love comes alive—online...

Visit us online at
www.eHarlequin.com

SINTMAG

If you enjoyed what you just read,
then we've got an offer you can't resist!

Take 2 bestselling love stories FREE!

Plus get a FREE surprise gift!

Clip this page and mail it to Silhouette Reader Service™

IN U.S.A.
3010 Walden Ave.
P.O. Box 1867
Buffalo, N.Y. 14240-1867

IN CANADA
P.O. Box 609
Fort Erie, Ontario
L2A 5X3

YES! Please send me 2 free Silhouette Special Edition® novels and my free surprise gift. After receiving them, if I don't wish to receive anymore, I can return the shipping statement marked cancel. If I don't cancel, I will receive 6 brand-new novels every month, before they're available in stores! In the U.S.A., bill me at the bargain price of $3.99 plus 25¢ shipping and handling per book and applicable sales tax, if any*. In Canada, bill me at the bargain price of $4.74 plus 25¢ shipping and handling per book and applicable taxes**. That's the complete price and a savings of at least 10% off the cover prices—what a great deal! I understand that accepting the 2 free books and gift places me under no obligation ever to buy any books. I can always return a shipment and cancel at any time. Even if I never buy another book from Silhouette, the 2 free books and gift are mine to keep forever.

235 SDN DNUR
335 SDN DNUS

Name	(PLEASE PRINT)	
Address	Apt.#	
City	State/Prov.	Zip/Postal Code

* Terms and prices subject to change without notice. Sales tax applicable in N.Y.
** Canadian residents will be charged applicable provincial taxes and GST.
   All orders subject to approval. Offer limited to one per household and not valid to current Silhouette Special Edition® subscribers.
   ® are registered trademarks of Harlequin Books S.A., used under license.

SPED02   ©1998 Harlequin Enterprises Limited

Silhouette

SPECIAL EDITION™

is proud to present:

BABY TIMES THREE

an exciting new miniseries from popular author

VICTORIA PADE

Baby Times 3

HER BABY SECRET
SE #1503, on sale November 2002

Paris Hanley needed to get pregnant—fast!—
without letting wealthy Ethan Tarlington find out
her plan! But after she gave birth to a baby girl,
passions flared between the single mother and the
business mogul. What would Ethan do when
he discovered Paris's string of secrets?

**Don't miss the other two upcoming titles in
the BABY TIMES THREE series, on sale
January 2003 and March 2003,
from Silhouette Special Edition.**

Available at your favorite retail outlet.

Silhouette®

Where love comes alive™

Visit Silhouette at www.eHarlequin.com   SSEBTT

#1501 GOOD HUSBAND MATERIAL—Susan Mallery
Hometown Heartbreakers
Kari Ashbury had burned him once…so why did Sheriff Gage Reynolds still have feelings for the gorgeous ex-model he hadn't seen in years? Then Gage uncovered a long-buried family scandal, and his world turned upside down. His past, his whole life, now felt like a lie. Was loving Kari a lie, too?

#1502 CATTLEMAN'S HONOR—Pamela Toth
Winchester Brides
Rancher Adam Winchester was used to getting his way, especially when it came to women. So when feisty divorcée Emily Major moved to town and refused to give in to his demands, the hard-as-nails single father felt outraged—then fell in love. The two could not resist their growing passion. But what would happen when their children got wind of the romance?

#1503 HER BABY SECRET—Victoria Pade
Baby Times Three
One wild night had left Paris Hanley pregnant with a longed-for baby girl. But Paris was terrified that if her baby's father, mogul Ethan Tarlington, ever found out, the take-charge billionaire would take away her beautiful baby. Then Ethan made Paris an offer she couldn't refuse. Would the single mom's big secret *finally* be revealed?

#1504 SUDDENLY FAMILY—Christine Flynn
True love happens only once, right? That was what widower Sam Edwards had always thought. Until free-spirited T. J. Walker came into his life…and swept the honorable single father right off his feet! But could Sam convince a relationship-wary T.J. that he was the one man she could count on?

#1505 WHAT A WOMAN WANTS—Tori Carrington
It was bad enough that Sheriff John Sparks had had a passionate affair with his best friend's widow! But now gorgeous Darby Conrad was pregnant…with *his* baby! The brawny bachelor wasn't exactly father material. But he hadn't reckoned on his powerful feelings for Darby… or the new family they were creating together.

#1506 JOURNEY OF THE HEART—Elissa Ambrose
Readers' Ring
The relationship between Laura Matheson and Jake Logan had always been a roller-coaster ride of joy and tears, yet the two couldn't deny the passion that was once again pulling them together. Then a cache of old letters was found, revealing an explosive secret long hidden. With the stakes high and emotions running deep, could Jake and Laura finally realize how important they were to each other?